The North Wing

SUSAN BUTLER

Copyright

DEDICATION

In loving memory of my mom, Nancy Colesworthy, my biggest fan in all aspects of my life. Her never-ending kindness and support of everyone around her was a wonderful inspiration for me as I wrote this book.

I'd also like to extend my appreciation to all my friends and family, who've been remarkably encouraging and helpful, and one by one joined me in this long but rewarding journey.

A huge debt of thanks to my brother, Bob Colesworthy, for his design assistance, my brother-in-law, John Cattin, for providing his invaluable input as my editor, my best friend, Jill Quinn, who read several of my early attempts, and convinced me nevertheless to stick with the project, and to my daughter, Lisa, whose comments reminded me entertainment is as important as style when creating a story.

Most of all, I would like to thank my husband, Brian, who stayed with me through the many days and nights I was parked in front of the computer, and patiently listened to my yammering about plot ideas, characters, and my continually evolving storyline. The truest form of love is that which is understanding, the love I've been fortunate and grateful to have.

ACKNOWLEDGMENTS

Cover photo, "Candlelit Corridor"
Courtesy of MaCall Potter
flickr.com/photos/macallpotter
macallpotter.tumblr.com

Original artwork by
Michael Colesworthy

A Work of Fiction

1

Life is seldom a simple or straightforward journey. Even in the best of circumstances, the future cannot be predicted, and no one can fully prepare for what may lie ahead. Any given event, despite how outwardly significant or trivial it may appear, has the potential to lead one down a new path. In some cases, for better or for worse, our lives are altered forever—there is no going back.

In the summer of 1887, shortly after her 19th birthday, an incident of this sort befell Abigail Parker. Months later, she boarded a train that would transport her to a new way of life filled with possibilities. When the train pulled into the station, she had reached her destination. Her true journey, however, was only about to begin.

The engineer braked to a full stop, and the resulting jolt roused Abigail from her nap. She rubbed her eyes and straightened herself to peek out the window. "Oh, my goodness, we're here," she whispered, her shoulders twitching and legs wriggling, prepared to spring from her seat the moment permission to disembark was granted.

Abigail regarded her fellow passengers, anticipating their shared enthusiasm, to find their expressions were largely disparaging. She shrank against her seatback in embarrassment, until she turned to see an elderly woman grinning at her with a glint in her eyes. *She's been in my shoes. Unlike these other stodgy people, she can understand why I'm celebrating so childishly*, Abigail thought. She returned the woman a grateful smile.

What the others hadn't guessed was the specific call Abigail had for her exuberance. The train had arrived in England, her country of origin. Travels for Abigail had begun in Austria where she'd resided the previous seven years. Although it had been a lengthy trip, the cause of her delight wasn't due to the physical and mental relief following a journey's end. It had nothing to do with the fact she hadn't returned to her homeland in a long while, and neither was it the prospect of visiting the places and pleasures she'd been missing. Typical reasons hadn't accounted for her euphoria. To understand her reaction would require learning the highlights of her past, the intertwining occurrences that led her to this point.

An only child born and raised near London until 1880, Abigail's family had moved in the fall of this year after her father accepted a prominent post at the University of Vienna. While enticing in certain aspects, for Abigail this had primarily been an intimidating concept. Relocating to a distant, foreign country could be daunting for anyone at the tender age of twelve, particularly for a person with Abigail's soft-spoken and shy disposition.

The Parkers had barely settled into their new home when the school term commenced. Abigail had faced her first day with an acute case of nerves, which had increased with every step as she'd walked through the campus, so stately and extensive she'd found it formidable. Of some consolation, the primary class she'd attended was comprised exclusively of children of the English department staff, and English had therefore been the spoken language. Regardless of this advantage, she'd entered the classroom trembling, and had clutched her books as the other children stared at her intently.

Despite the passage of many years, whenever Abigail reflected upon the events which followed, she was able to relive each moment, each sensation with distinct clarity, starting with meeting her teacher, Miss Hammond. Her strict and dour demeanor had done nothing to placate Abigail's anxiety. She had flinched when the teacher grasped her shoulders and pulled her to the head of the room.

"Children, this is your new classmate, Abigail Parker, who's recently arrived from England," Miss Hammond announced. Never desirous to be the center of attention, Abigail fidgeted while her fellow students perused her over. At best they appeared disinterested; more likely annoyed to be distracted from each other. "I would encourage all of you to make her feel welcome." She indicated to Abigail her place and nudged her away.

Abigail remained shaky when she seated herself, the security of her books so comforting she forgot she yet held them.

"You'll find it difficult to use your texts until you place them on your desk," Miss Hammond admonished. Many of the children snickered, and Abigail was mortified that a mere few minutes into the day she had a strike against her.

Following the morning lessons, the luncheon break began. As the children filed into the dining hall filled with small tables, Abigail wished for an invitation to sit with one of the groups, though no one extended her the courtesy. Soon the room was animated with the chatting and laughing of the youngsters, apart from Abigail. She ate alone, hardly tasting the food which may have filled her stomach but did little to allay the hollowness of her soul.

Her emptiness lingered as the day drug by slowly, a condition which didn't improve after dismissal. While everyone else scampered home with their friends, she plodded along, her legs heavy with the burden of rejection.

At home, Abigail found her parents were preoccupied with their own responsibilities and did her best to appear cheerful. She considered it pointless to disturb them, having a good idea the brand of advice they would offer: "Be patient; everyone requires time to adjust to an unfamiliar circumstance. You'll find each day will be better. Before long, all will be well." Although she wanted such wisdom to prove true, she was far less than optimistic.

Days passed, and the dismal pattern had persisted. Companionless and miserable, each night Abigail would recall the fun times she'd shared with her former school friends. She longed to be reunited with them rather than remain trapped in what she'd deemed a wretched existence.

By the school week's end, she was devoid of hope. She lay on her bed and stared at the ceiling, her tears dripping onto the pillow. In the morning she was on the verge of crying at school but managed to prevent it, thankful to have spared herself from any added ridicule her classmates were likely to inflict. Her one solace was the weekly respite which would begin the next day. Any time apart from the children who had shunned her she took as a blessing.

Abigail was seated at her desk the following week in a gloomy frame of mind when a student she wasn't familiar with entered the classroom. She could never have predicted it, but her introduction to this girl was to have a profound and indelible impact on her life.

It was soon obvious the child was held in the highest esteem by her classmates. Many of them hollered out "Anna!", and phrases such as "you're here!" and "where've you been?" were repeatedly echoed.

"Welcome back, Anna," the teacher said. "We're relieved you've made a full recovery from your influenza."

"Thank you, Miss Hammond," the girl replied with a spunky grin. She turned briskly, her skirt twirling to and fro as she sashayed towards her desk, the twinkle in her eyes indicating she enjoyed the limelight immensely. She took her seat across from Abigail and scrutinized her new classmate with blatant curiosity.

"Who are you?" Anna asked under her breath.

"I'm Abigail."

"Where are you from?"

"England."

"How did you…" Anna started when the lesson began, and Miss Hammond preempted her with a cross look. Anna appeared obedient, smiling as she placed her folded hands decorously on the desk. She waited until the teacher's back was turned to sneer at her, and then mocked her with a silent imitation of her words.

The other children giggled in response which prompted Miss Hammond to whip around, Abigail the target of her stern glare. "There will be no disruption in my classroom," the teacher told her. Indignant to be falsely accused, Abigail was too intimidated to lodge a protest, and hence said nothing.

At luncheon time Anna sat with her friends, Gerta and Elsa, who'd shown they could be boisterous. After whispering awhile with her companions, Anna stood to approach Abigail, who cowered in anticipation of a hurtful comment.

"Would you like to sit with us?" Anna offered.

Entirely surprised, Abigail perked up. "Yes, I would, very much."

Anna picked up some of Abigail's things and placed them on her table.

Abigail moved the rest. She'd barely seated herself when the girls inundated her with simultaneous questions. Her eyes flittered amongst them as they chirped incessantly, unable to offer a single word while she listened to banter such as "how far away is England?" asked by one, and answered with "I'll bet it's very far," by another.

The children at the other tables took note of the encounter, astonished by the interest the new girl was being afforded. When luncheon ended, Abigail's classmates regarded her far differently. Abigail then understood it was Anna's approval she'd been lacking to gain their esteem.

After school, Anna invited Abigail to walk home with her group. Abigail accepted and followed contentedly while the others frolicked along the campus pathway. Although it remained difficult to add a word to their conversation, for the first time since her arrival in Vienna Abigail was truly happy— no longer friendless in her unfamiliar world.

*****

Subsequent to that day, Abigail spent a great deal of time with her newfound companions, and they'd become nearly inseparable. Elsa had quickly proven herself to be a predominantly silly youngster, and Gerta, while clever, possessed an impish nature. As anticipated Anna emerged as the definitive ringleader, a position she openly relished.

Gerta and Elsa adored Anna's fun-loving, mischievous ways, and always followed her lead without question. When it became apparent Anna sought to surround herself with those she could manipulate easily, Abigail reasoned she'd been invited to join the group as a result, rather than in spite, of her timidity. This enlightenment had been of no consequence to her, for having close friends and the admiration of her fellow classmates was a state she found vastly preferable to being disregarded and lonesome.

During the remainder of their childhood, the girls enjoyed a variety of activities, a number of which entailed trouble. Fearing the loss of her friends, Abigail had agreed to participate in their mischief. She was surprised to discover breaking the rules could be an exhilarating form of entertainment, until an incident when Anna sought to take vengeance against Miss Hammond.

Several days beforehand, the teacher had imposed upon Anna what she considered to be an unmerited punishment. Anna, desiring retribution, convinced Abigail, Elsa, and Gerta to sneak into the classroom with her after dismissal, their design to cover Miss Hammond's chair with chalk dust. As they were set to enact the prank, the teacher returned, and the girls narrowly avoided detection by fleeing into a closet. After the teacher departed, given the close call, Abigail was flabbergasted to learn the others were bent upon continuing. Since she anticipated a severe chastisement if they were discovered, even her friends' goading couldn't convince Abigail to place herself in further jeopardy. She elected to run home.

The following morning, when Miss Hammond stood to approach the blackboard, the students snickered uncontrollably. The teacher inspected herself, incensed to find the back of her dark blue dress covered in the stark white chalk. She demanded the perpetrator confess, or she would have the entire class remain after school to give the room a thorough scrubbing. Regardless of her threat, no one would admit to any knowledge of the deed, and the teacher enforced her stringent ruling.

Later in the day, the episode was a frequent topic of conversation on the playground. With the consensus their amusement was well worth the discipline they'd received, Elsa bragged to several of her classmates about her involvement.

"You did this?" a boy asked in astonishment.

"I did, with the help of Anna and Gerta, but Abigail bolted which proves what a goody two shoes she is," Elsa said.

Abigail, who stood nearby, was caught off guard. She pursed her lips, too tongue-tied to vindicate her actions.

"That's not surprising. She is a namby-pamby," a girl said.

"Abigail's a namby-pamby, a goody-two-shoes namby-pamby," a child chanted. When others joined in unison Elsa didn't participate, appearing contrite to be the cause of the ruckus, and yet she made no effort to counter their gibes.

Unable to thwart their affront on her own, Abigail stood quivering while the taunting continued as her eyes filled with tears.

"And now she's going to cry like a baby," a youngster chided.

Anna and Gerta, who'd taken a lavatory break, approached the group.

"What's happening here?" Anna asked.

"Elsa told us the three of you put the chalk on Miss Hammond's chair, while Abigail ran off like a scared tot," another child informed her. "How do you bear this cowardly custard?"

"I do not *bear* anything. Abigail is my dear friend. You'd best stop your insults at once," Anna warned them.

7

"Don't be mad at us. It was Elsa who first called her a goody-two-shoes," a boy defended.

"Unlike the rest of you, she was teasing. The four of us tease each other now and again, all in good fun, but you're being cruel. Unless any of you want to become an outcast, you'll treat my friends nicely," Anna snapped. "Come, girls, today we'll play elsewhere."

Abigail smiled when Anna took her arm, and they jaunted away as Elsa and Gerta followed. This was to be a defining moment for Abigail. She recognized in Anna not merely a companion, but an unreservedly loyal ally who could be counted upon to stand by her through thick and thin.

*****

As the years passed, the girls' friendship remained strong and continued to be so when they'd entered the University. Having outgrown childish games, Anna, Gerta, and Elsa expressed their excitement regarding social occasions that would include boys. Abigail hadn't shared in their enthusiasm, preferring sedate activities such as reading, studying, and attending musical events.

Academics hadn't concerned the rest of the group in the least. Their interest in the University was to find the best possible candidate for marriage. To this end, parties and dances were their favorite events. Despite her protests, the girls had frequently coerced Abigail's attendance. "You cannot keep your nose stuck in the books all of the time," was the sort of contrivance they'd used to persuade her.

Anna, the first of them to blossom physically into womanhood, had grown more beautiful with each passing year. Her curly golden hair and buxom body were traits men obviously considered desirable. At an early age, she'd mastered the art of dressing and adorning herself to take full advantage of her attributes. Still the decided center of attention, upon entering any gathering Anna was surrounded rapidly by eager young men, and soon she'd honed the skill of flirtation. Elsa and Gerta, each attractive in her own right, had followed her example. When unsuccessful with Anna, typically boys weren't hesitant to turn their attention towards them.

Maturity had done little to change Abigail's bashful tendencies. She felt ill at ease in spirited situations, commonplace for her to sit and watch while her cohorts enjoyed their long list of dance partners. The occasions Abigail had danced usually took place at her friends' request. After a brief inspection, most of those solicited would comply, drawn to the appearance of the pretty, petite, waiflike blond with soft blue eyes and delicate features. More often than not Abigail's subdued demeanor became tiresome to the boys, who would as promptly dismiss her as a bore.

As their school years were ending, Anna, Elsa, and Gerta had acquired numerous suitors, but Abigail had none. During that time there were occurrences Abigail found aggravating, later amazed how the events had culminated to alter her destiny.

One such incident occurred at a summer party prior to their final year at the University. In an attempt to secure a relationship for her friend, Anna tried to coax her studious acquaintance, Peter, to offer Abigail a dance.

"Abigail is most intellectual. Should you become better acquainted, the two of you would have an enjoyable time."

"Ask that piece of milk toast to dance?" Peter scoffed; his back to Abigail who was sitting within earshot. "I did once and found I might as well dance with an empty dress," he mocked and strode off to extend his offer to someone else.

Anna sat by Abigail, who was snarling at his boorish comment. "Dearest, you cannot blame him for his opinion when you make no effort to be appealing or enjoy yourself."

Abigail huffed. "I don't care one bit about his opinion. I recall dancing with him. I have no desire to join him again either. He holds no traits I find attractive."

"Nor does any other man, it would appear," Gerta said. "Really, Abigail, you must follow our lead, and try to allure men rather than constantly push them away."

"I cannot change my perceptions or interests," Abigail said.

"You don't have to change anything, simply adopt the appearance of being enthralled by them," Elsa explained. "This is what we do."

"How then do you suggest I proceed when this *appearance* vanishes?" Abigail asked tartly.

Gerta shook her head. "It doesn't matter, once you've received an offer of marriage. You must find a way or risk becoming an old maid."

"Please refresh my memory, for I don't recall any of you entering into an engagement," Abigail retorted.

"We haven't yet, but we expect to receive offers shortly," Anna said. "We won't accept any proposal straight away since we have the luxury of selecting from the most favorable choices."

"This is true," Elsa agreed. "You must act hastily or be left with the dregs no other girl will have."

The music played, and the first dance began. To Abigail's relief, the conversation came to a halt when her friends were escorted to the floor.

"Appear enthralled indeed. I doubt worse advice has been offered to anyone," Abigail grumbled and witnessed her companions enact what she believed was a reprehensible, underhanded scheme.

*****

Abigail was dismayed, far more than surprised when the subject of marriage resurfaced two weeks later at her nineteenth birthday party, the last place she wanted to have the matter broached. There was, however, no preventing it, for many in attendance were atwitter with what they considered astounding news.

"Have you heard, girls? There's an eligible bachelor who arrived in town recently. He's residing nearby," Anna said. "I've heard he's the most handsome man a girl has ever seen, and wealthy beyond all reason. Reportedly he's in his twenty-fifth year, undoubtedly seeking marriage. We'd best hurry since he's expected to remain in Vienna only a few months. Afterward, he'll return to what's being touted as a magnificent estate in England."

"Why did he travel so far to find a bride?" Elsa asked.

"I don't suggest his visit was for this purpose exclusively," Anna told her. "He has business here at the University. My point is we should take advantage of the situation before it's too late."

"If he's handsome and rich, why do you suppose he remains unattached?" Gerta asked.

"I haven't the answer for that. Likely he hasn't found the right woman just yet. There's no reason it couldn't be one of us," Anna said.

"How will it be possible to become acquainted with him?" Abigail asked. "His society must be very grand; surely, there won't be an occasion for us to meet him."

Elsa rolled her eyes. "There's a ball Saturday night you goose."

"It's a ball for faculty members and their families, a function I cannot imagine he would attend," Abigail shot back.

"Rumor has it he will, as supposedly he has connections with the host. I for one will double my efforts to look my best," Anna related. "Hopefully Mama will grant me a new dress for the occasion. When I explain the circumstance, I've no doubt she'll consent."

"If he may be present, I won't attend," Abigail stated.

"Why on earth not?" Elsa asked.

"I've experienced enough humiliation from the men in this town. I needn't more from a man who must be entirely beyond my reach."

"This shyness of yours has reached the limit," Gerta said. "What is the harm in your attending? If you'll stop being a wet blanket, you might enjoy yourself."

"I have a proposal," Anna said. "Let's fetch Abigail early, and prepare her ourselves. Since you don't take advantage of your attributes, we'll show you how it's accomplished. That will set you in the right direction."

"There's no need," Abigail protested. "My appearance doesn't concern me. Changing it won't be of any help."

Gerta appraised her with disparagement. "We don't want to hurt your feelings, but you do need our help. Any improvement will make a difference."

"I'd rather you didn't bother yourselves. It'll be a waste of your time and energy," Abigail said in the hopes of dissuading them.

"Don't be a ninny," Elsa chided. "We'll help you in this whether you want us to or not. You're sure to discover it's for your own good."

*****

Since her friends repeatedly refused to take no for an answer, several days later Abigail found herself reluctantly entering the ball. They had transformed her image significantly, giving her the appearance of a confident, engaging woman. But the false front had only served to escalate her uneasiness, and Abigail couldn't fathom the reason she'd given in to their design.

The girls removed their outer garments and promenaded down the main staircase. Anna, Gerta, and Elsa held their heads high, their posture graceful as they discreetly surveyed the room for the mystery man. Abigail, as usual, was unsteady. She proceeded with slumped shoulders, clinging to the banister to avoid a fall.

After what seemed ages to Abigail, they reached the floor. Happy to have at least remained on her feet, she followed the others awkwardly while they sauntered through the gathering, still on the lookout for the stranger.

They joined Anna's mother at the far side of the ballroom. Attending as chaperone, she'd entered ahead to secure a table, and to ensure all attention was directed at the girls, her daughter in particular.

"We didn't see anyone we're unfamiliar with, Mother," Anna said. "Do you think the man has decided not to attend?"

"Don't worry; he'll appear soon enough. It's considered fashionable by those of high society to arrive late."

The longer they waited, the more Abigail's nerves rose, to the point she could barely hold still. In secret, she hoped he wouldn't come. "Are you certain this guise suits me?" she asked Anna.

Anna smiled and smoothed her friend's hair. "You're simply lovely this evening, dearest."

"You'd be lovelier if you wouldn't fidget," Elsa reproached her. "For heaven's sake, Abigail, take a breath and calm yourself."

As it happened the opportunity had ended, for at that moment the man in question entered. Abigail was taken aback by the reaction of her companions, their normally unflappable composure overcome, staring at him in awe while he descended the stairs.

He was an attractive gentleman; tall and dark, his deep blue eyes the highlight of his handsome, elegant features. Even from a distance, one could tell his attire was impeccable, the latest fashion of the finest quality materials. The perfect fit of his tailcoat accentuated his broad shoulders and tapered down to his trim waist. When he arrived at the floor he was greeted by the party's host, who introduced him individually to the gathering.

"My goodness, he's almost here," Anna exclaimed when they drew near. She giggled along with Gerta and Elsa before they turned to address one another, to render the impression they weren't particularly interested in the approaching guest.

"Ah, Mrs. Feldman," the host, Mr. Kruger, addressed Anna's mother. As her ensemble turned in acknowledgment Abigail was amazed, for they now appeared collected. "Allow me to introduce Mr. Darrell Lewis of Northampton, England."

"A great pleasure, madam," Mr. Lewis greeted. He kissed the hand she offered.

"A pleasure for me as well," Mrs. Feldman returned.

"Mr. Lewis owns a substantial amount of property here at the University and is currently engaged in the construction of the new science building," Mr. Kruger related.

Mrs. Feldman appeared impressed. "*Science;* what a noble pursuit."

"Although it is, of course, don't grant me undue credit in this arena. I'm merely overseeing the project," Mr. Lewis explained.

"Such modesty you have. I find it a most admirable quality," Mrs. Feldman said.

"He is an exceedingly modest gentleman," Mr. Kruger confirmed. "While he's not touting it, a large part of the venture has been funded from his own pocket."

"A remarkably generous endeavor, the ball must in truth be in your honor," Mrs. Feldman suggested.

"You're too kind; however, the honor belongs to this institution, and its exceptional faculty," Mr. Lewis insisted. "Now, please tell me, who are these winsome young ladies who accompany you this evening?"

"May I introduce my daughter, Anna Feldman, and her dear school companions; Gerta Friedrich, Elsa Groman, and Abigail Parker."

"A pleasure to meet you, sir," Anna said, oozing her most flirtatious charm.

"The pleasure is entirely mine," he replied.

Gerta and Elsa followed suit and extended their greetings with equally marked poise and allure. When Abigail received her introduction, her manner was nothing of the sort. She met his gaze briefly and then stared at the floor. "I'm pleased to make your acquaintance, sir," she uttered, her mouth dry and her breathing shallow.

"It's a *great* pleasure to make your acquaintance," Mr. Lewis said. His tone of voice held such enthusiasm Abigail peeked up and found his eyes were smiling into hers. "It appears the dance is about to begin. Miss Parker, may I have the honor of engaging you for the first turn?"

Her cohorts were stunned he'd bestowed his favor upon Abigail. Convinced she hadn't heard correctly, Abigail didn't react. The other girls gestured vaguely at her, but she didn't notice until Gerta poked her ribs with her elbow.

Abigail released a muted grunt before she finally said, "The honor would be all mine."

Mr. Lewis grinned, apparently amused by their antics. "Until later, my dear ladies."

Abigail tried to compose herself while he led her to the floor. As they danced, she didn't face her partner, quivering to the extent she feared it was discernible.

"Abigail Parker isn't an Austrian name," he cited.

"Indeed, it's not," she confirmed, her voice barely audible. "My parents and I resided in England until I was twelve, when my father accepted the post as dean of the English Language and Literature School, here at the University."

"I presume, then, you read a great deal?"

"Yes, I enjoy doing so, very much."

"A pastime well-disposed to your temperament, I believe."

His assumption caused her to wince.

"My comment wasn't intended to be an insult," he assured her.

She was skeptical about his earnestness but was unable to come up with a clever rebuttal on the spot.

They were silent for several minutes before Mr. Lewis attempted to revive the conversation with more of the usual introductory questions.

Given her labored speech, Abigail kept her answers succinct, often replying with a simple *yes* or *no*. As the questions ran their course she glanced at her friends for help. Although they motioned for her to be more engaging, she found herself at a loss.

The first dance was nearing the end. Abigail was certain, and to an extent relieved she would sit out the remainder of the ball until Mr. Lewis leaned close to her ear.

"Propriety dictates I dance with your companions, to avoid injuring them with insult," he whispered. "Afterward, I'd be most pleased if you'll dance with me for the remainder of the evening."

She was unable to conceal her astonishment, and he smiled kindly at her as he escorted her back to the group.

She sat by Mrs. Feldman who patted her hand.

"You did well, my dear," Mrs. Feldman said with a "better luck next time" connotation.

Mr. Lewis offered the next dance to Elsa, who returned noticeably pleased with her performance. After Gerta received her turn, she appeared convinced she'd taken the lead in what they blatantly considered a contest.

When he approached Anna, she accepted his offer with her usual aplomb. Her dress swayed with the rhythm of her hips as they walked towards the floor, she a little in front of him, evidently to ensure her movements caught his attention. She glimpsed back and winked at the girls, relaying her intent to steal the show.

Her mother placed her fingers to her mouth, beaming with pride. "His actions make sense now. He asked her last intentionally so they may dance together for the remainder of the evening."

Abigail watched them tolerantly, convinced Mr. Lewis had changed his mind. She was accustomed to being passed over, and therefore it didn't surprise or truly upset her. The circumstance was of her own making, as her friends had rightfully noted. It would be impossible for her to blame him if he admired attributes in the others she lacked.

At the end of the piece, Anna shone brightly while she clapped, circling with flourish and yet maintaining her position, plainly in expectation of another round. To her evident shock, Mr. Lewis offered her his arm. Her smile deflated into a grimace when he led her back to the group.

He assisted Anna with her chair, and then stood before Abigail, who blinked up at him in bewilderment.

"Miss Parker, may I impose upon you to join me in another dance?" He extended his hand to her.

Her companions regarded one another in marked disbelief when he escorted her away.

"He's decided to offer you each another turn, a kind gesture in my estimation," Mrs. Feldman said.

After Mr. Lewis remained with Abigail for several more numbers, it was obvious her speculation had been incorrect. Despite the many admirers with whom they danced, the other girls sulked to be out of the competition for their eagerly sought prize.

For her part, Abigail was sure she'd entered into a dream world, unable to believe this enigmatic man had chosen her over her captivating friends. Her bashfulness eased until he attempted to pull her closer, and her shoulders tensed involuntarily in resistance.

"There's no need to keep your distance. I'm not a wolf, you know," he teased.

The shine in his eyes suggested tolerance, not aggravation, and she relaxed her arms to allow his advance. When he placed his hand on her back a spark tingled the length of her spine, and yet his touch felt protective.

She became more compliant as the evening continued. For the first time, she was comfortable in a man's arms, and there was no mistaking Mr. Lewis was smitten with her.

"It would seem we did too good a job in her transformation," Anna muttered as she danced by Gerta and Elsa. They smirked behind their partners, their disappointment evident.

The party was winding down when the final selection was performed. Abigail felt like Cinderella with the clock about to strike midnight.

Mr. Lewis offered her his escort for the last time. On their way to the table he said, "Miss Parker, may I have your permission to call upon you at your home tomorrow, presuming your parents will approve?"

She jokingly wondered if he would bring the glass slipper. "I imagine they will. We have no plans I'm aware of."

"I'll make arrangements to arrive after luncheon unless this should prove to be inconvenient. If such is the case, please inform Mr. Kruger as early as possible. He has the ability to notify me."

"Likely it won't be necessary, but my parents will appreciate your consideration."

"Thank you, then, for the lovely evening. I'll look forward to our visit tomorrow," Mr. Lewis said.

They met the rest of her group who'd begun to gather their things. Mr. Lewis kissed Abigail's hand and wished the rest of the group a good night before he departed.

"Well, well, *well*. Our timid Abigail has at last transformed into a desirable woman, and what a fortunate time for you. We've never seen you act in this way," Gerta remarked, her attitude surly.

"I behaved no differently than I ever do," Abigail defended.

"Then I suppose he's the sort of man who prefers a meek, quiet little mouse; therefore, let him have one," Elsa gnarled.

Abigail flinched at their harsh words, her feelings hurt since her friends had apparently turned against her. "I find him patient, for me a pleasant change of character from the men I've encountered previously."

"They merely tease you," Anna said. "Admittedly we're jealous, and yet we are happy for you, are we not?"

"Yes, the fact is we are," Gerta agreed.

"I'm sorry we sounded unkind. After all, you won him fair and square," Elsa said.

"We must leave, girls," Mrs. Feldman directed.

They went upstairs to collect their coats and then headed to the carriage.

Given her friends' frame of mind, Abigail thought it best to conceal Mr. Lewis's request to call upon her. Inwardly, she glowed with the enchantment of her secret the entire trip home. When she exited the carriage, her feet didn't seem to contact the ground, as if she was supported by a cloud as she glided into the house.

"It appears you had a nice time," Mrs. Parker said. "You've seldom returned from a party in such a joyful state."

"I had a wonderful time, Mother. Do you recall the gentleman Anna described at my birthday party; the handsome and eligible bachelor?"

"I certainly do."

"He did attend the party. I must admit I was nervous when we first met, and so you'll scarcely believe how the evening progressed. He requested *I* join him for the first dance. He did grant the others their turn but afterward chose me alone to be his partner. And Mother, he wants to call upon us tomorrow. He's a polite man, for although I presumed you would consent, he suggested his visit take place after luncheon, allowing time to notify him if it isn't agreeable with you and Father. Please, may he come?"

"I have no objection," her mother said, looking to her husband for confirmation.

"Naturally he may call upon us. I've heard he's donating a great deal to the University. We dare not dismiss a man who's a generous benefactor," he agreed light-heartedly.

"Thank you, dearest Father."

Abigail gave him a kiss on the cheek and her mother a hug before she bounded up the stairs to her room. After changing into her nightgown she squeezed her pillow, twirling several times before she fell onto the bed. She closed her eyes and recalled her magical evening over and over until the memories of it were swept into her dreams.

*****

When the knock on the door of the Parker's home came at two o'clock the following afternoon, the maid ushered the urgently awaited guest to the parlor. "Mr. Darrell Lewis," she announced, and they all stood.

Abigail was reminded afresh of his striking appearance and prominence, doubly impressive in the confines of this smaller, quieter space. To her dismay, she trembled as when they'd first met, and her stomach clenched in a nervous knot.

"Good afternoon, Miss Parker," he greeted, his benevolent manner in stark contrast to the dominance of his physical presence.

"Good afternoon," Abigail replied, hoping her jitters weren't noticeable. "Mr. Lewis, these are my parents, Mr. and Mrs. Parker."

"A great pleasure, sir, madam," he said.

"The pleasure is all ours," Mr. Parker returned.

"Please, would you care to have a seat?" Mrs. Parker suggested.

"I'd be delighted. Your home is beautiful."

"You're most kind," Mrs. Parker thanked him.

"Mr. Parker, your reputation as dean of the English school has been related to me by Mr. Kruger. He tells me you've quite turned around a department which once had more than its share of struggles."

"It was good of him to say. It seems I owe you a compliment in return. Everyone here is astounded by your generosity regarding the construction of the new science building. I understand your ancestral home, Rochester Manor, is in Northampton. If you'll forgive my curiosity, what prompted your interest in our university?"

"The impetus was my great-grandmother, who was of Austrian descent. She persuaded my great grandfather to purchase a large amount of property in the vicinity, the advancement of education being a dear cause of hers. Evidently, she had family members who graduated from the University of Vienna. It was her fondest hope her children, along with those of future generations, would obtain their education at this institution. Sadly, she died young. Without her influence, the course she desired wasn't pursued. I learned of the University's outstanding reputation from Mr. Kruger, whose family had connections with hers. Although I didn't attend school here, I decided it would be fitting to honor her other aspiration—the construction of buildings on our property."

"What a gratifying story," Mrs. Parker said.

"And a lovely tribute to your great-grandmother," Abigail added.

"You, on the other hand, have been well educated here, I suspect?" Mr. Lewis asked Abigail.

"She has indeed," her father answered. "She's our most dedicated student."

"Dear Papa, how you exaggerate. I will admit I find my studies enjoyable."

"I notice Miss Parker is the only young person here. Might I inquire, is she an only child, or has she siblings who reside elsewhere?"

"Abigail is our only child," her father explained.

"Plainly a beneficial circumstance, in this instance," Mr. Lewis said.

Her parents beamed while their daughter lowered her eyes.

"Do you have brothers or sisters?" Mrs. Parker asked.

"I have a sister, Catherine, who's a few months older than your daughter."

"What of your parents, Mr. Lewis? Do you and your sister yet reside with them?" Abigail asked.

A sullen air enveloped him as he said, "My parents are deceased."

Abigail recoiled, mortified to have made a social blunder. "I'm terribly sorry."

"How sad you've lost them," her mother said. "They must have been rather young, I would suppose?"

"They were. A tragic carriage accident took them from us, far too early."

"How dreadful for you and your sister. Was it a recent occurrence?" Mrs. Parker asked.

"It's been some time now," he recounted vaguely.

"A difficult time for your family, I've no doubt," Mrs. Parker assumed.

"Yes, quite difficult; however, one adjusts; what else can one do?"

"Nothing more, of course. We do extend our regrets for your loss," Mrs. Parker said.

Abigail gave him a smile of sympathy.

Mr. Lewis entered into a state of somber reflection, and Abigail worried her mistake had been egregious. To her relief, it wasn't long before he perked up.

"I'm greatly enjoying my time here. The University is more impressive than I could have imagined."

"Is this your first trip to Vienna?" Mr. Parker asked.

"In fact it is. In light of what I've seen, I may now visit frequently." Mr. Lewis glanced at Abigail.

He refers to the beauty of the region, not me, she thought.

"How long have you been in town?" Mrs. Parker asked.

"I arrived two weeks ago."

"Have you had the opportunity to tour the city?" Abigail asked.

"I've been fully entrenched in the early stages of my project, and therefore I haven't, a status I hope to remedy promptly. What I've encountered along the way is nothing short of magnificent. I'm looking forward to devoting more of my time to pleasure soon."

"While it's hardly Vienna's most impressive sight, we could begin your tour with a stroll through our garden," Mr. Parker proposed in a witty fashion.

Mr. Lewis joined in the humor. "A splendid idea. Undoubtedly it will be a marvelous introduction to your fair city."

The ladies collected their shawls before they all exited the house by way of the back door.

"This is a lovely garden," Mr. Lewis said.

"We enjoy it, though it isn't grand as other gardens may be," Mrs. Parker admitted. "You'll see it's composed primarily of wildflowers and indigenous greenery."

SUSAN BUTLER

"I find nothing deficient about nature. Many beautiful settings are chiefly natural," Mr. Lewis said.

Abigail smiled at his congeniality. They strolled side by side and shortly were several paces ahead of her parents.

He regarded her with evident admiration. "I do find much lovely about this setting, even that which is not indigenous."

She blushed and turned away, unable to shake off her tremulous sensation.

"Have I said or done something to offend you, Miss Parker?"

"No, you haven't in the least."

"And yet you've been rather standoffish towards me."

"I beg your pardon; it wasn't my intention."

"Please don't apologize. I merely wanted to learn the reason for your change of mind."

"I've had no change of mind. I wish I could explain my behavior, but to be honest, I'm not certain what's come over me. There's something about you I continue to find…overwhelming."

"You needn't be overwhelmed by me. I'm the same as any other man who's been attracted to the attributes of a most charming woman."

"You're very obliging." Her crooked lips and puckered brow signified her lack of conviction.

"You doubt me, perhaps due to the frequent compliments you've heard me extend. While I find the practice gratifying, I never flatter. This sentiment I cannot abide. Whenever I offer praise, you have my assurance it's nothing other than heartfelt and genuine."

They stopped strolling, and Abigail peered into Mr. Lewis's eyes. "I believe you. Somehow, I can sense your sincerity."

"Then please accept you've no cause to be intimidated by me, none whatsoever."

The corners of her mouth curled up as her discomfort faded away. When he returned the gesture, she caught her breath, for once again his eyes were smiling into hers.

They turned away from each other when her parents caught up with them.

"Tea will be served shortly. We should return to the house," Mr. Parker said.

"Mr. Lewis, would you care to join us?" Mrs. Parker offered.

"It would be a pleasure."

Abigail suppressed her desire to skip with joy as they returned to the house.

Back in the coziness of the parlor teatime was an amicable event. The Parkers related facts and details about Vienna and the University. Mr. Lewis spoke of the magnitude of the tasks involved in the construction of a building.

The conversation was lively, but as the afternoon grew late, Abigail's bright mood dimmed since Mr. Lewis would soon leave. Although it appeared he was enjoying his visit, and he continued to fawn over her, she wondered if she'd ever see him again. For some reason she doubted it, and so she was relieved by the answer he provided as he prepared to leave.

"Mr. Kruger was kind enough to procure four tickets to the theater tomorrow evening, apparently a fine production of 'Much Ado about Nothing'," Mr. Lewis said. "I'd be enormously pleased if you would agree to accompany me."

Abigail was unable to contain her enthusiasm. "Shakespeare; I adore his work! Are you fond of his plays?"

"My favorite playwright," Mr. Lewis claimed.

Her father rekindled the frivolity. "Obviously you have excellent taste. We'd be honored to accept your invitation."

"I'll arrive at six o'clock to collect you if that's suitable?"

"It will suit us admirably," Mr. Parker said.

Following their farewells, Abigail sighed, wrapped up in the pleasure of the moment. *This will be such fun. Mr. Lewis has interests similar to mine. Even so, I do wonder why he should find any interest in someone the likes of me. I must admit, I'm entirely intrigued by him and I do hope his interest in me will continue to grow.*

*****

Abigail was in a feverish state the next evening while she listened for the clipity-clop sound of horse hooves. She was seated in the library, near a window which provided a good view of the drive, where she'd been waiting for half an hour prior to Mr. Lewis's scheduled arrival time.

Finally, she noted the warning clatter and poked her head out the window to verify it was him. She hurried to inform her parents. "Mother, Father, Mr. Lewis has arrived."

When the door was answered, the Parkers went to the foyer to greet him.

"Good evening Mr. and Mrs. Parker, Miss Parker," Mr. Lewis said.

"Good evening, Mr. Lewis," they each returned.

"You ladies are stunning," their guest remarked.

"Why thank you, Mr. Lewis," Mrs. Parker said.

"Yes, thank you," Abigail echoed awkwardly.

Mr. Lewis checked his pocket watch. "As it appears everyone's prepared to depart, we should head to the carriage straight away," he said and led the way there.

They arrived at the theater thirty minutes later. The men stepped out of the carriage to assist the ladies. Mr. Parker took his wife's hand as she stepped down and Mr. Lewis took Abigail's.

"Miss Parker, may I offer you my escort?" he asked when she was on the ground safely.

"Thank you, Mr. Lewis."

He smiled warmly when she placed her hand on his arm. "We are fortunate, Mr. Parker, are we not, to have such attractive ladies accompany us this evening?"

"Assuredly we are," her father agreed.

His daughter blushed bright red.

They entered the theater, and after their coats were checked found their seats to await the play's start.

The performance was as reported a splendid rendition. When the curtain fell, the actors returned to receive their ovations. The applause died down, and the theater began to empty.

Mr. Lewis retrieved their coats before they returned to the carriage. Abigail thought they would head straight to the house and the evening would end until Mr. Lewis suggested they dine at one of Vienna's finest restaurants. To Abigail's delight, Mr. Parker accepted his hospitality.

While sharing a lovely meal, they discussed the play in depth. Abigail and her father expounded upon the merits of Shakespeare's work, and Mr. Lewis seemed pleased to benefit from their extensive knowledge. When they'd finished dessert, Abigail presumed another cup of coffee or brandy would be ordered; instead, Mr. Lewis consulted his watch and said due to an early start he must end the evening immediately. Given his sudden compulsion to leave, Abigail was convinced he'd begun to find her company boring. She believed once again she'd chased a man away, which made his question at their front door entirely unexpected.

"Mr. Kruger has informed me he's hosting a party for his son's birthday on Saturday. Will you by chance be in attendance?"

"I've replied to their invitation, confirming our intention to join them," Mr. Parker related.

Abigail was filled with happiness and relief.

"I'm very glad," Mr. Lewis said. "Thank you for joining me this evening, and indulging me graciously. I'll look forward to meeting you at the party."

"It is we who must thank you for your generosity," Mrs. Parker insisted.

"Indeed," Mr. Parker said. "Good night, then."

"Good night, Mr. Lewis, and thank you," Abigail said.

Her father guided her and her mother inside. When the door was secured, Abigail gave him a hug.

"Are you looking forward to the party?" Mr. Parker teased. "I quite understand. He is an amiable young man, particularly for one of his stature."

"Isn't he, Father?"

"He does convey a kindly and unassuming nature, not what one expects from a grand gentleman," her mother said.

"What a shame his stay is temporary. Well, it's late, so off to bed with you, Abigail."

"Yes, Mother. Good night, Father," she said, her mood now somber.

She gave them a kiss and trudged up the stairs. Her mother's comment had reminded her of the reality regarding Mr. Lewis, an admonition which was a bitter pill to swallow.

Abigail closed the bedroom door and leaned against it, her head hanging in despair. *I've met a man whose companionship I enjoy, who doesn't seem off-put by my temperament, and yet not only is his status far above mine, his time here will be short-lived. Why then does he show any interest in me? Am I merely a diversion for him while he's in Vienna? Or does he taunt me as a perverse form of amusement?*

She sat at her dressing table, her mirror image marred by gloom, and brooded as she contemplated the potential fate of the individual before her.

"There's nothing for it," Abigail said aloud. "Whatever the reality, I cannot deny my desire to be with Mr. Lewis. If he continues to seek my company I may as well agree; what else have I to do? But it must be in the spirit of an acquaintance *only*. If I relinquish my heart, his departure will be painful. It will be painful enough as it is, and I mustn't allow matters to become worse."

Abigail nodded to bolster her resolve and then stood to prepare for bed.

*****

Subsequent to the Krugers' party, Mr. Lewis did suggest another outing with Abigail and her parents, and soon another. Such invitations continued; their frequency increasing as the weeks passed. Initially, her parents were in attendance until they were sufficiently satisfied with the young man's character to allow his escort of their daughter alone.

Once their outings weren't chaperoned, it became obvious Mr. Lewis's interest in her was advancing beyond friendship. He was flirtatious, which caused Abigail to further question his motives. Nevertheless, given his allure, she found battling her emotions was useless. In the end, she surrendered her heart to the man whose charms she could no longer resist.

Convinced she was utterly yet futilely in love, Abigail glared at the woman in the mirror she thought had offered her words of wisdom. "The worst has happened, for when Mr. Lewis returns to England my heart will crumble into pieces. What say you now, dear advisor, how do you intend to atone for your failure?"

Words from the poetry of Alfred Lord Tennyson came to mind; "'Tis better to have loved and lost than never to have loved at all".

"You've had a taste of love. Offer yourself a kindness, and end this at once," her counselor decreed. Even as she said it, Abigail shook her head. "I'm wasting my breath, aren't I? Then bury your feelings deep inside. Don't allow yourself to fall prey to what could yet be a ploy. At the moment you still have your self-respect and the respect of others. This you must protect at all costs."

*****

After another week had passed, Mr. Lewis, though his desires were clear, had proven himself to be nothing other than a gentleman. For Abigail, this was both a relief and a burden since his forbearance had served to intensify her love. Of greater concern, she'd begun to entertain the idea he may be in love with her, and her determination to hide her affection was waning.

Most recently, Mr. Lewis had invited her to take an afternoon stroll through the botanic gardens of the University. His mood seemed odd to her: tense and distracted, he had shown little interest in what she'd said or done. She was afraid his attention had been captured by another and visualized him devoted to a woman of far greater stature and appeal than she. Whether this was the case or not, it was evident something was praying upon his mind. She hoped he would reveal it before she became overwrought with worry.

Following a lengthy walk, they spotted a bench where Mr. Lewis suggested they rest. When they sat, Abigail's back stiffened in preparation for the worst.

"I believe we've become close, Miss Parker. Would it be audacious of me to address you by your Christian name?"

His request provided her some reassurance. "Not at all."

"*Abigail*," he said tenderly. "I regret to inform you I must return to England hastily. I have concerns regarding my business which compel me to leave Vienna much earlier than I'd planned." Her face fell in despondency, for it appeared her suspicion was founded. "Considering it was your ancestral home, would you be disposed to the idea of returning there, or would you never wish to leave Austria?"

"I haven't returned in a long time. I'd love to visit."

"And what if the duration were far longer? Would you object to living there permanently?"

"I can't imagine how this would be possible."

"It seems I must explain myself fully; for there's an obvious way it could occur. Abigail, I'd like your permission to ask your father for your hand."

She was pleased to discover she'd been wrong about his intentions, and yet boggled by a proposition of this magnitude. "I…don't know what to say."

"I'm in love with you, Abigail, desperately in love. I thought you were a bit in love with me, though now you give me the impression it may not be so."

"Then I've given a false impression. I am in love with you, Mr. Lewis, more than a bit. I love you urgently, but I've attempted to hide my feelings. A marriage proposal from you never entered my mind, and I was certain my love for you was pointless."

"Why do you say this, Abigail? Have I said or done something which has caused you to doubt me? I thought my feelings for you had become apparent."

"Although I cannot deny they have, it seems incomprehensible I'm the person you'd choose to marry when your choices must be many."

"They are; however, I choose you, for you are the woman I love; you and no other."

Abigail envisioned entering his world. She had severe qualms it was within her capability. "Your wealth and position are frightening prospects for me. Surely you're aware yours is a life of which I'm unfamiliar."

"Over the years, women have claimed to love me, in the pursuit of a life such as mine. The fact it frightens you leads me to believe you'd love me, even if I were of lesser means. How would you answer me if that was the case?"

"I would say yes."

"Please, then, say yes to the man before you, the man who loves you in a deep and passionate way. Don't permit the circumstance to sway you. Say yes to who I am, regardless of what I am."

Abigail looked away to hide the answer she knew her eyes would betray.

Mr. Lewis turned her face gently towards his, as he'd done at the ball. "I'm still not a wolf you need avoid."

She laughed softly but said nothing.

"I beg you, don't leave me in suspense."

She lowered her eyes to think for a moment before she returned to his gaze. "Yes, Mr. Lewis, I will agree to marry you."

He smiled and kissed her hands repeatedly. "Thank you, Abigail, my darling. Thank you for making me very happy!"

Numerous people were strolling nearby, which prevented their chance for a proper kiss.

"Since time is short, we should go to your father at once."

"A sensible suggestion, Mr. Lewis," she teased.

"In light of our new relationship, I'd prefer you'd address me as Darrell."

"You mean what will likely become our relationship. I doubt my father will be prepared for our news, but I can predict his answer. My parents have become fond of you."

"As I am of them, particularly if they'll grant me this beautiful gift."

"You see me as a gift?" she jested.

"I see you as an amazing and wonderful woman, one I've fallen madly in love with to the point I can no longer fathom any happiness in my life without her."

"Oh, *that* sort of gift," Abigail joshed again. "I do love you, Mr. Darrell Lewis."

"You cannot imagine how ecstatic this makes me, and to be honest relieved, for I wasn't convinced of your feelings or your answer. Now it's resolved, we should return to your home."

Mr. Lewis helped her rise. He held Abigail in a far more intimate manner than he had previously as they walked to the carriage and then drove to her home.

When they entered the house, they happened upon her mother, who was in the hallway.

"Good afternoon, Mrs. Parker," Mr. Lewis greeted her. "Is Mr. Parker available? There's a matter I wish to discuss with him, at his earliest convenience."

"He's in his study. At the moment, he shouldn't be overly preoccupied."

"Thank you." Mr. Lewis knocked on the door. He awaited permission before he entered.

Mrs. Parker scrutinized her daughter. "Is he about to...has he...?"

"Yes, Mother, he has. Would you have thought it possible?"

"I'm not completely surprised since he's obviously come to admire you, but I wasn't aware of the depth of his feelings. You, on the other hand...well, let's say your emotions have been apparent for some time."

"It's been obvious? I was attempting not to be transparent."

"You were, though perhaps only to me. I'm happy for you, my darling daughter. He's a fine, upstanding young man."

"He truly is. The full impact of his proposal has yet to strike me, and I fear I'll awaken to find this has all been merely a dream."

The door to the study opened. Mr. Parker entered the hallway with his future son-in-law.

"Well, Abigail, it seems you would marry this young suitor, and I have granted my permission."

She leaped into his arms. "Thank you, Father!"

Her mother gave Mr. Lewis a squeeze. "Welcome to our family. It will be wonderful for us to have a son."

"Thank you, ma'am, sir; it's my great delight I'll be amongst you."

"I need to inform you, Abigail, of my stipulation regarding this event, a point upon which I refuse to yield," her father alerted her. "Your young man has requested you arrive at his home in advance of the wedding, to arrange the various plans and select your dress. Given my faith in your judgment, and his promise you'll remain chaperoned prior to the wedding, I will consent… on the condition, you finish your schooling first. You're mere months away from completion, and I won't allow you to depart prior."

"Yes, Father."

"I agree wholeheartedly with your terms, sir, for I'd accept nothing less myself," her betrothed said.

"Very well; and now, let us arrange a celebration feast for tonight," Mr. Parker said to his wife.

"Yes, we must have this," Mrs. Parker agreed. She left to consult with the cook while the others retired to the parlor.

*****

Following dinner, the family returned to the hallway to see the young man off. After saying their goodbyes her parents stood in the doorway, permitting Abigail to walk with him alone to the carriage.

"I suppose I may now refer to you as Darrell."

"Please do so." He took her hands in his. "My dearest Abigail, I regret to tell you I have back-to-back projects which will prevent my return to Vienna, prior to your arrival at Rochester Manor."

"But…that will require us to be apart for over half a year."

"It will, my sweet. At the moment it seems a long time; however, once you're there, we'll have the rest of our lives to spend together."

"The thought of it makes me so happy, and yet it's difficult for me to consider the future fondly while my heart is aching."

"Permit me, then, to leave you with a remembrance, a symbol of our eternal love."

Darrell removed a small box from his pocket and opened it to reveal a dazzling pearl and diamond engagement ring. Abigail emitted a "huh" when he slipped it on her finger.

"Does this token by chance ease your pain?"

"My gracious, it's hardly a token! It's stunning, perhaps too stunning for me."

"Nothing can compare with the beauty of my bride, but my intention is to please you with beautiful things."

"Any gift I receive from you, large or small, I'll cherish forever."

Darrell smiled and held her face as he gave her a gentle first kiss. "Promise me you'll keep yourself well."

"I promise I will."

He gazed into her eyes and kissed her once more before he boarded the carriage. "Goodbye, my darling."

"I'll write to you often; will you write to me in return?" Abigail asked through the window.

"I will, of course," Darrell said with an affectionate grin.

"Have a safe journey," Mrs. Parker called out. She waved as the carriage departed. Mr. Parker lifted his hand.

Abigail stepped towards the carriage to keep it in her sight a few moments longer. "Goodbye," she whispered, and soon

Darrell was out of view. She put her fingertips on her mouth, her lips still moist with his kiss. Although her first experience of intimacy had been exhilarating, combined with her sadness it was a strange mix of conflicting emotions.

She walked back to the house and raised her hand, so her parents may inspect the ring.

Her father patted her hand.

"It's lovely," her mother said as tears streamed down Abigail's face. "My dear child." She held her and rubbed her back soothingly. "Don't cry, the time will pass quickly, you'll see."

2

Waiting has the potential to be one of life's most tedious and undesirable activities. For Abigail, the seven-month interval to be reunited with her fiancé had been a hardship and the reason she'd celebrated her arrival with such enthusiasm. With her wait behind her, she waltzed down the stairs of the train. As she stepped onto the steamy platform, she heard footsteps and saw a lad was approaching her through the haze.

"Are you Miss Parker?" he asked.

"Yes, I am."

He tipped his hat. "I'm Robert, miss. I was sent from Rochester Manor to collect you. Please, follow me."

He gathered her bags and hoisted them onto the luggage hold of a luxurious carriage. He then offered his hand to assist her inside.

Once seated, Abigail leaned back with a sigh of contentment. She glanced at her hands folded on her lap, her attention caught by the sparkling of her engagement ring. The gift had, as promised, often been a source of comfort for her. When she'd had difficulty sleeping, she would gaze at the ring, able to relive the sensation of her first kiss, and the love she'd seen in Darrell's eyes when he'd placed it on her finger.

The carriage drew away. She was antsy with anticipation, for the short drive ahead was the only remaining barrier between her and Darrell. While they drove, Abigail reminisced about the vehemence with which she'd opposed attending that fateful summer ball. If Anna, Elsa, and Gerta hadn't convinced her to participate she wouldn't now be engaged, a fact they'd reminded her of frequently.

The first time her friends spied the ring entered Abigail's mind. A great deal of Elsa and Gerta's envy of her had been reignited, and Abigail could picture the scene as clearly as if it had transpired yesterday.

"You're engaged? I cannot believe this has happened! Why ever did we insist you attend that dance?" Elsa grumbled.

"And we turned you into a beautiful swan to boot," Gerta chimed in. "Anna; this was your idea, thereby *your* fault the rest of us lost out."

"Well, I for one am proud of any assistance I provided which helped secure my dear friend's happiness," Anna said. "You two must cease your moaning, and congratulate Abigail. This is a joy she rightfully deserves. There are still plenty of prosperous men available from whom we may choose."

"I suppose. Congratulations on your *vast* good fortune," Elsa offered with thinly veiled spite.

"Our very best," Gerta added halfheartedly.

Abigail smiled at them. "There is an important matter we've yet to discuss: I've no wish to get married without bridesmaids to attend me at the wedding."

"By all means," Elsa exclaimed. "We may then travel to England for the ceremony and stay at the Lewis's grandiose estate."

"This will afford us some consolation," Gerta said.

"I'm happy you've agreed. Hopefully, Anna, whose help I appreciate with all my heart, will be my maid of honor if you'll accept the role?"

Anna gave her a hug. "Dearest; how can you think I would consider turning you down? It will be my immense privilege."

The carriage took a sharp turn onto the drive of Rochester Manor. Abigail leaned out the window to catch the first glimpse of her new home. As they came around the final bend, the house loomed before her.

"Oh, my heavens," she muttered.

Despite her expectations, the estate was larger and grander than she'd anticipated. The front was an impressive sight, composed of two exaggerated stories of light-colored stone brick, boasting bayed sections on either side. Detailing under the steep roof of blue tile, along with the twenty-four arched windows, created a majestic effect. Single story wings extended past each of the bays and then turned at ninety degrees towards the back of the house.

The drive circled around a grassy area near the front entrance, in the center of which was a huge fountain. Abigail visualized the line of coaches which would form prior to sizable events, carrying guests who donned extravagant attire, furs, and jewels. Until this minute, she'd given little consideration to the probable caliber of Darrell's acquaintances and family. She wondered how they would react to her modest background and envisioned herself cowering upon each introduction. With her scant knowledge of the topics and habits prominent people practice, she worried they would think her a fool.

More troublesome to her, as hostess, she would have the task of overseeing the details of these gatherings, an alarming prospect for a girl who'd never arranged a party. She hoped Darrell's sister, who she presumed would currently be in charge of such matters, would offer her help; although, Abigail reasoned her ignorance pertaining to this would be a strike against her.

They stopped at the entryway, where the driver assisted her to exit from the carriage. He seemed aware of her intimidation and gave her a kind smile as he knocked on the door. When it opened, Robert again tipped his hat. "Best of luck to you," he said before he climbed back on board and drove away.

"Welcome, miss, we've been expecting your arrival," the man at the door said. He stood aside to allow her entry.

It came as no surprise when she found the interior of the house was as lavish as the exterior. Over the floor of inlaid wood hung an enormous crystal chandelier, which extended from the second story. At the foyer's end was a balcony, where the staircase began on either side and converged at the landing to descend as one long case. The stairs were covered in rich blue carpeting, with handrails of dark wood supported by an intricate iron structure.

I truly am Cinderella, arriving at her prince's castle for the first time, she thought and pictured herself negotiating the staircase attired in a ball gown and tiara. *I'd best practice carrying myself gracefully. I doubt the guests will be impressed should I stumble my way to the floor.*

"Mr. Lewis requested I escort you to his study directly," the servant related.

As he led Abigail down a passageway, she observed the light-colored walls adorned with ornate moldings, from which hung numerous portraits and paintings. Recognizing many of the artists, she supposed their value was indeterminable.

At the study, the footman knocked on the door. Abigail's heart soared when the person whose voice she'd been yearning to hear granted his permission to enter.

"Miss Parker, sir," the man announced and bowed to take his leave.

Darrell was seated behind his large desk of mahogany, the character of this room dark, with wood paneling and maroon upholstery. He stood and held out his arms. "My dearest love, you've arrived at last."

Abigail rushed to enter his embrace. "I've been counting the minutes, Darrell. Our time apart seemed an eternity. I wasn't certain I could survive."

"But you're here now, safe and sound," he said. He kissed her gently. "Have you been well since your last letter? Please tell me, how are your parents?"

"We've all been quite well."

"I must say at the moment you appear exhausted. Of course, you'll want to bathe and recuperate from your journey. I'll call for your maid."

"You would call her when I've just arrived?"

"My apologies, dearest, there are a few pressing matters I must address prior to dinner. And it will do you good to have some rest."

He rang the nearby bell rope.

"What of your sister; isn't it rude to neglect our introduction?"

"Catherine is resting as well. You'll meet her at dinner."

A knock came a short while later. After Darrell opened the door, a young woman entered, lanky yet sprightly with dark red hair. Abigail estimated her age was close to her own; if anything, she appeared to be a tad younger.

"This is your personal maid, Mary Harrison," he said.

The girl curtseyed, and Abigail nodded.

"Take Miss Parker to her quarters. See she's settled in comfortably."

"Yes, sir."

"As it's past tea, Harrison may deliver a tray to your room if you're in need of refreshment," he told Abigail.

"Thank you," she replied in a somber tone.

Darrell kissed her cheek. "Rest well, my darling."

He returned to his desk and sorted through some papers.

Abigail begrudgingly followed the maid, wincing from the sting of his abrupt dismissal. In light of their seven-month separation, it was difficult for her to believe he couldn't spare a bit more of his time.

He didn't appear overwhelmed to see me, she thought. *Something must be wrong. Perhaps his love has diminished, or he's met a woman he'd prefer to marry. If this is so, why hasn't he broken the engagement? Being a man of honor possibly he's decided he won't; at least, not yet.*

They arrived at her bedroom, which Abigail surveyed with a tinge of disappointment. The relatively small room, far less impressive than her own in Vienna, could be perceived as belittling to a woman in her position. The furnishings of rosewood were practical for a house of this magnitude, including a desk, a short dressing table, several unpadded chairs, and a sleigh bed topped with a nondescript coverlet. Two windows, flanked by sensible white curtains, had a view of a courtyard but provided merely sufficient illumination. Pastel flowered wallpaper added a modicum of cheer to a room which was otherwise bland.

Mary, it seemed, could sense her disillusionment. "The master wanted me to explain this room is yours only for a while. Once married, you'll move into his suite on the other side of the floor. He had the wing renovated, and left your chambers empty to furnish as you please. He must love you very much to offer such an extraordinary wedding gift."

Abigail found a level of solace in her assertion. "It sounds most generous. Did he restore the rooms of the late master and mistress of the house?"

"No, miss, they remain intact on the first floor."

"That's understandable, given the tragedy he's suffered."

"Far and away he has. Would you like to see the apartment you'll occupy?"

"You've been there?"

"I have."

"Surely the master will mind?"

"Since the rooms are to be yours, I can't imagine he would. As long as we're careful, he'll have no call to mind," Mary said slyly.

Ordinarily, Abigail would have considered it improper to inspect the suite without first consulting Darrell. Caught up in the excitement of her co-conspirator her curiosity overruled her judgment. "Very well; let's see it."

They snuck down the hallway, pausing to peek over the balcony to confirm no one was nearby. With the coast clear, they scampered to the door at the far end. Mary flung it open with a dramatic gesture.

Abigail's jaw dropped at the sight of the enormous room, lined with windows which covered two walls. The late afternoon sun made the space all the more impressive.

"Is the master not thoughtful?" Mary asked. "He saved the corner room for you, being the largest and brightest. Come and see your view." She opened a balcony door.

Abigail gasped when she stepped outside. Much of the property could be seen, in one direction the front lawns, and the other a path leading to well-manicured gardens.

Back inside, Mary guided her to the opposite wall. "In here is your bathing and dressing area. It's nearly as large as your bedroom and incredibly splendid," she said as she unlatched the concealed door.

Her description wasn't an exaggeration. The room was elaborate, with an ornate tub, a large dressing table topped with a gold framed mirror, and huge armoires situated at the side walls.

From there they entered a joint sitting area, already furnished with stylish chairs, sofas, and a small desk. These fabrics were rich in jewel-toned patterns, welcoming for both a man and a woman. Abigail assumed they'd been selected for that purpose.

When Mary continued, Abigail became alarmed, certain the next rooms would be Darrell's. "We mustn't venture in there."

"Maids and his valet are allowed. Since you're to be mistress of the house, there's no reason you shouldn't be."

"I'm not mistress yet."

Mary grinned coyly and entered.

Abigail recalled her friends' advice: *don't be a wet blanket.* She mustered her courage and followed Mary.

Although she considered it wrong to invade Darrell's privacy, she was fascinated by his possessions. His dressing robe was hung by his wash basin, the touch of the fabric soft as Abigail caressed it with her fingers. To her surprise, she imagined him wearing the garment and wondered how he would appear when he removed it. The beating of her heart quickened.

The door to his bedchamber was open. With her curiosity at a peak, Abigail stole inside. The heavy dark wood

41

furnishings and materials of amber and green in this room were distinctly masculine.

Mary gave her a sassy wink, indicating the large bed.

Abigail, on the point of hyperventilation, rushed to her room.

Her maid followed her. "Are you alright, miss?"

"This is overwhelming. I haven't the slightest idea how to furnish rooms of any size, and mine are massive. However shall I choose when the choices must be nearly endless?"

"The master can't expect you to tackle the project alone, and you've plenty of time. Would you care for some tea now, or would you prefer to rest?"

"At the moment, I've no appetite whatsoever."

Mary removed Abigail's travel clothes before she led her to bed. "Shall I return at seven o'clock to help you wash and dress?"

Abigail nodded. After Mary left, she held her forehead, assuming she'd taken leave of her senses when she'd agreed to become mistress of the estate. *Perhaps Darrell has reconsidered the wisdom of our marriage, and the furnishing of those rooms is meant to be a test of my ability, not a gift. He may foresee my failure, which would grant him just cause to break the engagement. If this is his plan, he needn't wait. He could save us both a great deal of trouble by ridding himself of me without delay!*

She rolled over and drew the covers over her head.

*****

Initially napping in a restless state, Abigail eventually drifted into an exhausted sleep. When a nudge startled her, she found Mary standing by the bed. She directed Abigail to the bathing room.

While she soaked in the warm water, Abigail attempted to calm herself. *It's irrational to form conclusions until I'm certain of the facts. I must appear confident when I meet Catherine. I doubt her opinion of me will be favorable if I act like a dunderhead.*

At eight o'clock Mary showed her to the library, where Darrell and Catherine were waiting.

Abigail was immediately struck by his sister's beauty. Her frame was curvaceous yet svelte, with a stature several inches taller than her own. She sported the same dark brunette hair as her brother, which was handsomely styled. Her eyes were so intensely blue, they matched the color of her exquisitely detailed sapphire gown. Abigail glanced remorsefully at her austere lavender dress, which she knew paled by comparison. Of greater consequence to her, Catherine exuded an air of maturity and sophistication she thought was lacking in herself, an observation which did nothing to improve her self-assurance.

Darrell took her hand and kissed it warmly. "Did you rest well, my darling?"

Abigail was consoled by the tenderness of his manner. "I did, thank you."

He raised his hand towards his sister. "Abigail, this is my sister, Catherine. Catherine, this is Abigail."

"I've been looking most forward to meeting you," Abigail said.

"A pleasure," Catherine returned coldly.

A servant entered to announce dinner was served.

"Shall we?" Darrell said.

He offered Abigail his arm. After he helped the ladies be seated, he sat at the table's head, his sister and fiancé at either side.

"How was your journey, dearest?" he asked Abigail. "I didn't inquire about it earlier, did I?"

"All in all it was pleasant. The Express d'Orient was lovely as ever; I'd nearly forgotten what a treat it is to ride. The other trains were nice, and thankfully on time. The only problem I encountered was the channel crossing. Rough waters delayed the journey, which didn't suit me since the duration of the trip was lengthier than I'd recalled."

Darrell's eyes sparkled as he smiled, but Catherine smirked. "I find it amusing you were in a hurry to arrive," she said.

Abigail was thrown off by her comment. Darrell was observably disgruntled.

"Are you pleased with your new home?" he asked, presumably to steer the discussion in another direction. "Of course, you haven't had the opportunity to take in much. Tomorrow I'll show you more."

"*More* you notice he says, not all," Catherine said insolently.

Abigail perceived tension was rising between them and thought it wise to interject. "I imagine a house of this size must be difficult to view in one day. What I've come upon is beautiful, and my room is most comfortable."

"Naturally your room is comfortable. Darrell wouldn't allow *yours* to be uncomfortable," his sister taunted.

"Catherine; there's no call to be rude," he said.

"From *your* perspective, perhaps," she scoffed.

"Is Harrison agreeable to you?" Darrell asked Abigail, his attempt to change the subject now clear. "Has her service been satisfactory?"

"Far beyond satisfactory; I believe we'll get along nicely."

"It would seem the two of you prefer to discuss only mundane things," Catherine groused. "How can you behave nonchalantly with all which takes place in this house?"

"This is my betrothed's first night with us. The conversation should be welcoming."

"Indeed, heaven *forbid* we'd broach a controversial topic, despite its importance," his sister retorted.

"If I take your meaning, you're well aware of my position. The topic won't be open for discussion, not at any time," Darrell said firmly.

Abigail listened in dismay. *Is this conversation about me? Does she think our marriage is beneath him? I believe she must.*

"Well then, dear brother, what shall we discuss, the size of your shoes? Is this sufficiently banal for you?"

"Speak impolitely another time, and I'll ask you to leave the table," Darrell warned her.

"There's no need," Catherine said. "Tonight, I'd prefer to dine with someone else."

"On this one occasion, it may be for the best, with the stipulation Jake and Eleanor attend as well. Should you choose to disregard my wishes, I will discover you."

"*That* you have made abundantly clear," Catherine said in irreverence as she stood. She lifted her chin in a haughty fashion before she left the room.

Tears trickled down Abigail's face.

"My dearest; don't permit my sister to upset you."

"Obviously, she doesn't care for me."

"I apologize for her conduct, but you mustn't take it personally. Please understand; she has yet to recover from our parents' death. Since then she's come to view outsiders as intruders. She treats all of our guests with the same audacity."

"Oh, I see. When did you lose them?"

"Barely a year ago. Their loss hit her particularly hard. Her temperament, which was once sweet, has become intolerant and disagreeable."

"I'm sorry, Darrell. I'd be devastated if such a tragedy happened to me. Is she terribly unhappy about our marriage?"

"Regrettably she is. I've been trying to convince her; your gentle nature will be beneficial to our family. While I was hoping she'd welcome your arrival, I was expecting too much too soon."

"I'll make every effort to befriend her, with a great deal of prudence. Perhaps one day she'll accept me and become more of the sister I never had. Although I would love this, you have my assurance I won't press the matter."

"It's kind of you to be patient. I'm optimistic another young woman in the house will provide her with the companionship she requires to recover."

"I'll do my utmost. I want to make you happy, which could prove to be challenging under the circumstance."

"You needn't worry. My love for you cannot be diminished by interference of any sort."

Darrell pressed her hand between his, his eyes smiling as they often had in Vienna.

Abigail was now ashamed to have questioned his love, or the intentions of his wedding present. She was also relieved she'd misunderstood his sister's conduct towards her. Reassured her fiancé's adoration hadn't faltered she was able to relax and enjoyed her first meal in her new home.

*****

Following dinner, Abigail retired immediately at Darrell's recommendation. While reluctant to part his company, she had to admit it was unavoidable. Her body was aching, her eyelids too heavy to remain open.

Exhausted as she was, with Catherine's harsh remarks ringing in her head Abigail had difficulty falling asleep. It was a disappointment to discover she couldn't rely on her help with the supervision of this imposing household. Merely winning the smallest bit of her approval seemed a tall order.

After tossing about for some time, it occurred to her self-pity wouldn't solve any problem. She focused instead on a solution and concluded the best option was to remain patient with Catherine, regardless of how she was treated in return. Ongoing tolerance, she hoped, would ultimately soften her posture. Perhaps they could then become allies.

With her mind settled Abigail rolled over. She was on the verge of nodding off when Catherine's desire to dine with another came to mind. *I wonder to whom she referred, and why Darrell insisted she didn't dine with this individual alone. Given the spontaneity, the person must have been in the house. If they were, why weren't they dining with us? I could ask Darrell; although, it would be prying into an obviously sensitive subject. Surely, I'll be introduced to whomever it is eventually; how could it be avoided?*

Despite her logic, this was a matter Abigail found hard to put aside. She continued to puzzle over it until fatigue won out, and she drifted into a sound sleep.

*****

Abigail's eyelids fluttered as they lifted slowly in the sunlight. For a moment she was disoriented until she recognized the furnishings of her new bedroom.

I've spent my first night at Rochester Manor, she thought. *Thank goodness it's morning; I long to be with Darrell, and the sooner, the better.*

Her urgency caused her to snicker. How childish she decided it was to be missing him, when unlike the mornings of the last seven months he was nearby, down the hall unless he was an early riser. She pictured him in the room where she'd stood the previous afternoon, rising from the bed Mary had winked at, while his valet assisted him with the robe she'd touched. Again she imagined him removing his robe, and speculated what would happen next. For her the idea was enticing and to a degree unnerving. A shiver coursed through her body.

A rapid knock startled Abigail back to reality. She sat up and shook her shoulders to ward off the effects of her fantasizing before she called out, "Come in!"

Her maid entered. "Ah, miss, you're up. Shall I prepare you to join the master for breakfast? He'll dine in about half an hour."

"Yes, Mary, please. Do you mind my use of your Christian name? I've never had a personal maid. Although I should use your surname, I'd find it more agreeable otherwise."

"Since I've never been a personal maid, I wouldn't mind in the least."

"With the two of us wading in uncharted territory, I believe we have much in common."

Mary seemed gratified by the affability.

Abigail walked to her armoire. She sorted through her clothes, determined to achieve Catherine's impressive appearance; at least to the extent possible.

"Mary, which dress do you suppose best suits me?"

"This blue dress will bring out the color of your eyes."

Mary placed the garment on the bed before she directed her lady to the dressing table.

Abigail rotated her head as she regarded her image critically. "Would a different hairstyle be preferable? Perhaps you could add ribbons or some such adornment?"

"We'll be certain you're most handsome, miss," she said with a knowing grin.

Once the preparations were complete, Abigail considered her reflection, pleased with the result. "You've done wonderfully, Mary."

"I'm glad you think so, miss."

She helped Abigail rise and opened the door for her.

As she descended the stairs, Abigail practiced carrying herself with grace. At the dining room, she smoothed her dress and ensured her posture was perfect prior to her entrance.

Darrell, seated alone, rose to embrace her. "Good morning, dearest."

"Good morning, Darrell. Will Catherine arrive soon?"

"She'll be taking breakfast in her room."

"She will?" Abigail asked with discernible disappointment.

"This isn't meant to be a slight. It's her habit to sleep late. You're especially lovely this morning. I believe Rochester Manor agrees with you."

"Thank you, Darrell." She knew there are men who wouldn't have noticed and appreciated the thoughtfulness of his acknowledgement.

He kissed her cheek adoringly while he helped her be seated.

"What may I bring you, my darling?" He indicated the sideboard.

"Whatever you're having, I will also."

After delivering their plates, he took his seat. "Did you sleep well, my dear? Was the bed sufficiently comfortable?"

"Utterly comfortable. In fact, I slept so soundly it took me a moment to recall where I was."

"Since you're well rested, with this pleasant weather I thought we'd begin your tour with a stroll through the gardens."

"I would never object to that. I should imagine the grounds here are exceptional, with perhaps a tad more than wildflowers?"

Darrell chuckled. "I must admit they are beautiful with the flowers in the early stage of bloom. You *will* find we have our share of wildflowers."

When they'd finished their meal, he opened a window. "The air is yet cool. You should wear a shawl."

"It will be warm shortly. I'll be fine without one."

"You mustn't risk a chill. I'll have Harrison bring it."

"There's no need to call her. It won't take a minute to fetch a wrap myself."

"It is the duty of a personal maid to assist you in this manner," he said as he pulled the cord.

Mary responded promptly, and Darrell assigned her the errand. "We'll meet you at the back door."

When he escorted Abigail there, she discovered a rear corridor. "I didn't notice the house had a third wing when I arrived."

"This is the east wing. It forms two courtyards in conjunction with the north and south wings."

After Mary returned with the garment Abigail and Darrell stepped outside.

"This is a lovely setting," Abigail said, noting the ivy-covered walls of the patio.

"I believed it would please you," Darrell said and offered her his arm.

They proceeded down the pathway which led to the gardens. As they passed an adjoining wing, Abigail was astounded to discover it had no windows. With patches of brick, different from the rest of the house in color and pattern where windows ought to be, she realized this was not an original feature.

"Why are these windows bricked over?" she asked.

Darrell hesitated, apparently in contemplation. "We suffered a terrible storm a while back. It destroyed all the glass in this wing, which is no longer used. Being subject to the brunt of inclement weather, I elected to encase them."

"A sensible decision," she claimed.

In truth, Abigail was unable to comprehend the concept. She considered the variance of the bricks unattractive and doubted storms of such power were so recurrent the windows' repair wasn't warranted. She knew he didn't lack the wherewithal to procure a qualified carpenter. Deeming it inappropriate to challenge his judgment regarding a house that wasn't yet hers, she kept her thoughts to herself.

Upon the resumption of their walk, she could tell Darrell was uncomfortable, his sheepish expression an indication he had lied. Whatever his reason, Abigail was convinced there were facts regarding the circumstance he didn't wish to divulge.

They ambled ahead through the lawns. In a while, they came across a stone staircase which overlooked various plots. This was a vista rarely seen in a private setting.

"How exquisite," Abigail exclaimed.

He grinned fondly.

She admired the view for several minutes before they descended the case. First, they entered a boxwood garden, where shrubs lining a pebbled path meandered through planting areas filled with flowers. Next came a rose garden. Although it was too early for the bushes to be in bloom, the space would undoubtedly be spectacular when summer arrived. Following this was an herb and wildflower garden, and off to the side, a vegetable patch.

Past these areas a large greenhouse emerged, comprised of massive windows supported by the same stone brick as the house. They wandered amongst the lush plants, flowers, and fountains until they found a bench, and decided to rest.

"This reminds me of the setting we were in when I proposed to you. Here, however, we have the advantage of privacy," Darrell said.

He gazed into Abigail's eyes, and she could see his desire to kiss her. When she leaned forward, he touched her lips with his. As their kiss built in intensity, their ardor grew. An unfamiliar tantalizing sensation enveloped her.

"Abigail, I adore you," he paused to declare.

"As I love you, Darrell, so very, *very* much," she said and returned to his embrace.

When they'd separated, the smoldering appearance in Darrell's eyes reflected her impassioned response to their first intimacy. Abigail laid her head on his shoulder while he caressed her back and kissed her on the forehead.

"We should return to the house," Darrell said.

He placed his arm around her. She clung to him as they walked outside.

They returned via the same path and again passed the wing with the bricked-up windows. His mystifying explanation of them reminded her of the mystery she'd set aside; the individual Catherine spoke of the previous evening.

Was it a romantic interest of hers, perhaps a nearby neighbor, Abigail speculated. *That would fit since Darrell insisted she dine in the company of chaperones. And it didn't sound as though he entirely approved of their meeting. Who other than a prospective suitor would be the cause of such concern?*

Intrigued, she put curiosity ahead of etiquette. "Darrell, I hope you don't mind my asking; with whom did Catherine dine last night? Was the individual in the house, or somewhere nearby?"

He halted and released her arm. "I do in fact mind. What would lead you to pose these rude questions?"

"I was merely curious."

"A flimsy excuse for ill manners. If your knowledge was essential, I would inform you."

Having never witnessed the slightest ill temperament in Darrell she was unprepared for the gruffness of his retort, particularly when he could have simply declined to answer. "Of course, you would. I beg your pardon."

He frowned, apparently chewing the matter over.

"Please, Darrell, it wasn't my intention to be discourteous."

He didn't respond for what seemed a long time. She wondered what he could be deliberating about.

"I accept your apology," he said at last. "I may have overreacted, but you mustn't repeat an infraction of this sort."

"You have my word, I won't."

"Then we'll consider the issue resolved."

Although Darrell offered Abigail his arm, a conspicuous strain lingered between them as they arrived at the house.

"It would be wise for you to rest until luncheon," Darrell said, in a manner which implied insistence.

"Yes, I believe I will. I am rather tired."

Nodding to indicate her dismissal he departed, without further comment or show of affection.

Abigail headed glumly to her room. *He's still irked with me. Why would he hide a person's identity, and become affronted to such an extent when I requested he reveal it? And what is the true reason those windows have been bricked up? Storm my foot!*

Another of Catherine's comments came to mind when she'd accused her brother of nonchalant behavior with "all which takes place in this house". *To what did she refer? What is the situation here? Whatever it is, I hope I'll find out soon. Given how upset Catherine was last night, it cannot be good.*

*****

When the luncheon hour arrived, Abigail returned to the dining room. She entered warily.

"Good afternoon, Darrell, Catherine."

"Good afternoon," Catherine replied curtly.

"Did you rest well?" Darrell asked; his cold delivery in contrast to the thoughtfulness of his question.

"I did, thank you."

He helped Abigail be seated, without taking her hand as he'd done previously.

"Did you view the house this morning?" Catherine asked snottily. "You're correct, Abigail, it will require more than a day for you to discover all there is…" she began, until Darrell scowled at her in a manner which appeared to be a warning.

"We explored the grounds. Your brother was kind enough to show me your lovely gardens and greenhouse."

"This is a good day for the gardens. Will you tour indoors this afternoon, Darrell?" Catherine's tone remained haughty.

Her inference evidently disgruntled him. "I may not have the time."

"That would be a shame, would it not?" Catherine sassed him.

Darrell's eyes narrowed. "The shame is your attitude."

Catherine snarled. Abigail sensed she wanted to comment additionally, but her brother's stern glares apparently prevented her. With the tension between the siblings growing, she thought it best to refrain from conversation.

When they'd finished their meal, Catherine said she would take a turn through the grounds alone. Darrell stated he had business which required his attention and didn't wish to be disturbed.

"Darrell, may I have a word with you?" Abigail implored. "I promise to take only a few moments of your time."

"Very well."

He escorted her to the study, where he stood with his arms folded.

"It's clear you haven't forgiven me for my rudeness earlier. Please, could you find it in your heart to pardon me?" she asked.

Darrell's expression softened. He took her hands in his. "I'm sorry, Abigail. I was short with you at luncheon. It must have appeared I remain irritated with you. In truth, I do not. It was unkind of me to treat you callously."

"Then, you do forgive me?"

"I do. I was far more cross than the incident warranted. Now, I must ask for forgiveness."

"There isn't any need. It was wrong of me to pry. You had every right to be aggravated."

"I hadn't the right at all. Your questions were common enough, and naturally, you'd be curious. I should have explained I cannot tell you rather than become annoyed."

Darrell held her for several minutes. "Are you better now?"

"Yes, much better."

"Would you care to continue our exploration?"

"You said pressing business matters may prevent us."

"There's nothing so pressing it cannot wait until tomorrow," Darrell confessed. "Come; let us begin."

Upon exiting his study on the north side of the house, he led her down the main hallway. While glad he had apologized, she was troubled by his terminology. *Why is it he **cannot** tell me this person's identity? If he spoke correctly, it would mean either he doesn't know, which is nearly incomprehensible or isn't at liberty to say, although; in this instance, he should have said he **may not** tell me. Otherwise, it's a matter of he **will not** tell me. He must know his grammar, and it's possible he used the term deliberately as a means of deception. I suppose it may have been a slip of the tongue, but after his harsh response when I raised the question, I doubt that was the case.*

They arrived at the foyer and crossed over it to tour the south side of the house. First was the formal parlor, followed by the library. Next was a long corridor leading to the doors of the single-story south wing, where he related the servants' quarters were housed. Beyond this came the dining room, pantry, and kitchen.

As they viewed the area, she met Mr. Williams, the butler, and Mrs. Williams, the head housekeeper. Mr. and Mrs. Williams turned out to be the "Jake" and "Eleanor" Darrell insisted accompany Catherine at dinner the previous evening. He told her they'd been with the family since before he and his sister were born, and were as a father and mother to them, even prior to their parents' passing. Given the fondness of their relationship, he explained they address one another by their Christian names.

Jake, a man of average height and stature in his mid-fifties, was in the pantry overseeing the care of the silver service. He conveyed an air of strict formality, his manner proper as he bowed upon introduction. "A distinct pleasure to have you with us, Miss Abigail."

"It's a pleasure to meet you."

Apparently a man of few words, he said nothing further. He excused himself to resume his duties.

Darrell and Abigail departed the pantry. They proceeded to the kitchen where Eleanor was attending to the staff in her charge. A few years younger than Jake, she was petite like Abigail and a little stocky, her appearance strong for her height. Unlike her husband, her personality was exceptionally jovial and outgoing.

She gave Abigail a warm hug. "Welcome, my dear. Darrell has described in detail how sweet, and pretty you are. I've been keen to meet you."

"My depiction wasn't exaggerated, don't you agree, Eleanor?" he asked.

"I agree completely."

Abigail was embarrassed. "Thank you. I'm happy to make your acquaintance."

"Are you settling in comfortably, I hope? Is Harrison performing her duties sufficiently?" Eleanor asked.

"She is and has already proven helpful to me."

"That's good to hear. You need only say if you require anything she's unable to provide. Should my staff fall short of your expectations, you must tell me at once."

"I don't anticipate difficulties. This household and staff are obviously kept in excellent order."

"A nice compliment, but please be warned some of these younger girls can be flighty and careless, regardless of how many times I reprimand them."

Abigail's spirits rose as Eleanor related additional information pertaining to the estate, evident to her this was a kindhearted woman whose assistance would be invaluable.

"We should carry on, having detained you long enough," Darrell said a short while later.

"It's been a pleasure to make your acquaintance. Thank you for making me feel welcome," Abigail said.

Eleanor patted her hand. "I'm glad you've joined us, such a sweet and charming young lady you are. You two run along now."

They made their way to the rear of the house, where the banquet room was located. Past this was the corridor which led to the east wing. Darrell explained it was comprised of typical guest accommodations. He suggested they not bother venturing in, which caused Abigail to wonder if the anonymous person was residing there.

Subsequent to the wing was the ballroom. After they took a peek inside, they ascended to the second story by way of the back stairs. These led to the ladies' wing where Abigail's bedroom, Catherine's bedroom, a boudoir, and bathing facilities were located. Since she was familiar with the area, they passed through and headed to the marriage suite.

When Darrell opened the door of the bridal chamber, it was plain he anticipated her astonishment. Convinced it would be difficult and devious to appear amazed she made no attempt to play act but hung her head in shame.

"Abigail, is something wrong? Does the room seem inadequate?"

"Not at all; it's beyond adequate of course. I must confess this isn't my first visit; I was here yesterday."

"How was that?"

"Harrison told me of your gift. I was impatient to see it and insisted she must bring me here at once."

"I instructed her to inform you of the suite, which would imply my permission. These rooms are yours to view whenever you like; although, I appreciate your honesty."

"I'm afraid this isn't all there is to the matter. I entered your rooms as well, a stark invasion of your privacy. That was categorically wrong of me. I've no excuse to offer for my insolence."

To her amazement, Darrell grinned. "Why do you believe the thought of you in my bedroom would displease me? It doesn't at all; in fact, I hope in the near future you'll invade my privacy frequently."

Abigail blushed. "I thought of you when I found your robe…" She stopped, too shy to reveal she'd touched it, and imagined doing so while he wore the garment.

Darrell pulled her into his arms and kissed her passionately until she trembled.

"When I claimed I'm not a wolf, it wasn't altogether true. There is a bit of the wolf in me, only I've been keeping him at bay until I may honorably unleash him." He kissed her once more before he released her. "Now tell me; are you pleased with your rooms?"

"They're beautiful. It seems to me you've been too generous, for I didn't expect them to be grand."

"Precisely the point. I knew you'd appreciate my gesture when others would insist on the grandeur."

"Thank you then, Darrell. It was thoughtful of you, but *others* would undoubtedly have the talent to furnish rooms of such magnitude. I have no skill for it. You may be disappointed with the result."

"You don't imagine I possess the talent? I related my preferences to those I hired for the purpose and allowed them to implement the details. Rest assured you'll have as much help as you require. When I'm here with you, I won't notice the furnishings. You need only consider what pleases you."

"It's kind of you to show patience with my uneasiness."

"There should never be any call for you to be uneasy. Come now, it's nearly tea time. Let's return downstairs."

Darrell took Abigail's arm and rubbed it affectionately as they departed the suite. In light of his tender attitude, she was glad she'd revealed the truth since it had been tempting to keep it hidden.

After descending the grand staircase, they returned to the north side of the house, bypassing his study to inspect the billiards room which followed.

When they left Abigail found his pace slowed considerably, as if he was reluctant to continue. They arrived at a dim corridor, where his face contorted in a peculiar manner. As with the south side wing, there were doors at the end of the hallway, but these he stared at in an aberrant fashion, his expression at the same time unsettled, morose, and distant.

"This is the north wing. My parents' rooms are located here." Darrell's tone matched his appearance. "Upon their death, I had it closed permanently. I refuse to have their belongings disturbed. No one, including the servants, is allowed inside for any reason. With my memories troubling, it's my wish you avoid this part of the house. Do I make myself clear?" His voice mimicked the sternness of a parent forbidding his child.

"I understand, Darrell."

"To ignore this would injure me, as one could wound me with a knife."

"I would never hurt you intentionally."

"Very well. Next is the conservatory. We'll have a quick look, and then head for tea."

Darrell opened the nearby door. The pleasant ambiance of the solarium surmounted the gloom of the north wing, which helped to ease the tension. Sunbeams showcased the many varieties of potted plants, while thickly cushioned chaise lounges beckoned one to relax.

"What a lovely setting," she said.

"The atmosphere is appealing. It's a room you may wish to enjoy often. When you do, enter by way of the back corridor only."

"I will," Abigail promised.

"Now, we'll retire to the library."

The vehemence with which Darrell had banned her concerned her greatly. She thought of Catherine's comment, her doubt they would tour the entire house, and it dawned on her she'd likely referenced the north wing. *This could explain her behavior. She may be bitter due to the denial of her parents' rooms. Perhaps she seeks access to her mother's possessions. To be deprived of them would be painful for me.*

It then struck her this was the wing with the bricked-up windows. Had Darrell inadvertently provided the true reason for their enclosure? she wondered. The moment the notion occurred to her she dismissed it since dark curtains would be an equally effective and simpler solution.

They arrived at the library to find Catherine was awaiting them.

"I gather you did acquaint Abigail with the inside of the house," she remarked in her usual surly tenor.

"I did," Darrell replied.

"Did you view the *entire* house?" she asked Abigail.

"*Yes,* sister, she did," Darrell answered. "With the obvious exception of the north wing, which I've explained is forbidden."

"And that's all you've told her, I suppose?"

"She's been informed of all which is pertinent."

"Then you didn't disclose everything, *did* you?" Catherine accused, her obstinacy increasing.

"I believe I've made myself plain; Abigail understands what she requires."

"How convenient for you."

"*Catherine, that will do;* this conversation is to be dropped, never to be broached again."

His sister leaned back in a huff and brooded as she drank her tea.

Although Abigail's concern was escalating, it was now evident Catherine's antagonism was targeted towards Darrell. In an attempt to alleviate the strain, Abigail offered compliments about the house and staff. The mood, however, didn't improve.

When teatime ended Abigail excused herself to rest before dinner. She sat on her bed and stared blankly, dazed by the numerous disconcerting developments which had surfaced following her arrival, barely a full day ago. Darrell and Catherine were at odds over some issue, and to her, it seemed a safe bet it had to do with their parents' death. *He claims his sister is terribly disturbed by the tragedy, but he's troubled as well. I want to help them, yet how can I when the crux of their dispute hasn't been revealed? I'm making mere assumptions, based on very few facts. At the moment, the only thing of which I may be certain is I cannot be certain of anything.*

Abigail lay back on the bed, too distraught to find any level of peace.

*****

As the days passed the stressful environment at Rochester Manor had continued, and Abigail hadn't any indication the condition may ease. She'd attempted to thwart the ongoing bickering between Darrell and Catherine by introducing light conversation, with minimal success. Given she'd provoked him regarding the identity of the mysterious dinner guest, it was obviously unwise to confront Darrell with the other strange matters; although, remaining in the dark had become increasingly frustrating for her.

On her fifth night at Rochester Manor, Abigail was awakened by the sound of a piano. For a moment, she wondered if she'd only dreamt it. When it didn't stop, she crept towards the stairs and leaned over the balcony to determine the music's origin. With the volume still low, she presumed it came from a distant part of the house. She was on the point of descending the stairs to investigate when someone startled her with a tap on her shoulder. She turned to discover Darrell.

"Why are you out of bed at this hour?" he scolded.

"I was awakened by the piano. I didn't see any instruments when we toured the house. Where is it located?"

"The servant's quarters. Several of the staff play. Mr. Phillips, the footman, is particularly accomplished. I'm sorry you were disturbed. I imagine they're unaware of how far the sound carries. Typically, they haven't the chance to practice during the day; however, I'll advise them not to do so at this late hour."

"Don't trouble yourself. I hadn't heard the music prior and was only curious. Truly it doesn't bother me; I find it soothing."

"Now that you have the explanation, please return to bed. You mustn't wander about at night when you could easily fall and injure yourself."

"It was foolish of me. It won't happen again."

Darrell took Abigail's arm and escorted her to her room. He kissed her cheek curtly, appearing more concerned than agitated as he closed the door behind her.

Back in her bed, Abigail listened with added attention to the hauntingly beautiful music.

Astounding, she thought. *If it is Mr. Phillips who's playing, he's exceptionally talented.*

Shortly thereafter, the song was interrupted. Abigail had little doubt whoever was playing had been instructed to cease. Mortified Darrell may have severely reprimanded one of the servants she hoped to find the performer and offer her apology. *I must assure whoever it was I'd no desire to halt the music. I wish it would have continued; in fact, I'd love to hear it every night.*

*****

Abigail awoke to a dreary morning, which seemed fitting given her equally dim mood. On her way to breakfast, she happened upon Mr. Phillips. She thought this was fortunate, for if it was him playing, she could make amends quickly. If not, he could likely acquaint her with whoever it was.

"Good morning," she said.

"Good morning, miss," he replied.

"We haven't been formally introduced."

"My apologies, miss. I've been visiting relatives and returned late yesterday evening. I am Mr. Phillips, the footman, at your service."

A tall man of average build in his late forties, his engaging smile expressed a kindly disposition.

"Yes, I remember you ushered me the day of my arrival."

"It's a pleasure to have you at the Manor."

"Thank you, Mr. Phillips. Everyone I've met has been graciously accommodating. And I've discovered there's talent here as well. I adore music, particularly the piano. It's my understanding you play beautifully."

"Whoever claimed it was far too kind on my behalf. I began recently, and my play is poor, even for a novice."

"Perhaps I misunderstood. With continued practice, you should improve."

"I'm not overly optimistic, miss. I don't seem to have any natural aptitude for it. Any improvement will take a long while."

"Could someone offer you their assistance; perhaps another staff member who plays well?"

"Regrettably there isn't. One of the maids is more accomplished than I; although, slightly at best. We haven't much time for practice or the means to obtain adequate instruction."

"Such a pity. I do wish you the best of luck."

"Thank you, miss. Is there anything else you require?"

"Nothing at the moment."

The man bowed to take his leave.

She placed her fingers to her mouth, her brows furrowed in perplexity. *Obviously, it wasn't Mr. Phillips playing last night, or any of the servants. Darrell must know none of them play well. He's hiding someone's identity again, likely the person he wouldn't reveal the other night, but for what conceivable reason?*

Doubtful it was appropriate or wise to accuse Darrell of deception, she suppressed her concern before entering the dining room.

"Good morning, my love," Darrell said.

His cheerful mood and tender kiss indicated he didn't harbor any lingering annoyance. Once he'd pulled out Abigail's chair, he prepared their plates, which had become his habit. "Were you able to sleep well after we parted?"

She assumed he referred to the cessation of the music. "I did, thank you," she lied to conceal her qualms.

"You appear subdued this morning. Is anything the matter?"

"Nothing, other than I fear I've created trouble for the servants. I hope you didn't chastise them harshly."

"No, no; I merely explained the situation, nothing more."

Sorely tempted to ask, "explained to whom?" she resisted the urge. "That's a relief to hear."

"My dear, I need excuse myself directly after breakfast. I have several critical business matters I must attend, which may engage me until dinner."

"Of course," she said.

"I regret Catherine has not yet become a companion for you. How will you occupy the hours?"

"I'm not certain. Likely I'll read for a while. Later on, I'll take a walk if the rain holds off."

"An agreeable enough plan. Luncheon won't be possible for me; I'll have a tray in the study. If I complete my work early, I'll join you for tea."

"That would be lovely."

In truth, Abigail preferred to have time alone. It was as though she'd been presented with a puzzle, one that would be difficult to solve with many of the pieces missing. She was certain her attempt to collect them would anger Darrell, and any activity to this end must be covert. Although reluctant to go against his wishes, she believed she couldn't help anyone while the mystery persisted. She contemplated how to proceed, without running the risk of arousing hearsay.

Mary, she thought. *She's already proven to be a trustworthy confidant. Even so, I don't know her well enough to reveal my predicament. I don't think she would gossip, yet I'll approach her in a casual way to be sure.*

*****

As she prepared for dinner, Abigail posed her questions to Mary in the context of small talk. "Have you been in service here a long time?"

"No, miss. I came only a few days before you did. I lived nearby and was offered the post when it was announced the master had become engaged."

"I see. Were you at all familiar with the family prior to your arrival?"

"Not terribly; mine had no connections here. It was a mutual friend of Mrs. Williams and my mother who recommended me. Why do you ask, miss?"

"I'd like to learn more about the household where I'm to be mistress. I've discovered so little I feel at a disadvantage."

"You might seek out Mrs. Williams. She's been here since before the master, and his sister was born."

"That's good to know."

"There, miss, you're all ready."

"Thank you, Mary."

Abigail wondered about Mrs. Williams. Did she dare speak with someone close to Darrell? Mrs. Williams had been kind and forthcoming during their introduction, and she could think of no one else to consult. She decided if she used careful wording it would be safe to proceed. To obtain answers, she believed she had no choice.

*****

In the morning following breakfast, Abigail entered the kitchen in search of Eleanor. She found her in the middle of frantic activity.

"Mrs. Williams?"

"Abigail, dearest, how are you this morning?"

"Very well, thank you. You, on the other hand, appear overwhelmed."

"Indeed, we are. We've much to do in preparation for Easter."

"I'd forgotten Easter is approaching. Darrell hasn't informed me how the family celebrates holidays. Do they engage in large celebrations?"

"The immediate family celebrates all religious events privately, here in the house."

"They don't attend church, or participate in any functions?"

"No, not since…the accident."

"I suppose that's to be expected given their grief. And the staff?"

"While some return to their families, many remain. On Easter day we set out a large feast in both the servants' hall and the dining room. Part of the staff has already left, and we're shorthanded."

"Goodness, it's a small wonder you're busy."

"Was there something you required this morning, my dear?"

"Nothing of any urgency. Perhaps I could be of assistance to you."

Eleanor chuckled. "It's kind of you to offer, but I can't have you pitching in with the staff."

"Truly, I wouldn't mind; I'd enjoy helping."

"Darrell would never permit an activity so unseemly on your part."

"Why should he object if the suggestion is mine?"

"In his eyes, it won't make a difference."

"Then I'll leave you to it if I'll only be in the way."

Eleanor smiled and cupped her cheek. "Such a lovely young lady you are."

Abigail left the kitchen even more bewildered. *From what Darrell indicated, their year of grieving should have ended. How strange they still elect to spend their holidays alone. I must discover the reason their disruption has continued. Unfortunately, I'll have to wait for things to return to normal before I speak with Eleanor.* **Normal***; that's not a word most would use to describe this household.*

65

*****

Holidays, such as Easter, which oftentimes bring families together, did nothing to alleviate the tension at Rochester Manor. It had in fact escalated, and temperaments had become raw. Catherine's animosity was openly mounting; at times she seemed on the brink of disclosing the issue Darrell insisted be held in confidence. He'd come to lose all patience with his sister. As a result, they'd squabbled incessantly.

With the added commotion Abigail's frustration was at a peak, to the point she'd been tempted to consult with Catherine. In the end, she thought better of it. If Catherine wanted to be rid of her, snooping behind Darrell's back would provide her with the perfect opportunity.

Shortly after Easter, Darrell informed Abigail Catherine had been invited to visit friends who reside in the adjacent county and expected her to remain at least a fortnight. Although his sister appeared pleased to be leaving, Abigail considered it likely he'd had a hand in this invitation.

Once Catherine had departed, the condition of the house improved immensely. Without the continual aggravation, Darrell's disposition relaxed, giving Abigail pause to risk upheaving the placid conditions. On the other hand, she thought it likely when his sister returned the tranquility would as quickly end. Since a temporary solution was hardly preferable to none, she decided to go forth with her plan to confer with Eleanor.

A week later, her chance arose when Darrell was to be away from the house until evening on matters of business. Abigail sought out Eleanor during a quiet time of day. She discovered her alone in the kitchen.

"Good afternoon, Mrs. Williams."

"Abigail, my dear, come right in. Would you care for a cup of tea?"

"Thank you, Mrs. Williams; I'd love one."

"Now there will be no more of this Mrs. Williams formality. I'm sure you're aware Darrell and Catherine call me Eleanor. I want you to do the same."

"Eleanor then, thank you," she obliged as she sat and was handed her tea.

"You're welcome. Darrell and Catherine are as a son and daughter to me. I can't tell you how delighted I am to attain another daughter."

"It's kind of you to say, Eleanor. Speaking of Darrell and Catherine, I've noticed a good deal of tension exists between them. Oftentimes they're at odds with one another."

"Regrettably, this is true."

"Does their quarrel stem from the tragedy?"

"The tragedy; yes, it does. It's a dreadful shame, for there was a time when they were all happy children, and as close to each other as one can imagine."

Abigail raised her eyebrows. "All?"

"Did I say all? I meant to say both, of course. I'm afraid my age is becoming apparent."

The lapse in Eleanor's composure gave Abigail the impression she'd attempted to cover a faux pas, not explain a misuse of terminology.

"They suffered a horrible misfortune, yet such trials may unite family members," Abigail suggested. "In their case, I sense a marked disagreement pertaining to their ordeal."

"There is a great deal of controversy."

"Does it involve the north wing? They seem very troubled in its regard."

"You're most perceptive; it is the source of their dispute."

Eleanor wrung her hands, apparently uncomfortable with the direction of the conversation.

"I hope you don't think my intention is to pry," Abigail said. "I want to learn more, only so I may attempt to ease the strain between them."

"I understand. I dare say no more, other than I hope you will be able to help, someday."

To avoid losing Eleanor's trust, Abigail moved on to new topics. For the time being, she was satisfied with the confirmation of one pertinent point; the north wing was the root of the problem.

*****

Abigail received word Darrell had returned in time for dinner. She met him in the dining room to find he was excessively wan.

"Darrell, are you unwell?"

"I am well, dearest, although it's been a trying day. Problems have arisen with my latest venture I'd hoped would be resolved by now; instead, they've become far worse. I must leave in the morning for London to rectify them. I hate to abandon you, since it may require days to hash the mayhem out."

"While it's thoughtful of you to consider me, I've settled in comfortably here. You've no need for concern on my behalf."

"My sweet Abigail. I knew you'd be tolerant, yet without companionship, I fear you'll be adrift."

"Being an only child, I'm accustomed to entertaining myself. Have my assurance I'll be fine, particularly since you'll return in a few days."

"This is a relief to hear. I can think of no one else who possesses your patience and generosity."

"You possess the same qualities. In light of the patience and generosity you've shown me, how could I offer you less in return?"

Darrell smiled and caressed her hand. "Unless it would press the matter, I need request another indulgence. I'll be departing at an early hour, long before breakfast. I should retire directly after dinner."

"Please don't suspect I view your measures as any sort of neglect. You're overly burdened as it is. You mustn't add to it with undue concern for me."

"Bless you, my dearest Abigail. I love you."

"As I love you. You'll grant me a favor by taking good care of your health."

Dearest Darrell, she thought. *I cannot explain, but I'll have no difficulty whatever filling my time. Your absence will, in fact, be most opportune. I'll be able to continue with my search, which is precisely what I intend to do.*

*****

Abigail finished her breakfast tray quickly and then instructed Mary to hurry with her preparations. This morning, with Darrell gone, she was in no mood to dilly dally. Likely she had ample time for her pursuit; nevertheless, she didn't want to waste a second of her opportunity.

She bustled down the stairs as though the house was on fire. When she was in the foyer, she stopped short and stared alternately down the hallways. Anxious to start; she hadn't exactly considered whom or what she sought. She didn't think Eleanor would divulge much more, and Jake was not one to chat. To spy seemed her only option.

Abigail roamed without direction until she happened upon one of the maids at the entrance of the east wing carrying bed linens and cleaning implements. It seemed probable the young woman could tell her if someone had been residing there.

"Hello," Abigail said.

The girl halted. "I beg your pardon, miss. I didn't see you were there."

"It appears you're to tidy the east wing. Have guests stayed with us recently, or are we anticipating someone's arrival?"

"No, miss, I'm attending to my regular duties."

"Then I suppose Mr. Lewis wants these rooms maintained for unplanned visitors?"

"We don't receive many guests. The master insists the rooms his parents occupied are kept in perfect condition. I tend to them each and every week without fail."

Abigail quavered but managed to maintain her composure. "Oh, of course...I do recall him mentioning this. You're headed there now?"

"Yes, miss. If you'll excuse me, I'll get right to it."

Abigail reeled as she watched her enter one of the rooms. Scarcely able to think she bumbled her way to the conservatory and plopped onto a lounge.

"If the north wing isn't where his parents resided, he *lied* to me about the reason it's forbidden," she spat aloud.

Whoever or whatever he was hiding, Abigail was convinced the circumstance was appalling. She was determined to discover the truth. If she couldn't before Darrell's return, she'd confront him with her findings.

She walked purposefully to the north wing. She heard a noise and was about to investigate when the passageway doors opened.

"Oh, my God!" she blurted out. She sped to the adjacent wall to crouch behind a chair.

Soon she heard the sound of a lock being secured, followed by footsteps. Whoever it was arrived at the end of the wing and turned in her direction. She found it was Eleanor, who passed by without spotting her.

The moment she was out of view, Abigail slipped down the corridor Eleanor had vacated. She positioned her ear against the door; however, detected nothing.

She heard someone's approach from another part of the house and lurched upright. Panic swept through her when she realized the person was too close and the hallway too long for any chance of escape.

With no furniture or alcove to provide shelter, her only option was to plaster herself to the wall closest to the direction of the sound. Abigail shuddered with each forthcoming step, her shoulders constricted as she pressed her body ever firmer against the wall. She shut her eyes in anticipation of what seemed inevitable.

The person neared the entryway. Abigail gathered her nerve to take a peek. It was Jake, who strode by via the same route as Eleanor. He was apparently focused on his destination and took no notice of her.

When his footsteps could no longer be heard she peeled away from the wall, faint to the extent she steadied herself to prevent a tumble. On rocky legs, she made her way through the hall, and out the back door.

Abigail collapsed onto a bench. *That was a close call; too close. If I'm to continue, I must be more careful, yet there's no if about it.*

After considering her limited alternatives, she determined the only feasible course was to keep tabs on the north wing. She crept cautiously there and hid behind the same chair she'd used previously. A few servants walked by; however, an hour later no one else had entered or exited the north wing. For the time being she relinquished her vigil, but repeated her surveillance that afternoon and evening, only to be disappointed with the same result.

Although Abigail continued with the routine for several days, nothing more of significance had transpired. It seemed she wouldn't learn anything new prior to Darrell's return, until one night when she was again awakened by the sound of a piano. Abigail was convinced this was the same masterful performance she'd heard previously. "There's no possibility it is Mr. Phillips who's playing," she harrumphed.

She tiptoed down the stairs. Unable to pinpoint the sound's location, she headed towards the servants' quarters to confirm her presumption. When the music became softer, she changed direction. Suddenly, she froze in her tracks. She'd arrived at the north wing, aghast to hear the music was coming from behind the doors.

Once the initial shock subsided, she debated whether or not to investigate. With the urge to learn the truth more powerful than her fear, Abigail entered the corridor. She stole to the doors, her heart beating so hard she thought it would pound right out of her chest. She glanced behind to confirm no one was there and knelt to peer through the lock. In the dim lighting, she perceived a shadow. Unsure if it was cast by a figure or object, she continued with her scrutiny.

Riveted in her observation, several minutes had passed. Without warning, someone grabbed her from behind. Abigail released a shriek when she was yanked to her feet and turned around. It was Darrell.

"What are you doing?" he demanded. He grasped her shoulders to the point of bruising. "I gave explicit instructions you were *never* to come here. Is *this* your idea of respecting my wishes; to disregard my rules when I'm away from the house? Now I understand why you forgave me when I told you I must leave. You had this planned all along."

Too petrified to answer, Abigail could only shake her head. She winced when he seized her arm and dragged her to her room. She entered in such haste her feet entangled. When she hit the floor hard, he loomed over her, his eyes replete with contempt.

"Please, Darrell, let me explain."

"There's nothing *to* explain."

"You must believe me, I only attempted ..." she started.

"Attempted what? Whatever you attempted, you've hurt me beyond all reason." He paced the room for a minute. "I must determine how I'll handle this. You'll stay in here until I call for you."

Darrell removed the key from the door. After he'd shut it, she heard it lock.

At first, she couldn't move. Devastated by his intolerant reaction, it paled in comparison to her abhorrence of the truth. *My God; there is a person, or persons, inside the north wing. Who could they be? Why are they locked inside?*

Now trapped herself, Abigail had no choice other than await Darrell's decree. She pulled her knees to her body, and pushed her forehead against them, quaking as her life seemed to shatter like glass hit with a hammer. She found the strength to rise and managed to reach the bed, where she curled herself into a ball. "This cannot have happened," she wailed. "Please, *please,* let me awaken to find this has all been a nightmare!"

*****

Abigail had barely been able to lie still that night much less sleep; although, she finally did out of sheer exhaustion.

In the morning, she was startled by a knock on the door. Abigail braced herself to face Darrell. To her relief, Mary entered with a breakfast tray.

"Are you unwell, miss? Mrs. Williams told me you were to remain in your room this morning. She gave me your key but didn't explain why your door is locked. She was horribly flustered. I thought something must be wrong."

"Oh, Mary, everything has gone wrong. I've upset the master to such an extent; I'm afraid your position here will end shortly."

"Why do you say this, miss? What's happened?"

"I ignored a rule he'd enforced upon me. The master caught me in the act last night when he arrived home without my knowledge. I'm certain he'll break our engagement and send me back to Vienna."

"Could things truly be so dire? Surely his anger will pass."

"He won't forgive me this."

"Why not?"

"You've been advised of the rules in regard to the north wing, where supposedly no one is allowed to enter?"

Mary nodded.

"Although the master forbade me to go near the wing, I sneaked there. I was spying through the lock when he discovered me. This is why I'm to remain in my room, and why I'm convinced he'll break the engagement."

"If he forbade you, why ever did you go there?"

"He told me the wing had belonged to his parents, which in his grief he didn't want to be disturbed. Recently I learned this isn't true; they resided in the east wing, and their rooms are well maintained. He's deceived me in several ways regarding the north wing. I was determined to find the reason. I wasn't able to ascertain much, until last night when I was awakened by the playing of a piano. Did you by chance hear it?"

"No, but I'm a sound sleeper."

"I heard someone playing another night. When I questioned the master, he claimed it was the piano in the servants' hall."

"The one in our hall is occasionally played, by Mr. Phillips mostly, though not very often, and never at a late hour."

"I discovered as much from Mr. Phillips. It didn't take long to verify this wasn't the instrument being played. When I followed where the music led, I found myself near the north wing. The sound was coming from behind the doors."

Mary's eyes widened.

"Someone, perhaps more than one person, is locked inside," Abigail continued. "Miss Catherine mentioned an individual the master has refused to identify. I think it must be them."

"My heavens. Are they being held prisoner?"

"It's entirely possible."

Mary appeared alarmed. "Miss, the master may not send you away. Since you've discovered something he went to great lengths to hide, he may keep you locked up as well."

"He couldn't. My parents would wonder where I am."

"I didn't think of that. What a burden this must be for you. Is there any way I could be of help?"

"If you would; please attempt to gather more information. Do so only if you may proceed safely. I wouldn't want you to become caught up in this mess."

"Don't worry about me; I can be as discreet as a shadow."

"Thank you, Mary."

"I'll get to it straight away."

When she returned with lunch, Abigail looked at her with anticipation.

Mary shook her head. "I haven't learned a thing. The house is like a tomb. The master has kept to his study. Only Mrs. Williams has entered to deliver his meals. This morning she stayed in there quite a while, but after lunch, she left immediately. I've heard nothing from her, and no one else seems to know anything, except that something is wrong. We're performing our duties as quietly as church mice. We speak in whispers and walk as if we're stepping on eggshells. Of course, I'll keep my eyes and ears sharp."

At dinner time Mary's condition was far different; so unsteady the dishes she carried were rattling.

"Miss, I saw Mrs. Williams enter the north wing with a tray. Someone is definitely in there. Who do you suppose it could be?"

Abigail grimaced. "I've no idea, Mary. I'm not certain I want to know."

*****

Another night passed in an agonizingly slow way for Abigail. Mary had nothing new to report at breakfast or lunch, but tea time was another story. She arrived empty-handed, her appearance grim.

"The master wants to see you in the library," Mary said.

Abigail rose. She found she had to force her movement towards the door. *This must be the sensation one has when they head for the gallows,* she thought, the figurative end of her life seemingly imminent.

Mary gave her a hug. "Good luck, miss."

Abigail went down the stairs. To her surprise, by the time she was in the foyer a sense of calm had overcome her dread. Whatever Darrell had decided, at least her wait would be over.

As she neared the library's entrance, she heard he wasn't alone. Catherine's was the other voice. Abigail hid behind the adjoining wall to listen.

"How much longer do you intend to torture her, Darrell? Hasn't this gone on long enough?"

"I won't have her learn the truth; not yet."

"Come now, what possible excuse could you use to explain the music she heard the other night? Do you consider her a fool?"

"She is more astute than I first thought."

"Is this why you chose her then?"

"My intention was to find someone who could be easily deceived."

"Since this isn't the case, why continue with the deception? Even if you want to, how can you?"

"I'll find a way, and don't you *dare* undermine my efforts. I truly love this woman. I won't take the slightest chance I may lose her."

"It's despicable to hide the truth until she can no longer change her mind."

"Perhaps; however, I don't care. I cannot live without her, and I won't. I must have her for my wife."

"Why not grant her the benefit of the doubt and tell her? I believe she loves you so much she'll accept the circumstance."

Abigail stepped into the room. Her piercing glare made it clear she'd overheard their conversation. "Tell me what?"

Catherine smiled triumphantly while Darrell covered his eyes. When he approached Abigail, she sneered at him and backed away.

"I cannot blame you for maintaining your distance," he said. "My treatment of you has been dreadful. Now, you've discovered I've been deceptive as well. Although you've every reason to think ill of me, I beg you to hear me out. When you've learned the truth, hopefully, you'll understand my actions, however deplorable, were done out of love; my intense love for you."

His sister smirked at him. "Go ahead, Darrell, tell her."

"Abigail." He paused to collect himself. "Catherine and I have a brother."

3

The jolt of a dire revelation can be overpowering. Like a cloak of icy cold chain mail, it may enshroud its victim, rendering them speechless and immobile. Abigail was frozen in the clutches of this form of shock as she awaited Darrell's explanation, though it was impossible for her to fathom how any justification could exist.

"I'd prefer to relate the situation in private," Darrell requested of his sister.

She nodded and closed the door after she departed the library.

"Abigail, please be seated." He indicated one of the chairs.

"I'd rather not."

"*Please.*"

Although incensed, given their relationship she believed she owed him the courtesy and complied.

Darrell pulled a chair close to hers and seated himself.

"Hidden in the north wing is my brother, Edward, who I regret to say isn't well. Sadly, he is insane, his condition devastating to the extent he can be dangerous to himself and those around him."

Abigail's eyes widened. "In what sense is he dangerous?"

"The threat stems from his desire to take his own life, which has at times led him to violent aggression."

"That's dreadful. I presume it's the reason he's locked inside."

"It is. Following several incidents, our parents were faced with the prospect of sending him to an asylum. They couldn't bring themselves to subject him to a place so abhorrent and decided to use the north wing as his shelter instead. I concocted the story about the windows, which were bricked up for the sake of Edward's safety. All hazardous items were of course removed from the wing, or so it was thought. In his mania to inflict harm upon himself, my brother was determined to find the means. His solution was to smash one of the window panes. By a stroke of luck, Eleanor had just entered the corridor. She heard the crash in time to prevent him from using a shard in the way he had planned, but she was hurt badly when she pulled it from his hand."

"How awful. Has he made attempts since?"

"With the windows secured he hasn't, yet the inclination continues. We employ the utmost precaution when in his company. Although disturbed, he's quite brilliant. At all times he's on the lookout for an opportunity."

"Edward, then, is the person I've heard playing the piano?"

"Yes, it was him. Mercifully, the pursuit affords him a level of peace."

"It's been said music has the capacity to soothe the soul. What I cannot understand is why you lied to me about this. Why did you resort to such lengths to deceive me?"

"I'm exceedingly regretful I did. My prior experiences with engagement caused me to employ drastic measures. Edward's condition is viewed as a stain upon our family; consequently, our social status has declined. When no family from this region would permit their daughter to marry me, my relations in other counties offered me their assistance. While these efforts did result in several commitments, each, in turn, was broken when it was revealed I have a brother who's mad. They were all stuffy, disagreeable peahens anyway. I'd had my fill of such arrangements and resolved the next time I would choose for myself."

"Why did you choose me?"

"I was thoroughly off-put by the traits those repugnant women possessed. What I came to desire was a woman whose nature was far different. When we were introduced, I could see at once you hold the qualities I sought. I fell in love with you, more than I can say. May God forgive me, in my desperation to ensure I wouldn't lose you, I chose to hide Edward's existence until after we were married. This is why Catherine has been contemptuous. She's been attempting to foil my selfish actions."

"I heard you say you chose me since I appeared dimwitted. Is this what you find superior, a woman who lacks intellect?"

"Dimwitted isn't what I said. You do not lack in intelligence. It's one of your finest attributes. You did seem trusting and naïve, which was in part why I began our courtship. These traits of yours, however, result from what I was seeking; a gentle and kindly disposition, not a lack of acumen."

"With my character as you describe it, I suppose you expect me to forgive you for everything you've put me through."

"Not at all. My behavior was deplorable. I've no right to appeal for your forgiveness, and less right to presume I could regain your trust. Should you come to understand my actions were done out of love, foolish though it may be, I hope you'll consider staying."

"Why should I trust in you, when you have no trust in me? At least not enough to confide in me."

"I wanted to, yet I was afraid to take the chance. However certain you wouldn't dismiss me as hastily as the others, I was afraid if you learned the truth you would."

"You believe I'll find the situation intolerable?"

"It's entirely possible. Edward's infirmity has made life difficult for Catherine and me in many aspects. I ask only that you meet him. Afterward, I'll explain the events which led to his madness. When you're acquainted with all of the facts, our future will rest in your hands."

"It's doubtful I need more facts. I can't imagine how you'll persuade me to tolerate your deceitfulness and elect to honor our engagement."

"Abigail, I beg you, hear me out in full before you impose your judgment upon me."

"In the interest of fairness, I'll grant you this one favor."

"Your abiding patience and kindness; these are amongst the reasons I love you dearly."

Darrell rose and offered Abigail his hand.

She shook her head. "Let's not get ahead of ourselves. I will follow you, and that's all."

He motioned towards the door with a sullen look. When she stood, he led the way to the north wing.

After unlocking the doors, he took a candle from the wall. Since their eyes weren't adjusted to the darkness, the candlelight was barely sufficient to make their way down the gloomy hallway.

They paused at the entrance to one of the rooms.

"This is Edward's library, where we should find him at this time," Darrell explained. "You'll be perfectly safe in my company; although, his appearance may startle you."

Abigail shivered as they entered the room. In the dimness, she saw the figure of a man, seated on a winged back chair, with only his left side visible. He looked wretched as if he held the weight of something terrible on his narrow shoulders. When he glimpsed up, he saw Darrell wasn't alone and turned away.

"Edward, I'd like you to meet someone," his brother said firmly.

While plainly reluctant, he seemed to consider the request a command. He turned towards them until his entire face was in view.

Abigail released a "huh" when she discovered the man's right eye was missing, the surrounding area marred by scarring.

Aside from this disfigurement, she considered his features handsome, as much as his brother's, other than his complexion which was ashen. Once he stood, she saw his frame differentiated greatly from Darrell's; only a bit shorter, but painfully gaunt.

Edward's demeanor suddenly brightened. He rushed towards Abigail. "Emily!"

She took cover behind Darrell and clung to his shoulder. "You're well aware this cannot be Emily," he admonished.

Edward halted. His face fell as if he'd been slapped.

"This is Abigail, the young woman I've spoken of."

"Hello," Edward greeted in a small, shy voice.

"How nice to meet you," she returned warily.

Edward glanced at his brother. When he received Darrell's nod of approval, he extended his hand to Abigail. Darrell nodded again, an indication she needn't be concerned.

She emerged from her shelter and offered Edward her hand in return. He used the tips of his fingers to support it, like a delicate piece of china he feared he may break.

"You are very pretty," he said.

"Thank you," she said. *There's nothing about his manner which appears threatening. He seems entirely meek and timid, and ... there's something else here; a trait I can't define.*

"Did you arrive alone?" Edward asked.

"Yes, I did; my family will join me later."

"You have a brother or sister?"

"I haven't; however, this will ... *may* soon change."

Darrell grimaced.

"It will be agreeable for you to have a sister, I would think?" Edward asked.

"Most assuredly, assuming I ... well, if such is the case, will I not also have a brother?"

"In name only, for I cannot be of much use to you."

Edward's remark, although heartrending, helped her identify his elusive quality; his air apologetic, as though he thought himself unworthy of taking one's time.

They stood in awkward silence until Edward approached Darrell with an expression which suggested a matter of consequence had dawned on him. "May I play the piano?"

"Yes, you may do so whenever you wish. You'll no longer require my permission."

Oh no, Abigail thought. *Darrell has denied him the activity, due to me. It was Edward who was performing the night the music ended abruptly. I owed my apology to him.*

Edward wrung his hands, apparently waiting to be excused.

"You may retire to the music room," Darrell said. "We must leave to take our tea."

"It was a pleasure to meet you," Abigail said.

"Thank you," Edward returned. He scurried out. Soon after, Edward was playing.

Abigail evaluated the brothers' relationship as she and Darrell walked the shadowy hallway. She considered their relationship not at all typical for brothers—Darrell in the role of a strict father, and Edward, the obedient son. Under the circumstance, she didn't think the disparity was surprising, and yet found it more pronounced than one would expect.

Abigail shaded her eyes when they stepped into the daylight. Darrell locked the doors with particular care. He pulled the knobs several times to test their security.

They went to the library, to discover Catherine hadn't returned. Darrell was about to send for her when the maid who brought the tray handed him a note.

"My sister relates due to her recent arrival she's tired and prefers to rest rather than join us."

He motioned to the servant she may pour the tea.

While they drank, Abigail listened in awe to Edward's performance. "Your brother plays with exceptional skill, doesn't he?"

"Indeed, he does. He was endowed with a natural talent. With ample time for practice, he's come to master the instrument impressively."

SUSAN BUTLER

"He seems sad and … lost; although, he doesn't appear menacing."

"Appearances are oftentimes deceiving. You mustn't allow his placid exterior to mislead you. He's far more disturbed than one may readily perceive."

"It's such a distressing plight for him. Has he always suffered from this tendency?"

"Not at all, we were at one time a happy family; I dare say happier than most. It was a grave tragedy that changed our lives forever."

Darrell pushed his tea aside and rested his hands on the table to lean forward.

"When I was a child, our closest neighbors were dear friends of the family, with whom we spent many pleasant hours. They had three sons and a daughter, all of our ages within a few years of one another. While their daughter, Emily, played with Catherine occasionally, more often she could be found in the company of my brother, happier to run and climb with Edward than to play with dolls or other games customary for girls.

"As the years passed, they became inseparable. When Emily was ten and Edward twelve, our parents agreed they'd be intended for each other. The announcement was made to them. Although too young to understand what marriage entails, they were delighted, so innocent to them it meant they could play together forever. We couldn't help laughing when they ran off to climb their favorite tree as a form of celebration, unsuspecting of the disaster that would soon befall us."

"A disaster; what happened?"

"All was well until Edward chose to climb higher than usual; high enough apparently the entire county was in view. He wanted Emily to share the panorama and coaxed her to join him. Despite her reluctance, she made an attempt. By his account, as he reached for her hand, she lost her footing and fell to the ground. He raced to her aid to find she'd hit her head on a boulder. When he rolled her over, he nearly passed out. In addition to the trauma from the rock, her eye had been put out by a tree limb. Blood was streaming down her face."

"Merciful heavens, it's unthinkable."

"We heard his screams and rushed to discover the ghastly scene. Edward was in a state of complete hysteria. Consumed with guilt and grief, he blamed himself solely for the incident, beyond consolation when he ran off while we tried to help Emily. It was immediately evident she had passed; there was nothing to be done, and so we carried her to the house. On our way we heard Edward shriek again, unprepared to face a second horror when we found he'd gouged out his own eye with a large knife."

"No," Abigail said, and covered her mouth.

"Edward would have died as well, but thankfully my parents arrived in time to save him. As I said earlier, he's made other attempts to end his life; therefore, his confinement was unavoidable. After ten years he's gone mad, living in darkness and insurmountable despair."

"The means to help poor Edward has never been attained?"

"Our parents made every effort. They solicited the advice of various doctors; however, the most that could be accomplished was to prevent him from harming himself."

Abigail shook her head. "What became of Emily's parents?"

"They were unable to tolerate living in the house which held many memories of their only daughter and moved away a short time later. Although they claimed they didn't blame my brother entirely, we never heard from them again."

"What a heartbreaking misfortune, for all of you."

"Yes, it truly is. You now have all the particulars concerning my deception. While I admit the circumstance doesn't excuse my actions, with the deepest humility I beg you to forgive me. Should you choose to break our engagement, due to my behavior or Edward's illness, I won't attempt to change your mind."

"I'm still disappointed you chose not to confide in me. Given your past refusals of marriage, I do find a measure of validity in your silence. The severity of Edward's illness also makes your reluctance to disclose the truth understandable, to a small degree."

"Had I told you the story prior to our engagement, what would your answer have been, do you suppose?"

"Supposing isn't necessary. I wouldn't have allowed the situation to stand between us. The tragedy and Edward's resulting illness is no fault of yours. It's despicable for anyone to lower their opinion of you or refuse engagement on these grounds. I would have said I'd be honored to join your family. The dishonor belongs to those who would inflict further injury upon individuals who've suffered tremendously as it is."

"*Abigail,* how foolish I was to question your generosity. I offer you the sincerest regret for my doubt and apologize profusely for my atrocious deeds. I've nothing left to say; I'll merely reiterate my admission I'm undeserving of you or a second chance. If you can find it in your heart to grant me the opportunity, I promise to devote myself only to your happiness."

"Provided your actions were strictly due to your fear of losing me, and you give me your solemn word you'll never again keep any concerns a secret from me, I'll give you another chance."

Darrell knelt on one knee and cradled her hand. "As God is my witness, I will never again deceive you. I'll do whatever you require of me to repair the damage I've caused. I love you, my dearest Abigail, with all my heart and all my soul. Will you please, *please* marry me?"

Her face shone as she said, "Yes, Darrell, I will marry you."

Tears formed in his eyes. "Bless you my sweetest, dearest love for your kindness. Bless you, so very much."

Darrell laid his head on her lap. Abigail bent over to kiss him on the temple, with tears the equal of his.

*****

Exhausted from the strain of her ordeal, Abigail returned to her room a short while later to rest.

Mary was there, awaiting her arrival. "Miss, do you have good news?"

"I have. You'll scarcely believe all I've discovered since I left."

She suggested they sit before she recounted the tale. Frequently Mary would shake her head or cover her mouth, incredulous of the facts Abigail could yet barely fathom herself.

"I have accepted his apology and elected to stay. I will become Mrs. Darrell Lewis," Abigail said in conclusion of the story.

"You must be happy this has ended well. What a shock to discover the person locked in the north wing is the master's *brother*. It's a small wonder he's disturbed, after that horrible accident."

"If only you could see him. He's a sad, desolate soul. It nearly broke my heart to witness an individual who suffers such torment."

A knock came. Mary opened the door to find Catherine.

Mary curtseyed. "Good evening, Miss Lewis. Do you need anything more, miss?" she asked Abigail.

"No thank you, Mary, that will be all for now."

Mary left and closed the door behind her.

"Good evening, Catherine."

"Good evening, Abigail. May I have a word with you?"

"Of course; would you care to have a seat?"

"Thank you. I've come to apologize for my untoward behavior since your arrival."

Abigail smiled. "It isn't necessary. I understand you wanted me to uncover the truth about Edward."

"I was appalled when Darrell informed me of his intent to deceive you. This wasn't merely a deplorable contrivance in regard to you; it hurt Edward since he forbade him to play the piano."

"Yes, I learned as much upon meeting him."

"Playing is the only activity from which he derives a measure of solace. It was no fault of yours; nevertheless, your presence is the reason he was denied."

"I'm glad I overheard your conversation with Darrell; otherwise, this might yet be the case. There is one point which remains a mystery to me; since you weren't to return home until next week at least, how is it you're here?"

"Eleanor sent the carriage for me. Her note detailed what happened the night my brother returned and caught you at the doors of the north wing. With the urgency of the situation, she requested my immediate return."

"And the night of my arrival, you dined with Edward?"

"I did."

"I recall Darrell insisted Jake and Eleanor be your escort; to shelter you from harm, I suppose?"

"This is *his* position."

"It's not also yours? You don't think Edward is capable of harming you?"

"Honestly, I don't. In his quest to injure himself he's hurt others. He never meant to, and I think he's abandoned the notion to prevent its reoccurrence."

"Darrell also said your dining with him doesn't usually meet with his approval. What did he mean by this?"

"He resents our brother for the damage to the family. He takes my desire to visit him an affront, as though it exhibits my preference. I must obtain Darrell's permission to meet with Edward, which allows him to monitor the frequency of our visits. Once when he refused, I went to the north wing regardless, and I was discovered. I needn't tell you how Darrell reacts when his rules are broken. While he rarely grants his consent, I daren't make another attempt. I wish I could spend more time with Edward. It grieves me to be denied his company."

"I'm sorry to hear this. And I have learned the consequences of going against Darrell's dictate. I've never encountered a person so agitated in my life."

"When aggravated he can become irrational, which wasn't the case prior to the incident. In those days, our older brother was highly protective of Edward and me. He had such a kind nature and gentle temperament he never uttered a harsh word. He won't admit it, but he was also profoundly changed by the accident. Since Edward cannot function in the world, his affliction is evident. Far less apparent is the extent to which Darrell is troubled. By keeping his wound hidden typically he manages himself well, yet it's always festering. When irritated, the person who provokes him will pay the price. The day Emily died I was visiting our aunt and was spared the agony. My brothers, however, still haven't escaped from their nightmare."

"It's pitiable after these many years they remain traumatized."

"It is. Abigail, the depth of your love for Darrell cannot be debated. Nonetheless, I must offer you a warning. Life in this house is at times difficult. Consider carefully your willingness to cope. You could forsake our family; it's not too late."

"Although I appreciate your concern, I am hopelessly in love with your brother. Now I think it would be wrong of me to abandon you when perhaps I can be of help."

"Then, as you are to be my sister…" They rose, and she gave Abigail a hug. "I'll let you rest prior to dinner."

"Until then."

Catherine closed the door as she left.

Abigail leaned against it. "My heavens," she said aloud.

She was dizzy, as though she'd been running through a maze of the psyche. *Thank goodness this ordeal is over. I don't think I could have survived much more.*

Abigail shook her shoulders to relieve her tension before she headed to bed.

*****

Refreshed from her nap, at eight o'clock Abigail strode to the library in contentment. Many weeks following her arrival at Rochester Manor, she was able to enjoy her first pleasurable meal in the company of her fiancé and his sister. Catherine's treatment of her continued to be accommodating. Darrell's affection had returned to that of the man she'd fallen in love with in Vienna. The interaction between the siblings was a different affair; more courteous than fond. Compared to their previous bickering, for Abigail, the change was a significant and welcome improvement.

Catherine retired directly after dinner, while Darrell and Abigail went to the parlor. He pulled her into his arms, holding her as if he may never release her.

"Thank you again, my darling, *thank you* for staying with me," he said. "I don't know what I'd have done had you left. The thought I could have lost you unnerves me beyond reason."

"I didn't want to leave," she confessed. "I'd be miserable without you."

"My sweet Abigail."

He placed his hands on her face and kissed her ardently. When he loosened his embrace, she sensed it was with more than a bit of reluctance.

"You need to acquire more rest," he said.

"It would be best. I believe all the upheaval has exhausted us both."

They clung to one another as they slowly ascended the stairs. At her door, Darrell gave Abigail a quick kiss.

"Good night, my dearest." He smiled and touched her gently under the chin.

"Good night, Darrell."

The corners of her mouth curled up as she watched him walk the hallway. She continued to observe him until he closed his door.

Abigail entered her room and dismissed Mary immediately. This evening, she wanted to be alone with her thoughts.

She pranced about in celebration while she prepar[ed] herself for bed. Upon tiring herself out, she slipped unde[r] covers and sunk into the pillow. She stared as scenes from [the] evening seemed to materialize on the ceiling, until her eyelids were too heavy to remain open.

Once Abigail's eyes had closed the images vanished, overshadowed by visions of Edward. How inappropriate it was to celebrate her good fortune, she thought, when downstairs a soul was suffering endless torment. She questioned how it was possible after ten years Edward had made no improvement and wondered how long it had been since anyone made an attempt.

Catherine's claim that Darrell harbored ongoing resentment against his brother also came to mind. Since she'd witnessed firsthand his dominance over Edward, Abigail found her assertion credible. *With his station in life, one could understand why for Darrell their loss of good footing was humiliating. Yet from the disparaging statements he's made regarding those of high society, it would appear he's surmounted their disdain to a considerable extent. There must be other factors contributing to his spite. Whether this is true or not, Darrell's attitude could be of hindrance to Edward's recovery.*

Abigail scowled at the idea. What had begun as a lovely evening had been dampened by a fresh array of worries. In need of sleep she rolled onto her side; however, her eyes, which she'd fought to keep open, now refused to close. Bombarded with these new concerns, she was awake long into the wee hours.

*****

A flock of birds near Abigail's window were chirping when she awoke; although, their merriment did little to dispel her qualms. She wanted to consult further with Catherine and sought her out after breakfast. She found her in the boudoir relaxing with a book.

"Why, good morning, Abigail."

"Good morning."

"You appear somber. Is something troubling you?"

"Yes, there is. Would you mind if we continued our discussion of Edward?"

"Not at all. How may I help you?"

Abigail seated herself on a nearby chair. "Last night I was basking in my own happiness when it occurred to me, I hadn't given much thought to your unfortunate brother. It felt wrong for me to celebrate while he suffers horribly."

"It's kind of you to consider him, though I'm not sure how I may ease your conscience."

"You told me Darrell resents him. I can't understand why this should be. The few details I've learned about the situation don't seem to fully account for his attitude. I think there must be more to his animosity than meets the eye."

"No doubt there is. Due to his bitterness, he won't confide in me."

"Do you suppose his dominance inhibits Edward's ability to recover?"

"It's difficult to say. He's so ridden with guilt I doubt he could return to us completely. You do, however, make a sound observation. Darrell's stance may well prevent the remotest possibility."

"Edward's seclusion must also be a significant obstacle. How much contact does he have with the outside world?"

"He receives several visits daily from Jake and Eleanor when they deliver his meals. We all dine together occasionally; although, as I mentioned not as frequently as I'd prefer. Jake typically spends little time with him. While Eleanor would like to offer more, she cannot devote too much with her many responsibilities. It angers Darrell when any of us spend what he considers to be an unwarranted amount of time with Edward, as vague as this is, so the length of our stay is usually brief."

"Does Darrell see him often?"

"Only rarely, and then primarily to dictate his authority."

"This is distressing. There's a barrier beyond the walls that separates this family. Obviously, it's a burden for you that impedes your relationship with Darrell."

"Undeniably it does. I'll admit I took advantage of your first evening here. Since he was keeping Edward a secret, Darrell couldn't prevent me from dining with him without disclosing the truth."

"It's rather ironic I was able to help at that time. I wish I could be of help now."

"It would be wonderful, but I know of nothing you could do."

"I'll give it more thought. This is a circumstance I cannot claim to comprehend; still, I won't accept there are no options."

"Please be certain you factor in every conceivable consequence before you take action of any sort. With Darrell's temperament, an impulsive move could prove disastrous."

"I appreciate the warning. If you'll excuse me, I'll return to my room until luncheon."

"I'll look forward to seeing you then," Catherine said.

In the solitude of her bedroom, it wasn't long before Abigail determined a quandary of this nature wasn't something she could handle on her own; it would require sound guidance. Her parents seemed the logical choice to consult. Since her only communication had been a telegram notifying them of her safe arrival, a letter to them was due regardless. She sat at her desk and wrote:

17 April, 1888

My dearest Father and Mama,
Please rest assured in a general sense I'm doing well, which I hope is true for you and my dear friends. I miss you all dreadfully.
While I don't want to cause undue alarm, I'm writing to seek your advice regarding a grim discovery I made yesterday. I'm certain you'll be shocked, as was I, to learn Darrell has not only a sister but a brother, Edward. Darrell's design was to withhold his existence until after we were married. He was concerned I'd call off the engagement

if I discovered his brother, for sadly he's terribly disturbed. His condition stems from an accident that occurred ten years ago, in which Edward's young betrothed died. Apparently, this poor individual blames himself alone for her death. Driven mad by guilt, he's attempted to take his own life on several occasions.

Of greater concern, Darrell allegedly resents his brother for the difficulty the family has endured as a result of his illness. Ostensibly too imbalanced to function in a rational manner, Edward has been locked away throughout the course of this time. Darrell claims he's beyond help, and therefore his confinement may continue indefinitely. Frankly, I question his contention. I've no idea how to proceed, or what steps to take to alter the circumstance...

Worried she wasn't explaining the situation sensibly, Abigail stopped to review what she'd written so far. *No, no, this account is too jumbled. How will I best describe this bizarre circumstance? It may not be possible within the confines of a letter. It may only serve to upset Mother and Father; perhaps to the extent they'll insist I break the engagement. To think of it, how much assistance could they offer when they've never faced a dilemma of this sort; few have.*

She tore the page, and took a fresh sheet to write:

17 April, 1888

My dearest Father and Mama,

I hope this letter finds you well. I'm getting along splendidly here at Rochester Manor. It seems an eternity until my wedding day will be near, and at last, you'll arrive. I miss you both dreadfully.

As I indicated in my cable this house is dauntingly grand, yet I'm becoming accustomed to its opulence, and am settling in nicely. Darrell has been remarkably generous with my wedding gift. He rebuilt an entire wing for our suite, setting aside the largest area for my rooms. The space is beautiful as well as vast. I'm to furnish it in whatever fashion I please. You can imagine how worried I am at the prospect.

Catherine is a dear girl. I'm certain we'll become close friends. The staff is gracious and helpful, particularly a Mr. and Mrs. Williams, who serve as parents to both she and Darrell. I feel most welcome, which is fortunate as I prepare to enter the role of mistress.

Please give my best to my dear friends. Relate how terribly I miss them also.

Sincerely,

Your loving daughter, Abigail

She folded the letter, believing this was a wise decision. When Abigail contemplated with whom she may confer Eleanor seemed her best alternative, and conceivably the only alternative. She would wait until Darrell was to be away from the house for at least several hours, to avoid the risk he may overhear their conversation. To succeed in her endeavor, she realized patience was the essential factor; a point she must keep in mind at all times.

4

Despite her young years, Abigail had experienced several cases of life's unpredictability, and yet nothing could have prepared her for the magnitude of her discovery of Edward. How strange she thought it was a cataclysmic event had improved her life at Rochester Manor; had nearly transformed it into what she'd dreamt of prior to her arrival. Her relationship with Catherine was becoming fond, close to sisterly. Darrell was in high spirits primarily. Although distinct friction lingered between the siblings, the atmosphere was generally tranquil.

Nearly, however, was the key descriptive term. Paradoxically, it was Edward's bleak situation which hindered her happiness. With Darrell doting upon her, after a week had passed, she hadn't the opportunity to confer with Eleanor, and Abigail was frustrated by the lack of progress.

Several days later during teatime, she noticed Catherine was unusually quiet and distracted. Evidently, a matter of importance was preying on her mind as well. When the maid had finished serving, Catherine fidgeted prior to revealing her thoughts.

"Darrell, may I have your permission to dine with Edward this evening?"

"Not tonight." His voice was gruff. "You should continue to dine with us, to become better acquainted with Abigail. At last, you've made her feel welcome. It would be rude to abandon her."

"The length of time since we reconciled may be short, yet we're becoming fast friends, aren't we, Abigail?"

"We are. We've enjoyed many activities since then. Only yesterday we took a nice stroll through the gardens."

"An encouraging start, though hardly sufficient to achieve a sisterly familiarity," he said.

"You pose a valid point," Catherine admitted, "but I haven't seen Edward in a long time. I would miss one dinner merely."

"Your last visit was the evening Abigail arrived, which I consider recent."

"It seems ages to me," his sister said, her appearance downcast.

Abigail sympathized with her plight. "It has been a number of weeks since her previous visit, and we'll be together tomorrow. I won't be slighted should you permit her."

Darrell looked annoyed. "I don't recall soliciting your input. Don't undermine my authority."

"I didn't intend to. With your concern on my behalf, I thought my position would be helpful."

"Clearly, there won't be a moment's peace with the two of you until I acquiesce. Very well, Catherine, dine with Edward if you're determined to do so. Abigail, I will see you at dinner."

He left abruptly and closed the door with a thud.

"Please don't create trouble for yourself over this," Catherine said. "The issue is between Darrell and me."

"I felt compelled to intervene, particularly since I didn't appreciate him using my presence as an excuse to deny you. His stance regarding your visits with Edward is unwarranted. His attitude must change."

"It would be wonderful, though highly unlikely. Eleanor has tried for years to change his mind, to no avail."

"Being new to the household, I can address the situation from a different perspective."

"Unquestionably; still, Darrell may not assess your efforts rationally. It could result in the severe consequences I've spoken of."

"Until he listens to reason our unsettled state will remain. It isn't agreeable for any of us to live this way."

"How very true. Now, I need to return to my room."

"If you've no objection, I'll come upstairs with you."

"In view of the support you've given me, how could I object?"

They walked to the ladies' wing and paused at Abigail's door.

"Thank you for your consideration today," Catherine said. "It means the world to me to be able to meet with Edward."

"You're most welcome. I'll see you tomorrow."

"Yes, tomorrow," Catherine replied and gave her a squeeze before she walked to her room.

Abigail grinned. *I believe I have a sister,* she thought.

*****

Abigail entered the library at dinnertime to find Darrell was yet in an acrid humor. Offering little of his usual affection, he escorted her to the dining room in a brusque manner. He snarled when they were seated.

"Are you unwell, Darrell?"

"I am *quite* well."

"You're perturbed Catherine isn't with us."

"Due to your interference."

"Please, you mustn't believe my purpose was to upset you. With her mood sullen, I was concerned our evening would be unpleasant. I thought tonight her absence would be for the best."

"While that may be true, I doubt it was your primary motivation."

"I'd be lying if I said otherwise. I admit I felt pity for her."

"How *very* kind of you to disregard my feelings, my wishes in the matter."

"I'm sorry you've found my suggestion inconsiderate. I was convinced the time apart would allow the situation to calm and do you both good."

Darrell's expression softened. "You're correct; we wouldn't have enjoyed our evening with her in a snit. This topic has been a continued source of conflict between us. Oftentimes she's been defiant towards me, which is why I'm reluctant to give in to her tantrums. I trust you had only kindly intentions; however, going forward I ask that you please not contradict me. I would value your full support."

"You'll always have my support. I apologize if it appeared otherwise."

"You've never given me cause to distrust your loyalty. I must bear in mind you cannot fully comprehend our situation. There's more to this than one may readily perceive."

It was on the tip of her tongue to request he expand upon his statement. Since Abigail didn't want to reignite his indignation, she censured herself and smiled to cover her apprehension. She decided this wasn't the proper time or place to confront him but wondered if a suitable moment would ever occur.

*****

In typical instances, validation in regards to an issue or fact elicits a considerable sense of self-satisfaction, for the party who's proven correct. Since the situation at Rochester Manor was anything but typical, Abigail would've preferred to have been proven wrong. Darrell had, however, confirmed her suspicion; there were more obscure points pertaining to the household discord. She hadn't obtained every puzzle piece after all. Some were still missing, and she was determined to find them. After contemplating the matter well into the night, in the morning she arrived at breakfast with a plan.

"Good morning, my darling. Did you sleep well?" Darrell asked.

"Eventually I did."

"Were you ill?"

"No, merely preoccupied."

"Something must be distressing you."

"Frankly, there is. I've been thinking about your brother a lot. It's regrettable, don't you think, how ill acquainted I am with the man who'll soon be my brother?"

Darrell's eyebrows furled.

"Catherine and I have become close, which I believe pleases you. Despite his condition, Edward is part of the family. We should meet again."

"You want to reassess your decision to stay."

"Not at all; the thought couldn't be further from my mind."

"Undoubtedly you've noticed how difficult it is to converse with Edward. With his level of disturbance, you could never become close to him."

"Of course not, yet even the smallest increase in our familiarity would be nice."

Darrell leaned his elbow on the table and rubbed his chin while he thought. "Since you were generous in your acceptance of my brother's condition, I should be generous as well. An early morning visit would best suit my schedule. I'll arrange for us to have breakfast with him tomorrow."

"A splendid idea."

This is perfect, Abigail thought. *Mealtime is the ideal opportunity for conversation. If I ask the right questions, perhaps something will slip out that will shed some light on the situation. With any luck, I'll discover enough to solve this puzzle once and for all.*

*****

Abigail stirred with the breaking dawn and smiling stretched her arms towards the bright sunshine. Her maid entered to find her lady in high spirits, filled with optimism.

Mary helped her rise and they chatted at her dressing table while she prepared Abigail for the day.

When she entered the library at the usual time to meet Darrell, Abigail's bright outlook dimmed. He was obviously in a foul mood. Barely extending to her a morning's greeting, he gripped her arm and escorted her to the north wing.

Edward, who was in his library, rose upon their entrance. In stark contrast to Darrell, his disposition seemed to have improved considerably since their previous visit.

"Good morning, Brother," Darrell said coldly.

"Good morning, Darrell, Abigail," Edward replied, bowing his head.

"It's a pleasure to see you again," she said.

"We've come to join you for breakfast," Darrell explained.

"Eleanor informed me I should expect you," Edward said. "Shall we move to the dining room?"

"We can't very well eat here," Darrell said. He took Abigail's arm.

She was taken aback by the crustiness of his comment and wondered if he'd been joking, as brothers are apt to do.

They situated themselves at the dining table. Eleanor arrived shortly thereafter with the breakfast tray. "Good morning, my dears." She placed the tray on the table. "Enjoy yourselves, now."

When she turned to leave, she gave Abigail a fond wink.

"You're very pretty," Edward said.

"Yes, yes; you complimented Abigail during our last meeting," Darrell snapped at him.

Abigail winced when Edward lowered his head ashamedly. A strained silence ensued.

"I've heard you play the piano," she said to revive the conversation. "You perform beautifully."

"Thank you," Edward said.

"Have you been playing a long time?" she asked.

"About ten years."

Abigail realized he must have learned shortly after Emily died. "You have a remarkable gift. Listening to you is a joy."

Edward seemed embarrassed and looked away.

Is he not used to praise, or does he believe he doesn't deserve admiration? she wondered.

"You're getting married," Edward said.

"We've discussed the event previously. There's no need to broach the topic again," Darrell admonished.

"You didn't say when you're to wed."

"The date isn't any concern of yours."

Abigail found this retort of Darrell's irrefutably dismissive. "We're marrying in mid-November, which is fortunate since there are many arrangements yet to complete."

Darrell sneered. A marked tension permeated the room.

Abigail wanted to ease the strain. "Edward, would you play for us when we've finished eating?"

"He cannot. I've business to attend," Darrell said.

"Another time, then," she said.

"I...would enjoy this," Edward said, visibly wary of his brother's reaction.

His concern was justified when Darrell scowled. "I've been detained long enough." He rose and pulled out Abigail's chair, his action so unexpected she was forced to place her fork and napkin on the table.

"It was a lovely breakfast. Thank you, Edward," she said.

He stood with notable disappointment. "The pleasure was all mine."

"Good day." Darrell smirked at his brother once more before he drew Abigail out of the wing.

"Never pose a suggestion to Edward without my permission," he said as he locked the doors. "It isn't your place to determine his activities."

"I'm sorry; it won't happen again," Abigail said.

"See that it doesn't." Darrell strode off.

That was a disaster, she thought. *At least I learned one thing; whatever the reason, Darrell has no patience or tolerance for poor Edward.*

When she walked towards the foyer, she happened upon Catherine.

"Good morning, Abigail."

"Good morning, Catherine. I've just come from the north wing."

"Eleanor told me you were dining with Darrell and Edward. It would appear it went badly."

"To put it mildly."

"What happened?"

"I thought it'd be pleasant if Edward played for us after breakfast and asked him if he would. Darrell was piqued by the notion and ended our visit when we'd barely begun to eat."

"That's hardly surprising. I would've been stunned if he'd agreed."

"He's cold towards Edward; I'd say to the point of cruelty."

"Indeed, he's utterly callous in his treatment of our brother. It's as though he wears a shield of armor; thick and impenetrable."

"Darrell is more troubled than he appears. During dinner last night, he admitted there are issues contributing to his animosity I doubt he'll reveal. I'm inclined to agree with your opinion of Edward also. He doesn't appear dangerous; he may possess the gentlest soul I've encountered."

"He's gentle and kind to everyone except himself, which is why Darrell maintains he's dangerous. While there is a level of truth here, I suspect primarily he wants an excuse to keep our brother locked away."

"If this could be Darrell's purpose, I must meet with Edward again. I haven't spent enough time with him to assess the severity of his condition."

"Before you are married?"

"I don't mean to imply I may break the engagement."

"You needn't hesitate to speak your mind in my presence. In any event, it's doubtful Darrell will agree to another visit."

"That's the idea. I want to observe Edward without Darrell's interference."

"Are you suggesting you'd see him without permission?"

"To learn the truth, I have no choice."

"You mustn't consider it. Darrell would be beyond irate if he discovered you."

"I'll wait for him to be away on business."

"Have you forgotten how unpredictable he may be? Don't you remember the night he came home without prior notice and caught you at the doors of the north wing?"

"How could I forget? I must have help to prevent it from happening. Do you suppose Jake and Eleanor would provide their assistance?"

"Jake is exclusively loyal to Darrell. He would never go behind his back. Eleanor, on the other hand, may be willing. It grieves her Edward is alone most of the time. Even so, she wouldn't let you visit by yourself."

"You could come with me. I know you'd like to see Edward if you don't mind the risk."

"I'm perfectly willing to take the risk, but we'll still need Eleanor's help. I don't have a key."

"Let's arrange then to speak with her privately."

"There's no harm in asking. She's too busy at this time of day. The afternoon will be better."

"Shall we approach her after tea?"

"That should be a good time. I'll slip her a note, and request we meet in her parlor."

*****

At teatime's conclusion, the girls hurried to Eleanor's quarters. They were excited, for Darrell had informed them of his plan to depart town in a few days. Already they had the perfect opportunity to visit Edward since Darrell estimated he'd be absent the better part of a week. Eleanor's initial reaction was, conversely, far less than enthusiastic.

"Oh dear, dear, dear," she said, shaking her head. "As much as I'd love to help Edward, this is a foolhardy venture. It may not matter if Darrell is away. Jake is his second set of eyes. I shudder to imagine the consequences if he were to nab us."

"Suppose Jake had to be away also; if he went to town before Darrell's return," Catherine suggested.

"When will Darrell depart?" Eleanor asked.

"In three days, on the afternoon train," Abigail said.

Eleanor was silent a moment while she considered their proposal. "Jake was to head into town tomorrow. Perhaps I could find a reason to delay him until Darrell leaves."

"It would be marvelous if you could," Catherine said.

"To pull this off, we'll have to plan carefully," Eleanor said. "One potential snag is the duration of Jake's trips. They vary significantly, depending upon the errands he must perform and the supplies we require. We'd have a few hours at best."

"Write a list which will detain him as long as possible. Be certain you add to it every imaginable item," Catherine said.

"I could send along my knives to be sharpened, and shoes which need cobbling. That should occupy him quite a while."

"This sounds like a good plan," Abigail said.

"Don't raise your hopes, my dears. First, I must convince Jake to delay. We can't proceed otherwise."

Catherine grinned. "I'm not worried, Eleanor. I have complete confidence in your ability to influence Jake."

*****

Fate, as it happened, was in favor of the ladies. Throughout the course of the next few days, the weather was inclement, which obliged Jake to postpone his trip.

The day following Darrell's departure the sky had cleared sufficiently for Jake to travel to town, his lengthy list in hand. As soon as he was out of sight, the women hurried to the north wing.

Eleanor peered around warily and then unlocked the doors. "Edward isn't expecting you. I didn't want to give him false hope in the event our plan fell apart. One person passing by could ruin everything."

After they entered the wing, Eleanor checked the corridor once more before she secured the doors.

They found Edward in his library. When he saw them, he dropped the book he was reading and rose with a confused expression.

Catherine gave him a hug. "Good morning, dearest Brother."

"Goo…good morning. Why are you here?"

"I wanted to become further acquainted with the man who is to be my brother," Abigail said. "I hope you don't mind."

"Not at all, only I don't understand how this is possible." Edward glanced around nervously. "Where is Darrell?"

"He's gone to London to attend to his current project," Catherine said.

"Oh." He fidgeted, apparently thrown off by his unexpected guests.

"Edward, do you remember what is polite to suggest when you have visitors?" Eleanor asked.

"Would you… care to sit?"

"We'd love to," Catherine accepted. "It's fortunate our lovely Abigail is joining the family, don't you agree, Edward?"

He wrung his hands. "Yes, she is….I do…and I hope…wish you all the best."

Abigail smiled, touched by his shy admiration. "Thank you, Edward. I was thrilled to discover Darrell has such a talented family member."

He looked downward. "Thank you, Abigail."

"Tell us more about your home in Vienna," Catherine requested. "Darrell hasn't provided us with many details."

"England is, in fact, my ancestral home," she explained. "We lived in Crawley until I was twelve when we located to Vienna."

Abigail saw Edward flinch. She recalled he was the same age when his sad turn of fortune occurred.

"My father had accepted the position as dean of the English department at the University of Vienna, where I studied when the time came. Prior to then, I attended a school established for the children of the faculty, where I met the three girls who to this day are my dearest friends."

She proceeded to recount tales of them, along with her family and the city itself. Edward evidently hung upon her every word, presumably engrossed by the account of a happier adolescence than he'd experienced.

When Abigail concluded her story, Eleanor rose. "Although I hate to interrupt this pleasant morning, I must get on with my day."

Edward appeared crushed.

"Catherine and Abigail may stay a while longer. I'll return when it's time for them to depart," Eleanor said. She stepped rapidly down the hallway.

"Edward, would you play for us?" Abigail asked. "We hadn't the chance during my previous visit. I'd love to hear you now."

"If you wouldn't mind my faltering. I'm unaccustomed to an audience."

"You needn't be uneasy. I've listened to you on numerous occasions. Likely you were unaware, yet you've been playing for a captive and appreciative patron," Abigail said.

"Is there a particular piece you'd like me to play?"

"Play what you prefer. I enjoy all genres of music."

He escorted the ladies to the music room. Abigail listened in awe, amazed not only by his performance but by the improvement in his demeanor. When absorbed in his playing he exuded the confidence and peacefulness she hadn't witnessed in him, as a hint of the man he may've become under different circumstances emerged. Catherine looked over at her and gave her a knowing grin.

After he'd performed several pieces, Eleanor entered. "Jake may return at any moment. I'm afraid the girls must leave."

Edward's expression became pained, his behavior that of a disappointed youngster.

"You played beautifully, Edward," Abigail said. "Thank you for sharing your talent with us."

"Will you visit again?"

Abigail smiled at him. "We hope to. Unfortunately, it could be a long while before we have the opportunity."

"I understand," he said. "Thank you for coming."

Eleanor and Catherine gave him a hug. Abigail offered him her hand, which he took in his usual gentle manner. She could barely feel the kiss he placed on it.

As they departed Abigail glanced back. Edward stood in the doorway of the music room, gazing at them in a wistful manner.

Once they were outside the north wing, Abigail saw Catherine was wiping her eyes.

"Why are you crying?" Abigail asked.

"Edward was so happy. It broke my heart we had to leave. We won't return for such a long time."

"I haven't seen him that well in ages. He was downright chipper," Eleanor said.

"Couldn't we find a way to visit him more often?" Abigail asked. "It's bound to help his morale."

"To be truthful, I no longer think it's terribly dangerous," Eleanor said. "When Darrell is away there's not much call for anyone, other than Jake and myself, to be near the north wing. When my husband is engrossed in his duties, he blocks out all else. He's such a creature of habit I can predict his whereabouts at any given moment. I believe if I maintain a watchful eye, you could continue with your visits throughout Darrell's absence."

Catherine appeared thrilled. "That would be wonderful!"

"We ought to continue then," Abigail said.

Eleanor nodded. "Tomorrow I'll alert you when Jake is in the thick of a task, and we'll give it a try."

"How will you explain our absence if Jake discovers we've gone missing?" Catherine asked.

"A good point," Eleanor said. "We must try to foresee each event which could spell disaster. Should he inquire, I'll claim you're having an outing. We must also take every precaution you're not spotted entering or exiting the north wing. If someone brought it to the attention of Jake or Darrell, I don't think I need explain how dire the consequence would be."

"We'll employ the utmost caution," Abigail said.

"Our stealth shall be unparalleled," Catherine agreed.

*****

The following day, Catherine and Abigail were nearing the end of luncheon when Eleanor burst into the dining room.

"Jake is attending to chores outside. Come with me quickly." She motioned for them to hurry.

Eleanor unlocked the doors of the north wing with shaky hands and nudged the girls inside.

They found Edward seated in his dining room following lunch. He appeared incredulous to see them. "You have returned! May you visit awhile?"

"I expect we'll remain until teatime," Catherine said, notably short of breath.

"My goodness, you're winded," he said.

"We did hurry here a bit," his sister explained.

"You shouldn't have risked injuring yourselves on my behalf, though it was kind of you. What shall we do this afternoon? Shall I play for you?"

"That would be delightful," Abigail said.

Edward escorted the ladies to the music room, where he helped them to be seated.

His manner has been nothing other than retiring and gentlemanly. It's difficult to imagine him behaving otherwise, Abigail mused.

During his performance, Abigail witnessed while Edward transformed into the contented individual who'd emerged the day before. She took note of Catherine as well, who was

108

radiating the fondest of pride in her brother. It did her heart good to see the siblings together in such a happy state.

Lost in their enjoyment the afternoon flew by, to the point they were startled when Eleanor entered the room.

"It cannot be time to leave?" Catherine protested.

"It's nearing teatime," Eleanor said.

Edward rose to say goodbye, his appearance downtrodden.

"May we visit tomorrow?" Abigail asked him.

"Please, while it's kind of you to offer, Eleanor tells me the weather has been fine as of late. You shouldn't miss out only to humor me."

Catherine took hold of his shoulder. "We don't consider visiting you a waste of our day. Since we may only come when Darrell is away, we'd prefer to take advantage of the situation, a great deal more than the weather."

"I agree, Catherine," Abigail said.

"You're too kind to me," Edward said.

"Until tomorrow then," Catherine said. She gave him a hug.

"Until tomorrow," he repeated.

*****

At bedtime, Abigail read a cablegram from Darrell Mary had recently delivered. It notified her he'd booked his return trip, and to expect his arrival in two days on the early morning train. For Abigail's part, the news was a mixed blessing. However regretful to disappoint Edward with his brother's premature return, she missed her fiancé. She sighed serenely as she held the cable to her heart.

Upon informing the others the following afternoon, while Edward was disheartened Catherine was downright perturbed.

"So, today's visit will be our last," she grumbled. "Naturally, on *this* occasion, he was able to complete his business promptly. Why wasn't he delayed instead?"

"Please, Catherine, don't be unkind," Edward said. "I'll miss you both, yet Abigail will be happy to have our brother at home."

"No doubt *she* will."

"Truly, I regret our visits must end; however, the circumstance is temporary," Abigail said. "It's reasonable to assume Darrell will travel in the near future."

"I hope it's the *very* near future," Catherine said with a sneer.

"Well now, shall I play for you?" Edward asked.

He smiled at Abigail, who regarded him with appreciation, obvious to her he'd made the suggestion to placate his sister. "As always, we welcome the chance to hear you perform."

He's considerate for a person who's suffered greatly, she thought. *More and more, I believe Darrell is wrong about Edward. He doesn't appear dangerous in the least. But I mustn't be too hasty in my assessment. I haven't any experience with the mentally unbalanced. I'd be wise to recall one cannot be certain what demons lurk in the mind of an individual who's disturbed.*

*****

Abigail awakened prior to the usual time and rung for Mary at once. She wanted to begin her preparations early, hoping to look her best in anticipation of Darrell's return.

Expecting he'd be awaiting her at breakfast, she hurried down the stairs, only to discover he hadn't arrived. She didn't find this overly surprising since schedule delays are commonplace. When luncheon and dinner also passed without word, she was worried something more serious had occurred.

The hour was growing late while she and Catherine awaited Darrell's arrival in the parlor. Abigail kept her mounting anxiety to herself as his sister related her displeasure.

"How thoroughly irritating," Catherine groused. "Had Darrell sent a telegram informing us of the delay, we could have visited Edward another time. Well, I've had enough of this. I believe I'll retire. Are you coming?"

"I'll wait here a while longer."

"Good night then," Catherine said.

Alone Abigail was entrenched in a stony silence, which did nothing to quell her sense of alarm. As midnight approached, she hunched over the armrest of the sofa and squeezed her damp eyes tightly shut. In her estimation, the remaining question was which disaster had befallen her fiancé and prepared herself to receive the horrible news.

When someone touched her shoulder, she jolted, astonished to discover she'd fallen asleep.

"Darrell!"

"Abigail, my darling, you haven't yet gone to bed?" He joined her on the sofa and gathered her into his arms.

"I'd no intention of retiring until you arrived safely."

"You should've thought of your health."

"My health was the last thing on my mind."

When he tightened his embrace, she noticed he was shaking.

"Is anything the matter? Did something happen?" she asked.

"No, all is well."

She pulled away to confirm he was flustered. "Something is wrong. You must tell me what it is."

"It's nothing, nothing at all."

"You're not being truthful."

"I give you my word nothing's happened. I'll admit I've been distressed, by nothing other than complete foolishness."

"I've never known you to be foolish. If you're troubled, you must confide in me."

"It's utterly childish. I had an unsettling dream a few nights ago. In it, I came home to find you were gone. I ran frantically through the house, searching everywhere to no avail. When at last I awoke I was overwrought to the point of tears. Fretful my nightmare may have been a premonition, I've been desperate to see you since. Upon my arrival, I rushed directly upstairs. With the door to your bedroom open, I saw you were

111

in fact missing. As in the dream, I sought you out, and have been in agony until I discovered you here."

She smiled at a vulnerability she hadn't witnessed in him previously. "I'm sorry you were upset, but you needn't be ashamed. We all harbor unwarranted fears at times. By now, you should know you'll never lose me."

"I do know. The fact I was unnerved by a dream is absurdly juvenile."

"You may be less embarrassed when I admit I've been distressed as well. I told myself your delay was a common setback, and yet I've been beside myself with worry. When the hour grew late, I was convinced a disaster had occurred."

"Your concerns were at least warranted. I was detained by unforeseen issues and departed much later than I'd intended. Normally I would notify you; however, I was uncertain when I'd be at liberty to travel. When at last I was able to leave I was in a rush to board the late train and didn't stop to send a cable."

"I understand. It doesn't matter, now we're together. I do believe only those who love each other deeply would worry to such an extent."

"I cannot argue with that."

Darrell brushed Abigail's hand with his lips. When he met her gaze, his eyes flared with passion. He kissed the length of her arm up to her neck, their breathing labored as they lay back. She was on the brink of succumbing until he sat up and touched her cheek caringly.

"It's late; we should retire," he said.

With her ardor inflamed she debated whether she wished to deny him; although, the sofa in the parlor wasn't her idea of a romantic first interlude. "I suppose we should."

Darrell's disappointment was evident as he continued to caress her face with his fingers. He lingered a few minutes before he took her hand and helped her to rise.

While they climbed the stairs, Abigail considered suggesting he take her to his bedroom, but couldn't bring herself to make such a bold request. She was also concerned if they fell asleep someone may discover them, and they'd be subjected to a humiliating scandal.

When they arrived at her room, Darrell kissed her cheek. "You'll never leave me, will you?"

"I'll never leave you." Abigail gave him a loving kiss and closed her door.

5

A bigail stood patiently as the bodice of her wedding dress was buttoned. When the veil was placed on her head, she turned around, stunned by the vision she saw reflected in the mirror. The woman gazing back was hard to recognize. She displayed a distinct elegance while wearing her low-cut gown of ivory satin, its fine beading sparkling which enhanced the stylish lace accents.

Cinderella has arrived, Abigail thought. She still doubted her ability to fulfill the expectations of the individual she beheld, by outward appearances a lady of refinement.

"Gracious, my dear, if you aren't the loveliest bride," the person assisting her exclaimed. Although she stood nearby, to Abigail, the voice sounded distant, as if she was a participant in a dream. "Mr. Lewis will be very pleased."

The woman removed the veil. "Please lift your arms so I may begin the fitting. The bodice needs to be taken in a tad, and we must raise the hem," the dress shop seamstress informed her.

"Are you certain the gown isn't overly elaborate?"

"Not at all, in view of the gentleman you're to marry. Try to remain still. I wouldn't want to prick you with the pins."

Abigail continued to appraise her reflection as the tucking and pinning commenced. *How I wish Catherine was here to reassure me*, she thought.

Although she'd agreed to accompany Abigail, Catherine had claimed a sudden ailment and reneged. Since she didn't appear unwell, Abigail assumed she'd angered her in some way.

This proved to be only the first in a series of slights Catherine was to inflict over the course of the next few days. Her callous behavior had disappointed Abigail, particularly since her previous weeks at Rochester Manor had otherwise been idyllic. Darrell had remained at home throughout, each day a romantic holiday for the couple as they'd spent much of their time together.

With Catherine's mood testy, Abigail had frequently inquired regarding her wellbeing. She didn't admit anything was bothering her, yet made her feelings plain by missing meals, refusing to participate in activities, and adding little to any conversation.

This continued until one day, as Darrell lavished upon Abigail his amorous attention, she saw his sister glaring at them. At this moment the probable cause of her sour attitude dawned on Abigail. She requested Catherine meet her in the boudoir to discuss the issue.

"You've been displeased with me as of late, and I imagine I know the reason," Abigail said. "I suppose you're upset with me because of Edward."

"I'm far more than upset. Evidently, while you've been entranced by the company of your devoted fiancé, you've managed to forget I have another brother."

"Why do you presume I've forgotten him? On the contrary, I think of him frequently."

"Why should I believe this when you haven't so much as asked after him in ages?"

"I made the assumption all was the same as before."

"In this, you're entirely wrong."

"What do you mean?"

"Eleanor confided in me Edward isn't well. She tells me as of late he's hardly touched his food and does nothing other than mope about. Hasn't it caught your attention we haven't heard him play in weeks? Recently Eleanor allowed me a brief visit when you and Darrell were taking a drive, in the hopes I could raise his spirits. I was shocked to the core by his appearance. He was happy to see me; however, it was obvious I'm not the person he's truly missing. Now I wish you'd never visited him. It turns out your fleeting attention was a crueler deed than leaving him be."

"I'm awfully sorry my idea has led to this. It never occurred to me he would react in this way."

"It didn't to me either. In fairness, it isn't your fault, but Eleanor and I are terribly concerned. He's dreadfully morose. We fear he's slipping into a hopeless state."

"Oh, no; this mustn't continue. Darrell mentioned problems have arisen with his current venture which may require him to travel. Have Eleanor tell Edward I miss our visits also, and we should be able to meet in the near future."

"I will. I hope you're correct, for the sooner this takes place, the better."

*****

The following morning, Abigail had good news to share with Catherine.

"Darrell's business troubles have worsened. He's to depart tomorrow and expects to be engaged for at least a fortnight."

Catherine appeared relieved. "Thank heavens."

"He feels bad he'll be away for a lengthy period. I'm to meet with him shortly. I'll see you at luncheon."

"Until then."

Abigail went to the study. She tapped on the door.

"Come in," Darrell called out. "My dearest love. I've concluded the preparations for my trip. My time is now yours. Shall we take a stroll prior to luncheon?"

"That would be lovely."

She took the arm he offered, and they left to walk the garden path.

"Dearest, there's a matter regarding my trip I've yet to relate. I've made arrangements for Catherine which I'm concerned may be a hardship for you."

"Arrangements?"

"I've taken the liberty of extending my drive in the morning to call upon the Kensington household."

"Who are the Kensingtons?"

"They're the friends my sister was visiting when Eleanor summoned her back unexpectedly. Since her stay was cut short, I've decided to make amends by escorting her there on my way out of town. I'd sent them a cable, and they're delighted to have her return. It will be nice for her, though I fear I may have been inconsiderate in your regard."

"You needn't be concerned about me. Catherine will be... excited I'm sure." She knew she'd be anything but.

"I presume she will. I've been awaiting the Kensingtons' reply prior to informing her, which fortunately came this morning."

She forced a grin. "How opportune."

"I thought so."

"Will she stay with the Kensingtons until your return?"

"I see no reason she shouldn't unless it will be a burden for you."

"How could it be? As you know, I'm used to fending for myself."

"I suppose it would be possible for you to join Catherine if you'd prefer. I doubt her friend or the family would mind."

"I wouldn't dream of imposing. Catherine should enjoy the company of her dear friends alone."

"Thank you, my sweet. Look ahead, there are buds on the rose bushes."

Abigail attempted to maintain her composure while they walked at a leisurely pace, from her perspective a great deal slower than usual. Having learned of Darrell's plan, she wished they wouldn't dally. To be unable to visit Edward was sure to upset Catherine. Since Darrell wouldn't understand why she'd be displeased to reunite with her friends, Abigail worried it would cause him to be suspicious, and if he pressed her for an explanation, his sister might let something slip. Abigail believed it was crucial to warn Catherine about the trip prior to luncheon, but with time elapsing, the opportunity to do so was running short.

When at last they arrived at the house, it was with only a few minutes to spare.

Please, Catherine, don't be early, Abigail thought.

To her relief, she wasn't in the dining room.

"Darrell, would you please excuse me? I'd like to freshen myself."

"Take all the time you need, my darling."

Abigail walked with poise until she was out of Darrell's sight. She then raced up the stairs and knocked frantically on Catherine's door.

Catherine opened it in alarm. "My gracious, Abigail, whatever is the matter?"

"Darrell has informed me of a plan he's devised. It's bound to upset you."

"What plan?"

"He intends to take you to the Kensingtons' tomorrow on his way out of town."

"What are you speaking of? He's mentioned none of this to me."

"He will at luncheon, which is why I wanted to notify you prior. He cabled them recently and received word today they're happy to have you return."

"How typical he made the arrangement without consulting me."

"His purpose is to atone for shortening your previous trip. He assumes you'll be delighted."

"Under normal circumstances, I would be. At present there's no choice in the matter; I must refuse."

"Upon what grounds? Any reason you offer he'll likely find suspect."

"I could claim it wouldn't be thoughtful to leave you without companionship."

"We've addressed the point. I told him I wouldn't mind."

Catherine looked exasperated. "What possessed you to say this? It would've provided the perfect excuse."

"Previously, I've assured him as an only child I'm capable of amusing myself. He may've found it odd for me to claim otherwise. I doubt it would've made a difference. I believe his mind was already set. Any protest will serve to annoy him."

"Set or not, we must address the situation with Edward without delay. Let Darrell become irritated if he's so inclined."

"Let's not be rash. If you refuse, we must concoct a defensible explanation."

"Nothing comes to mind. He may roar the house down, but he cannot force me to leave."

"A moment here," Abigail said when a thought occurred to her. "There's no need for you to object. If you depart with Darrell, what would prevent me from visiting Edward?"

"Only that Eleanor must keep watch. You'd have to meet him without an escort."

"I don't see why I shouldn't."

"You aren't afraid to be alone with him?"

"There's nothing to fear. I'm convinced he's no longer dangerous."

"Abigail, I'll be honest with you. His mental state has deteriorated since you last saw him. There's no guarantee you'll be safe in his company."

"As you rightfully pointed out, his decline was a result of *my* interference. Since it's my fault, I must at least try to help him."

"I want you to help my brother, and yet I won't forgive myself if he's regressed to the extent he harms you."

"If I thought him capable of harming me, I wouldn't offer my assistance."

"I hope you're correct. I'll agree, on the stipulation you promise to take the utmost precaution. You should maintain your distance at first. If his behavior appears at all threatening, run away. Pound on the door if you must. Your discovery would be preferable to the alternative."

"You have my assurance, I'll proceed carefully."

"Bless you, then, for this kindness, dearest Abigail. You are a sister to me, in the truest sense."

"I'm glad to hear it. I've always wanted a sister. Goodness, look at the time! I told Darrell I would freshen myself. He must be wondering what's detained me."

"Since you've gone beyond the call of duty in regard to Edward, I'll take responsibility for your delay."

Catherine gave Abigail an affectionate hug and took her arm before they headed to the dining room.

*****

Eleanor and Abigail shaded their eyes from the late morning sun and waved as the carriage with Darrell and Catherine on board pulled away.

"Are you certain you want to attempt this?" Eleanor asked.

"I'm quite certain."

When the carriage was far down the drive, they went to the north wing.

"I haven't told Edward to expect you," Eleanor said. "You may yet change your mind."

Abigail shook her head. "My mind hasn't changed."

"I should accompany you inside. Edward is frail; however, a determined spirit can overcome physical weakness. He may yet have the ability to overpower you."

"Thank you, Eleanor, it won't be necessary. Your keeping watch will provide the protection I truly require."

Eleanor turned the key. "Edward will assume I've locked the doors. I won't in case you must flee. Don't hesitate if you're uneasy."

"I won't delay."

Eleanor handed her a candle, and Abigail entered. As she crept along the hallway, the light flickered eerily, which created a disquieting atmosphere. Suddenly, the warnings she'd taken in stride rattled her nerves. In addition to the advice of

Catherine and Eleanor, Darrell's assertion she'd be safe only when in his company came to mind. The further she progressed, the more fearful she became. With each step a chore, she paused to reconsider the wisdom of her actions. She reminded herself in the past Edward had been nothing other than meek and kind towards her. Without her help, she was concerned his present unhealthy condition would deteriorate. She determined it would be her responsibility if the worst happened; therefore, she must proceed.

She gathered her courage and continued on tiptoe. Despite her attempt to remain brave, a shiver raced down her spine as the hairs on the back of her neck rose. Touching them, she loosened her decorative comb. With its sharp prongs, it occurred to her the typically innocuous item could be used to inflict injury, and she thought it best to remove it. She shoved it behind the handkerchief in her pocket in the hopes Edward wouldn't notice it was there.

Near the library, she heard his movement and peered around the corner. She covered her mouth when she saw how painfully feeble he'd become. With her mouth dry and breathing shallow, she took a step into the room.

Edward glanced up and leaped from his chair. On the verge of bolting from the room, Abigail changed her mind when she saw his expression of elation. Regardless of his appearance, her shoulders stiffened. She held the doorframe for support in the event he tried to grab her.

"Abigail!" He extended his hand to her.

She hesitated before offering hers. To her relief, he held her hand as gently as ever. The whisper of a kiss he placed on it provided her further assurance there was nothing to fear.

"It's a pleasure to see you, Edward." Her voice was raspy.

"No, no; the pleasure is mine. I presume Darrell is away?"

"Yes, he and Catherine left a short while ago. We're expecting their return in a fortnight."

"I see. Would you care to have a seat?"

"I would, thank you. I hope you'll accept my apology for my lengthy absence. Had it been possible, I'd have come sooner."

"You needn't trouble yourself. I understand why you must wait for my brother to depart. You're kind to visit when I've little to offer in return."

"That's not true. I enjoy our meetings and take particular pleasure in your playing. May I ask why we haven't heard you as of late?"

"I haven't had the desire, with no one to perform for."

"I've mentioned before I can hear your performance from outside the north wing. I've been missing it tremendously."

He looked contrite. "I had forgotten. How inconsiderate of me."

"You weren't really. I do hope since I've reminded you we'll hear you more often."

"I promise you will."

"Would you play for me now?"

"I'd be delighted."

Edward escorted her to the music room. As she'd witnessed previously, his spirits seemed to rise the moment he sat at the piano.

It was obvious he was enjoying himself greatly until he'd played a few selections, and Eleanor entered the room.

"Must Abigail leave?" he asked.

"I'm afraid she must. It's nearing luncheon time. She'll be expected in the dining room shortly. Since Jake will soon be on his way with yours, it would be dangerous to delay."

"Thank you, Edward, for sharing your talent with me," Abigail said. "As usual, your performance was astounding. I'd love to return tomorrow if you'll have me?"

He grinned. "I'll find a way to manage."

Abigail offered him her hand. "Until tomorrow, then."

After he kissed it, she and Eleanor walked to the corridor doors. Once they were back in the daylight, Eleanor secured the locks.

"I gather he wasn't any trouble?" Eleanor asked.

"None whatsoever. I was shocked by how feeble he's become. I don't believe a few visits will help him significantly. If he's to make true progress, I must come here frequently."

"It would improve his health tremendously if you're willing to make the effort."

"It's no effort. After all, I'm currently in need of companionship as well. Perhaps I could visit him on a daily basis."

"Such a dear, sweet girl you are. If this is to be a daily occurrence, I'll provide you with a key. For safety's sake, we'll set a schedule for your visits. The house is typically quiet between the hours of two and four. At those times, I could easily keep the area clear."

"An excellent suggestion."

"I'll have the key copied today and hide it in your dresser drawer."

They heard footsteps approaching.

"That will be Jake," Eleanor said. "You must hurry along, my dear."

"Thank you, Eleanor," Abigail said and scurried out of the corridor.

*****

The following afternoon at two o'clock, Abigail tucked the newly made key into her pocket. For the first time, she was able to enter the north wing of her own accord.

Not surprisingly, Edward was ecstatic when she explained the plan she and Eleanor had devised. During the course of the next two weeks, Abigail witnessed with pride the steady improvement in his health. Not only did he gain weight and stamina, but she also found the advancement in his mentality remarkable. By the time Darrell was due to return the awkward, childlike individual had all but vanished, as an engaging adult had begun to take his place.

In view of his progress, when the day of their final visit arrived, Abigail faced with reluctance the task of notifying Edward; although, he acknowledged it first.

"Darrell will return home tomorrow, I believe?"

"This is when we're expecting him."

"I'll miss our visits, very much."

"As will I. It's been a pleasure to have become better acquainted with you. You're in every sense a brother to me, and not in name alone; I've become fond of you."

"Thank you, Abigail. Goodness knows I couldn't ask for a lovelier or more caring sister."

"Our time apart is a temporary state. Since Darrell travels frequently, it shouldn't be long before I have the opportunity to return."

"Please don't be concerned for me. I'm aware of the circumstance. I appreciate the kindness you're willing to extend me."

"The comprehension of a situation doesn't make its endurance easier. My fondest wish is one day we'll no longer need to meet in secrecy. When you're sufficiently recovered, I hope to convince your brother to unlock these doors and allow you to rejoin the family."

"The locks aren't detaining me. I wouldn't leave if the doors were unlocked."

Abigail stared at him in disbelief. "Edward, why do you say this?"

"In light of my horrendous deed, I must remain in the north wing until my dying day. It's what I deserve."

"You cannot mean it. To believe this is absurd."

"It's not absurd in the least. It's my fault Emily fell."

"You weren't the cause of her demise."

"Of course, I was."

"How did you arrive at this conclusion?"

"Quite easily, since I forced her to climb higher than she should have."

"In what way did you *force* her?"

124

"On the upper branches, the view was astounding. We were celebrating, and I wanted her to share it with me. She was frightened, but I urged her relentlessly until she gave in."

"This sounds like encouragement, not force."

"I goaded her into it, by accusing her of behaving like a ninny."

"Even so, if she thought herself incapable, name calling alone didn't force her. She had the option to refuse."

"She didn't want to disappoint me."

"People have been known to disappoint one another by choosing to follow their own counsel."

"Why do you continue with this debate when the facts are straightforward? No rationale can change them. It cannot be denied what I did was inexcusable."

"In hindsight, you would've done otherwise, yet you couldn't have foreseen she would be seriously hurt. Many children in their day have fallen from trees. It was merely a dreadful misfortune her injuries were severe."

"*Merely* a misfortune; how dare you claim this? Emily wasn't *merely* injured; she *died,* as a result of my foolishness."

"I understand your sense of responsibility to a point. Still, what transpired was an accident; you meant her no harm."

"My intention makes no difference. She's gone, due to my selfish conduct."

"While her fate was grievous, it doesn't follow you should be punished, particularly in this harsh manner."

"Not only do I deserve punishment, a sentence worthy of my transgression doesn't exist. At a minimum, I must remain in this darkness, and consider each day how heinously I've hurt everyone I love."

"This simply isn't true. You mustn't continue to think in this way."

"You would presume to tell me how I must think? You know nothing of the matter."

"I know enough to conclude your viewpoint is unwarranted. If you permit me, I may be able to help you."

"No, no. I'll listen to you no longer."

It was clear he was becoming agitated.

"Please, Edward, I don't want to upset you. Just hear what I have to say."

"Stop this, stop this!" he shouted.

He traipsed the length of the room, wandering back and forth while he yanked at his hair. His sanity seemed to abandon him when he snatched a small chair and threw it. It hit the fireplace grate, breaking off one of the legs.

She stood dumbfounded when Edward leaned over, panting as he glared at the broken chair, presumably contemplating his options. In a trancelike state, he picked up the detached leg. He gripped it in the manner of a mallet before he turned towards Abigail.

Moving with a surreal slowness, he stepped in her direction. A wave of panic seized her, like a thousand demonic fingers grasping at her body. With Edward between her and the doorway, escape didn't appear possible. She opened her mouth to cry for help, but her throat clenched. She couldn't produce a sound.

He drew nearer. Abigail shuddered violently while thoughts raced through her head. *Darrell warned me of this; why didn't I believe him? What'll I do? If I run now, he'll capture me easily. I must wait… wait until he's closer, and then try to duck under his arms. Dear Lord, I beg you, give me the ability to escape!*

By this time, Edward was a few feet away. She was bracing herself to make her move when to her surprise he turned the chair leg on its side. He offered it to her with both hands.

"Please," he said.

"Please, what?" she asked hoarsely.

"Please, release me from my torment."

"I don't understand."

"*Please.* If I knock myself out, I won't be able to finish the job."

Abigail's eyes widened. "Edward, no…this isn't the answer."

He thrust his hands towards her. "I beg you!"

She reached for the leg cautiously. He smiled when she took the piece from him until she placed it on the floor and kicked it away.

"I'll do no such thing, and neither will you," she said.

Edward broke down. He fell to his knees, shaking with the force of his sobs.

Abigail held her chest in relief. She knelt next to him and placed her hand on his shoulder.

He flinched and looked up, his face distorted in anguish. "Her hand was there, almost touching mine." He extended his in demonstration. "Had she been a fraction nearer… a mere fraction nearer…"

"Edward, I'm sorry, terribly sorry."

"Why, Abigail, why did this happen?"

She shook her head. "I don't know. Sometimes things simply go wrong. But what choice have we other than to accept life's risks? Whether for entertainment or necessity, in every activity lays a level of peril. To live fully, we cannot avoid them all."

"Climbing trees is nothing other than foolishness."

"If this were true, your parents would have forbidden you. They must have been aware of the potential danger, more so than you."

"They did encourage us to engage in sport. Both Emily's parents and mine accepted our love of climbing."

"Many climb for the sheer pleasure of it; adults as well as children. There are those who climb, ride, run or shoot, despite the possible consequences. We're meant to enjoy our lives, not merely stay alive."

"Most employ measures to minimize the peril, which I did not. It was irresponsible of me to be careless."

"You were a child at the time. You shouldn't have subjected yourself to adult accountability."

"I wasn't a small child, I was twelve. My age doesn't exonerate my actions; don't you agree?"

"Perhaps if you view the matter from another perspective, you'll find the answer. Suppose Emily had persuaded you to climb higher, and it was you who fell. To follow your line of reasoning, you'd expect her to be punished by spending the remainder of her days in a dark prison."

"No, I wouldn't; not at all."

"You'd be upset if she treated herself with such cruelty, wouldn't you?"

"I cannot bear the thought of her suffering in this way."

"Then you must recognize in your heart Emily would be grieved by the way you've treated yourself. Hiding from the world doesn't honor her memory; it's quite the opposite. To honor her you must live your life fully unless you imagine she'd want you to suffer."

"She wouldn't. She was the sweetest girl who ever lived. It was never my intention to dishonor her."

"Of course, it wasn't. I imagine penitence has been a means for you to survive the agony of her loss, as well as atone for the burden of your guilt. While blaming ourselves is easy, forgiveness is often far more difficult to attain. I suspect Emily would want you to forgive yourself and put an end to this punishment. The question is; do you believe it?"

Edward wept softly. "I do." Upon regaining his composure, he wiped his tears with his sleeve. "I'm sorry I frightened you."

"No harm was done," she said.

"Except for the chair. What will I tell Jake when he arrives? I cannot claim this was an accident."

"I'm afraid not. If we hid it, do you suppose he'd notice it's gone missing?"

"It's unlikely he would."

"Is there a closet where we could bury it, perhaps one used for storage?"

"At the end of the wing is a room which isn't used anymore."

"Then let's hide it there."

Edward carried the chair, while Abigail followed with the broken leg. He stuffed the pieces behind some other items. She draped it with a dust cover she'd found.

She brushed her hands and began to walk away.

He took her arm gently to stop her. "Abigail, thank you."

"It should be hidden sufficiently."

"Not for the chair. Thank you for releasing me from my torment."

"You're most welcome, dearest Edward."

He gazed deeply into her eyes. They were lost in the enormity of the moment until the clock chimed four.

"I'd no idea of the time. I must leave," Abigail said.

Edward escorted her to the corridor doors, where he took her hand.

"Until we meet again, promise me you'll take care of yourself, my dear brother."

"Please do the same, my dear sister."

"I'll return as soon as I can."

"I'll look most forward to seeing you."

Abigail glanced at her hand which he was yet holding.

Edward quickly released it. "I'm sorry."

She opened the door. "Goodbye for now."

"Goodbye," he returned. He smiled warmly before she left.

Merciful heavens, she thought as she locked the door. *What an afternoon!*

As frightening as the encounter was, it was hard for Abigail to comprehend how well it had ended. Edward had made significant progress. If he was able to recover fully, she believed it was possible he would one day rejoin the family.

Don't get ahead of things, she cautioned herself. *Take matters a step at a time. If Edward regressed before, he could regress again. Only time will tell if this family can truly become whole.*

*****

Abigail had entered her bedroom to retire for the night when a knock came at her door.

"Come in, Mary," she called out, though it wasn't her. "Why, good evening, Eleanor."

"Good evening, my dear. We've each received a telegram from Darrell, which you'll want to read without delay." She handed the page to her. "Would you mind if we sat a moment?"

"Please; let's do so." Abigail surveyed the cable. "I see he's having great difficulty with his venture. He'll be away another two weeks at a minimum."

"Which is most opportune, given the change in Edward's attitude, don't you think?"

"His improvement is noticeable?"

"It's remarkable. When I delivered his dinner, I found him in astonishingly high spirits. Since today was to be your last visit, I asked him why he was so perky. He told me what happened this afternoon."

"What did he say precisely?"

"He said you explained the circumstance surrounding Emily's death in a way no one else had. At long last, he agrees it was an accident. Thanks to you, his guilty conscience has been eased."

"I'm glad he didn't change his mind after I left. Now that I may continue my visits, I hope he'll make further progress. Maybe he'll improve enough to live with the family."

"Oh no, my dear, I'm afraid I don't foresee this."

"You don't believe he can recover sufficiently?"

"That remains to be seen. My chief concern here isn't Edward, it's Darrell."

"*Darrell* concerns you? Are you implying he wouldn't release Edward under any circumstance?"

"It's highly doubtful."

"Why do you find it doubtful? Darrell is a reasonable man. Surely whatever stands between them could be addressed."

"He is reasonable, except in his opinion of Edward. Resentment may be a persistent ailment, particularly when the wound is deep."

"You know the issues, apart from the obvious, that adds to his resentment, don't you?"

"No… not specifically."

"Eleanor, you mustn't hide anything from me. I must learn the truth."

"I give you my word; I know nothing more than you."

"Since you claim to be unfamiliar with the particulars, you must concede to reunite them isn't out of the question. If Edward could be helped it's possible Darrell can be helped as well, don't you agree?"

"Your accomplishment with Edward was extraordinary. Still, it's bound to be a greater challenge where Darrell is concerned."

"For the time being, to argue is useless. The point will be moot unless Edward recovers completely. Frankly, I don't see how it can happen if he must remain in the north wing. When you think of it, we have a paradox on our hands. To recover he must be away from there, but there's no chance of his release until he recovers, unless…"

"What's going through your head?"

"Perhaps we could take him out of there, if only for a few hours. Any amount of time away would be helpful."

"It's a daft idea. Even if we were willing to take the risk, we mustn't with Jake in the house… but… he *won't* be in the house tomorrow! He's to run the household errands."

"Do we dare attempt it? What of the other servants?"

"I could offer them an afternoon's holiday. With Darrell and Catherine away, the workload is light."

"It would be wonderful for Edward if you don't think we're being foolish."

"For his sake, I believe it's worth a try."

"We should; in fact, we must. He's been in that awful place far too long."

"We're in agreement then?"

"We are."

"I'll inform the staff at once and make the necessary arrangements."

"Would you permit me to inform Edward? I'd love to see his reaction."

"Certainly, my dear. You've more than earned the privilege."

There was a tap at the door.

Mary entered. "Forgive me, Mrs. Williams. I'd no idea you were here."

"It's no trouble, Mary. I was on the point of leaving," Eleanor said. "Good night, my dear Abigail."

"Good night, dear Eleanor," Abigail returned.

Mary closed the door behind her. "Everything is well?"

"Everything is well, very well indeed," Abigail said.

*****

Abigail entered the north wing the following afternoon, grinning from ear to ear.

Edward jumped from his chair. "Abigail, why are you here?"

"Hello, Edward." She attempted to suppress her excitement. "Darrell sent word business difficulties will detain him an additional two weeks, if not more."

"How marvelous…forgive me, you must be distressed about this."

"Do I appear distressed?"

"No, you seem happy. Is there a particular reason?"

"There is. I have an invitation to extend to you. I believe you'll find it astounding."

"An invitation? To do what?"

"I cordially invite you to take tea with me today," she said in a droll manner.

"How can this be?"

"Jake is out of the house attending to numerous tasks. He isn't expected to return until evening."

"Then it will be my immense pleasure to have you join me."

"I'm afraid you misunderstand. I'm asking you to join *me*."

"I don't take your meaning."

"Eleanor has arranged for us to have our tea in the parlor. Not this parlor, the one in the main part of the house."

She awaited his ecstatic response, stunned to find he looked grim.

"This cannot be. I'm not permitted to leave the north wing."

"You may today. Darrell and Jake are gone, and the staff is on holiday."

"Darrell would never grant his approval, and neither would Jake."

"Those who may object need never learn of this. There's no one in the house who could report to them."

He shook his head. "Thank you for the kind offer, but I cannot accept."

"Why do you refuse?"

"I wouldn't know how to behave."

"You needn't worry about etiquette. No one other than Eleanor and I will be in attendance."

"While I appreciate your gesture, my answer remains no."

"Edward, I don't understand your refusal. I thought you'd be thrilled to at long last leave this horrible place."

"I'm sorry to disappoint you."

"At least grant me an explanation."

"I've already explained my position."

"You haven't provided the true reason."

"The reason is of no importance."

"If you'll confide in me, perhaps I could alleviate your concern."

"You must excuse me. I've no desire to discuss it."

"If you'll decline my offer so be it, but to deny me an explanation is rude."

"I don't intend to be rude, it's simply my position cannot be altered."

"Even so, to address the matter would be beneficial for you."

"You cannot help me with this."

"What an unfair presumption. You should grant me the opportunity."

"You haven't the slightest notion what you ask of me."

"Obviously, I don't. Please, you must tell me."

Edward went to walk out of the room; instead, he turned back. "I'm afraid," he said, his fists clenched. "Are you pleased to hear me admit it? Was this *helpful* information you've gained at my expense?"

"Oh, Edward…"

"Say no more," he cautioned.

"Fear is nothing to be ashamed of. If you'll explain…"

"Huh," he cut her off again. "You've no idea when to leave a matter alone, do you?"

"Only since I wish to offer my help."

Edward smirked while he shook his head. "If I tell you, will you promise to leave me be?"

"First tell me."

"Since you won't relent I will, though I doubt you'll understand my feelings. If I leave here, everything on the outside will remind me of Emily. All the pain, all the torment I've endured will return. I'll be forced to relive each minute of my nightmare."

Abigail regarded him with compassion. "Although you may not believe me, I do understand."

"You understand nothing."

"It's true; I cannot comprehend the strain you're experiencing. Nevertheless, you should make an attempt. My father taught me it's best to face our problems, not hide from them."

"This isn't a mere *problem* to be swept neatly away."

"No, it isn't; however, we've confronted your burden of guilt. To leave this place is the logical next step in your recovery."

"How dare you claim this is logical? Logic doesn't factor into this equation, not in any way."

"Logic was a poor choice of terms. I have a suggestion, which I don't make lightly. Permit me to escort you to the main parlor. If you find anything upsetting to the smallest degree, we'll return here at once."

He dropped his head, his resolve apparently weakening.

"Please, Edward. Emily would be proud of your accomplishment."

"Possibly," he muttered.

"If you won't do this for yourself, do it for my sake."

He considered the idea before he spoke. "If it'll make you happy, I'll try."

"Thank you, Edward."

She stepped towards him. He allowed her to take his arm, trembling as they made their way slowly through the hallway. Several times he paused, and Abigail tugged him to continue. At last, they were at the door.

Eleanor was awaiting them outside. "The coast is clear," she said.

After he hesitated for what seemed a long while, Edward took a step out of his dark world and into the illumination of the corridor. He stood there, squinting from the daylight he hadn't encountered in many years.

"Abigail," he said in a shaky voice.

"I'm here." She took his hand.

He glanced around nervously while the ladies led him to the parlor. They assisted him to the sofa and sat by him on either side.

"Nothing much has changed," he remarked. "It appears to be a beautiful day."

"It certainly is," Abigail said.

"The same as...that day," he added, sounding grim.

Abigail looked at Eleanor, who signaled her readiness to respond if he became unhinged.

Edward stared at a place on the floor. "Emily sat here when we would play games..." He surveyed the rest of the room. "I also remember Mama and Papa, and Catherine and Darrell. We came here every night after dinner."

"Those were wonderful times," Eleanor said. "We've many fond remembrances in this room. Do you recall the

Christmas tree, which always stood in this corner?" She indicated the place.

He smiled. "And all the presents we would open."

"Often too many, in *my* opinion." Eleanor chuckled.

"I received a sailboat one year. It was my favorite present."

"It still rests on the chest of drawers in your room," Eleanor said. "Do you recall the time Darrell ran off with Catherine's new doll?"

"Oh, yes. He was angry with her for nabbing one of his toys and threatened to throw the doll into the woods. Mother and Father forced him to return it and apologize. He was sincerely regretful when he found Catherine was sobbing. She was merely five, after all."

Abigail listened while Eleanor and Edward continued to share stories, relating joyful and entertaining accounts of various holidays, birthdays, and other cherished events. Edward laughed at one of them, the first time she'd heard him do so.

The afternoon sped by. As the sun descended, Eleanor glanced at the clock. "It's getting late. We'll have to end our visit."

They rose to leave the parlor. Abigail held Edward's arm as they walked to the north wing. On the way, it occurred to her it could be cruel to confine Edward to his jail following his taste of freedom.

"You may accompany Edward inside," Eleanor said when they arrived, as though reading her mind. "You mustn't remain more than a few minutes."

"I won't stay long," she said.

"I never realized how dark it is in here," Edward remarked upon their entrance, which amplified Abigail's concern.

"Would you care to sit a moment?" he offered when they arrived at his library.

"Thank you. I hope it isn't too great a trial to return to this dreary place. Will you be well?"

"I'll be well, more than well. Please, forgive my boorish behavior from earlier."

"You weren't boorish. Undoubtedly it was rude of me to press the matter, yet I suspect things turned out for the best."

"To be honest, facing the outside world wasn't as daunting as I'd built up in my mind. Without your guidance, I would never have made an attempt."

"The anticipation of a situation is often worse than the reality." She checked the clock. "The staff will return soon. I must leave."

Edward escorted Abigail to the doorway.

"We'll find another opportunity for you to have a respite from this place," she said.

"As always, you're kind to be concerned about my welfare. Have my assurance, I'll be fine." He kissed her hand. "Thank you, Abigail."

"You're most welcome." She kissed him on the cheek, and his face sparkled. "We'll see each other tomorrow," she said before she stepped into the hallway.

"Until tomorrow," Edward called after her.

"Goodbye, Edward," she replied.

She secured the door. Successful as the afternoon had been Abigail felt drained and went to her room to rest.

A half-hour later, a knock came at her door.

"Come in," Abigail called out. "Ah, Mary, how was your afternoon?"

"The day was lovely, miss. Thank you for allowing me."

"It was no trouble."

"I have a cable from the master."

"You do? I didn't expect to hear from him for some time." She opened the page. "Oh dear."

"Is the news bad, miss?"

"The master won't be detained as long as he previously anticipated. He and Miss Catherine will return by the end of the week, which is good news aside from…"

"Aside from?"

Abigail was on the verge of confiding in her but decided she must not. "It's nothing."

"Would you care to rest a bit longer?"

"Yes, Mary, I would."

Abigail was deep in thought as Mary covered her with a blanket. Regardless of the change in plans, Abigail's mission was set. She hadn't come this far only to give up; she would risk anything to help her newfound brother. But if Darrell learned of her liaisons, and elected to chastise her in some way, she feared anyone with knowledge of her actions may also face a severe consequence. *This is a risk I will not take. Those of us already involved have accepted the chance we are taking, but it would be terribly unfair to endanger anyone else. I must censure what I say in front of others, and not allow even the smallest hint of our undertaking to slip out.*

*****

Edward's possible reaction was a worry for Abigail when she broke the news to him the next afternoon, but he accepted it graciously.

"I'll be fine. I yet have four days to look forward to," he'd told Abigail.

Although his attitude was encouraging, she was frustrated they would have to suspend their meetings, given his health was progressing steadily. With the uncertainty of Darrell's travel requirement, she feared it may not occur soon enough to prevent Edward from having a relapse.

On the day of their return, it was approaching teatime when Abigail received word of Darrell and Catherine's arrival. She met them in the library, to find they appeared exhausted. While Catherine elected to retire immediately, following his long absence Darrell wished to remain with his fiancé.

"My darling," he said, and extended his arms.

Abigail entered his embrace. "Gracious, you can barely stand. Are you certain you won't rest?"

"The tea will refresh me adequately."

"Please, then, you must be seated." Abigail helped him to the sofa. "It is good to have you home."

"It's good to be home. I apologize for the delay. I assure you it was unavoidable."

"You've no need to be regretful. It wasn't excessive after all."

"Likely it seemed longer to me, due to the trials I've faced. I thought I'd pull out my hair on several occasions since the majority of the problems could have been avoided. The difficulties stemmed from poor planning, by far less than competent individuals."

"I can tell your nerves are frazzled."

The maid entered with the tray.

"I'll pour today; you may be excused," Abigail said. She prepared Darrell's cup and handed it to him.

"Thank you, my darling. This was thoughtful of you. I've missed your kindness immensely."

"Now you're home, all will be well."

"All will be well with my beloved beside me, upon whose tenderness and faithfulness I may always rely. You are the one person who'll never disappoint me."

His assertion caused Abigail a twinge of guilt. She doubted he would say this if he knew of her recent activities. She hated to go behind his back; however, believed she had no choice. *One day, when Edward is entirely well, I'll convince Darrell to release him. The family will be whole, which will benefit Darrell as much, perhaps more, than anyone. It cannot be healthy to live with bitterness and resentment; therefore, the ends must justify the means. Drastic times call for drastic measures. It's simply the way of things.*

*****

Having spent the remainder of the day with Darrell, it was late evening when Abigail entered her room to prepare for dinner.

A short time later, she returned to the library. Catherine was there, appearing refreshed from her lengthy nap. Darrell, by contrast, staggered into the room on the verge of collapse. Abigail took his arm for support as they walked to the dining room.

Following a large meal and several glasses of wine, it was evident Darrell could no longer fight his fatigue.

"Dearest, while it pains me, I must retire. I hope you'll forgive me."

"Please, you must. Your eyelids are so heavy, I doubt you'll remain awake another five minutes."

"Thank you for your indulgence."

He escorted the ladies to the parlor and said his good nights before he departed.

"I'm glad he was forced to retire early," Catherine said. "I've been dying to ask about Edward. Were you able to visit him while we were away? Was he of any trouble?"

"He was no trouble whatsoever. I met with him every day."

"Every day; how wonderful. However did you manage it?"

"Eleanor provided me with a key. We set a routine where I joined him at two o'clock and departed at four. She ensured no one was near the north wing at those times, which made the chance of my discovery minimal."

"A clever plan. To visit him daily was extraordinarily kind of you."

"It wasn't an act of kindness; I enjoyed our time together. Edward played for me each afternoon. I loved every minute."

"That must have raised his spirits enormously."

"His spirits weren't merely lifted; I would claim his entire outlook has changed in a profound way."

"What do you mean by profoundly?"

"He's far more content and…confident I suppose one would say."

"*Confident?* His playing had such a dramatic effect?"

"It wasn't to do with his playing alone."

"Whatever else then?"

"A great deal has transpired, which entails a rather long account."

Catherine shrugged. "We have all evening."

"Oddly enough, it began when Edward made an admission I found disturbing."

"What admission?"

"He told me it wasn't the locks that detained him in the north wing. He believed his imprisonment was deserved, due to a misguided sense of negligence. I was shaken to my foundation by the notion, and insisted he explain himself."

"You cannot imply Edward discussed the accident. He won't speak of it with anyone."

"At first he refused. He became excessively agitated. Mercifully, he calmed down. Afterward, he confessed the reason he blamed himself for Emily's fall. I pointed out life entails risks we all must accept, though it isn't unusual to harbor guilt when an accident occurs, regardless of fault. I convinced him Emily would be upset by the way he's punished himself and hiding from life doesn't honor her memory; it discredits her benevolent nature."

"This is an astounding insight; how did you acquire such wisdom?"

"Frankly, I'm not certain. It struck me when Edward revealed the underlying flaw in his reasoning."

"Am I to understand, are you indicating at long last he's accepted the truth?"

"He has, yet I've more to relate."

"*More;* what you've described is beyond belief; what else can there be?"

"Edward took tea with Eleanor and me a few days ago…"

Catherine leaned forward. "Yes, yes?"

"…not in the north wing, but here, in this very room."

"He left the north wing…he saw the light of day…" Catherine put her hand on her forehead as if she felt faint. "That's not possible."

"I'm afraid it is; he sat right here." She indicated his place on the sofa.

"Abigail, you wonderful, amazing, dearest girl; I cannot say what this means to me. I'll never be able to thank you for your compassion, at least not adequately."

"You've no need to thank me. I did it for myself as much as anyone. My ambition is for Edward to recover sufficiently to reunite with the family."

"I doubt that will ever happen."

"You're referring to Darrell's viewpoint?"

"I am. It's unlikely his attitude towards Edward may be altered."

"You and Eleanor share this contention, but I won't accept it. I've been witness to a vulnerable side of Darrell's character, which presumably neither of you has."

"Please recall, you've also been witness to his bitter and unyielding conduct towards Edward. Don't misunderstand me; I'll gladly eat my words if you prove me wrong. At the moment, I'm so happy for Edward I can scarcely think of anything else. I cannot wait to see firsthand his improvement. Tomorrow, I'll request Darrell's permission to visit him."

"You imagine he'll grant his approval when you've just arrived?"

"I think he will. He seems of a mind to please me lately."

"Don't you consider this an indication Darrell is capable of change?"

"Towards me, yes; however, where Edward is concerned the situation is entirely different."

"We cannot judge Darrell's capacity for tolerance until the final verdict is revealed. Now, please tell me about your trip."

Abigail wanted to change the subject. She saw no need to belabor the issue with Catherine when it would only serve to aggravate her. By hook or by crook, she was determined someday, somehow, she would reunite Darrell and Edward, and their relationship would return to brotherly. The only thing that mattered to her was the outcome, not the perception of certain persons who would undermine her efforts with what she believed to be unwarranted skepticism.

6

It has oftentimes been said hope is an emotion which springs eternal, and never did a person hold dearer to this notion than Abigail Parker. Presently, she had good reason to be hopeful. Every member of the Rochester Manor household was in a cheerful frame of mind. Catherine was pleased Darrell had granted her request to dine with their brother an unprecedented three times in the two weeks following their return. Darrell was gracious and even-tempered with everyone, in particular, Abigail, whom he continually showered with gifts and romance. The servants went about their tasks in a lighthearted manner, openly chattering, whistling, and on occasion singing. Jake's typically staid continence had eased considerably, and as such, he'd permitted his staff leniency in this regard.

The singular hiccup during this time frame happened the morning following Darrell and Catherine's homecoming. Refreshed from a good night's sleep, he and Abigail were sharing a pleasant conversation at breakfast when he asked a question she was unprepared to address.

"Tell me, my darling, how did you manage to entertain yourself with Catherine and me absent for such a lengthy period of time?"

"I…took walks and read a great deal. With her duties less taxing, Eleanor and I spent a lot of time together. It was nice we had the chance to become better acquainted."

"Did you take any drives into town?"

"No, I didn't."

"Why ever not? This is an ideal season for an outing. It must have been tedious to remain here the entire time."

"The thought never occurred to me."

"I'm surprised Eleanor didn't suggest it. You may've found items suitable for your new rooms."

"I wouldn't want to select pieces without consulting you. You may not approve of my choices."

"I believe I made it clear you need only please yourself. Have you begun the project at all?"

"I haven't since I've been waiting for your return."

"Then you must, or your rooms may not be completed prior to the wedding. What in heaven's name is wrong with Eleanor? She has information regarding the persons who may assist you. I cannot understand why she didn't prompt you to begin when there was ample spare time."

"You shouldn't reprove Eleanor. It wasn't her duty to implement a chore for which I'm responsible."

"A chore? Do you view my gift as an ordeal I've imposed upon you?"

"Of course not, it's merely…"

"Merely?"

"I'm nervous, for if they turn out badly furnishings of this caliber must be difficult and costly to replace."

"If you continue to harbor doubt, I'll reaffirm my position. Where I'm concerned, you cannot make a mistake. You mustn't delay any longer. Please consult with Eleanor at her first available moment."

"I promise, I will. I'm sorry I gave you the wrong impression. Chore was a poor choice of terminology to describe your lovely present."

"In fairness, you did advise me of your intimidation. While you're unaccustomed to an undertaking of this sort, my intention was for you to find pleasure in the venture, not strain. It may help to bear in mind your bedroom is simply a room, and this is only a house, no more."

"This isn't an ordinary house, it's a mansion. My rooms aren't typical, they're exceedingly grand…"

"*Abigail,*" he interrupted, "this is a *house*. Your rooms are the same as any other. I'll grant you our home is larger and more opulent than most, yet in function, there's no difference; we have walls and a floor and a roof to keep us dry. What matters to me here is *you*. My greatest desire is your happiness. I hope you'll never doubt this."

"I've no doubt whatsoever. The patience you've granted me regarding my foolish misgivings is clear evidence."

"My darling, you're anything but foolish. Your willingness to humor me is part of why I love you dearly."

"As I love you."

Darrell's eyes smiled when he leaned over to kiss her. "Would a drive after breakfast be agreeable? We could head into town. Perhaps together we'll discover items for your rooms."

"That would be wonderful."

Abigail was tempted to take advantage of his benevolent mood to reveal the truth about Edward; however, she quickly thought better of it, given how unrealistic it was to anticipate Darrell would react favorably to her admission of deceit.

Stay patient, Abigail, she thought. *The day will come I'll have to address the matter, but it must be done in a way that won't injure Darrell or destroy his faith in me.*

"Was there anything else on your mind?" he asked.

"Only my belief I'm a fortunate woman; most fortunate indeed."

*****

As uplifting as hope can be when dashed the resulting sting of disillusionment can be pronounced. Unfortunately for Abigail, after many idyllic weeks, she was about to experience a blow of this sort.

She'd been awaiting Darrell and his sister at teatime on a sunny, peaceful day when he entered the library in a disgruntled state.

"The nerve of that man," he said.

"The nerve of what man?" Abigail asked.

"My darling, I didn't see you were there. It's my brother. I met with Edward at his request. Since this is a rare event, I thought it strange enough until his purpose was revealed. It's nearly beyond my comprehension."

She quivered. "What do you mean?"

"As outrageous as this is, he asked my permission to leave the north wing, and allow him to live with the family. When I accused him of another suicide attempt, he denied it emphatically, claiming he no longer contemplates the act. He must think me a complete fool to suggest that out of the blue he's overcome his madness. The very idea of such audacity is galling."

Abigail closed her eyes and pictured the scene painfully. How could she side with Edward, she wondered, without adding fuel to this fire? "Well, ten years is a long time. Perhaps his attitude has changed."

"Highly unlikely, when previously time has been of no consequence."

"The adage time heals all wounds oftentimes prevails. The fact it may've taken a while doesn't necessarily mean it couldn't happen for Edward. Perhaps you should give him the opportunity to prove himself. If he is being dishonest, you could return him to the north wing immediately."

"Were I to release him, even briefly, he may harm someone. I refuse to take that chance. How could I forgive myself if he hurt you?"

The fallacy of his statement made her grimace. "Your point is well taken yet mustn't we allow there's a possibility he's telling the truth?"

"There isn't the remotest possibility. You don't know him as I do. Mark my word, he'll take advantage of the situation, and attempt something sinister. I've mentioned before, he can be very clever."

"It seems unjust to simply presume his mental state hasn't improved."

"Abigail, please *end* this banter. If you wouldn't mind pouring my tea, I'd be grateful for the opportunity to soothe my temper."

"Of course."

She stood to prepare his cup.

"Thank you, my dearest," Darrell said as she handed it to him.

Abigail poured for herself and sat next to him. She drank pensively, teetering on the brink of a confession. She opened her mouth; however, the words wouldn't form. *How may I speak honestly when this will hurt him, possibly beyond any hope of repairing the damage it would cause? Yet if I say nothing, Edward will continue to suffer.*

While she agonized over the situation, Darrell regained his composure. "Forgive me, my sweet. It's Edward who's provoked me. I'd no call to be short with you."

He's calmer now. I must tell him what I've done and pray for understanding.

She was gathering her courage when Catherine entered the room.

"Good afternoon. What's wrong with the two of you?"

"Nothing, my dear sister. I had a bit of a quarrel earlier. It's behind me now."

"With one of those idiotic persons you oversee, I suppose?" Catherine asked.

"In this instance, the trouble stemmed from deceitfulness," Darrell explained.

"Those dunderheads will be the death of you, my poor brother. Abigail, you look pale. Are you unwell?"

"I'm rather shaken by the incident."

"Such a shame, but all will be resolved soon, I hope?"

"It has already," Darrell said.

"Thank heavens for that. You're in dire need of a respite," Catherine remarked.

As Catherine spoke, Abigail realized her confession could be problematic. *I cannot tell Darrell what I've done. It isn't me alone he would view as disloyal. He would hold Edward accountable, as well as Catherine if she admitted her participation in my defense. The truth could cause the calamitous outcome she's warned me of. I'll have to find some other way to convince him of Edward's recovery.*

"You do look wan, my dearest," Darrell said. "Perhaps you should rest."

"Yes, I believe I will," Abigail agreed. *Rest; how can I possibly rest? I need to find a solution to this impasse. I'll have no peace until I do.*

*****

As Abigail had expected, throughout the remainder of the day she'd been unable to ease her troubled mind, irritated to be caught in a trap of her own making. That night she couldn't sleep as she envisioned the afternoon's encounter between the brothers repeatedly: Edward pleading to be released from his prison and an incensed Darrell who flatly denied his request. The longer she considered it, the more concerned she became that Edward would inflict upon himself the harm Darrell had predicted.

She glanced at the clock to discover it was one in the morning. Although she knew the inkling was unwise, she considered visiting Edward right then. After tormenting herself another half hour, she threw her covers off with a jerk. However misguided the notion was, she had to be certain Edward had done nothing rash.

Abigail poked her head out the door to check the hallway before she tiptoed to the north wing. In the silence, the lock seemed to make a terrible racket. She paused to listen for any indication someone had been awakened.

When the house remained still, she entered the wing and closed the door as quietly as she could. It was darker at this hour with the sconces on the wall unlit. As she felt her way down the hall, she saw light coming from the library. She found Edward there, fully dressed, his appearance surprisingly calm as he read a book.

"Abigail! Why are you here?" he asked when she entered the room. "Darrell cannot be away."

"He's in the house, but it's late. Everyone retired long ago."

Edward, apparently unaware of the time, looked at his watch. "*Abigail*, why have you come?" His tone was softer.

"Darrell informed me you asked his permission to leave the north wing, and he refused. That must have been a cruel blow. I've been worried about you ever since."

"There isn't any need. I doubted he'd grant my request. Although I'd prefer to leave, I'm used to my surroundings. I'll be fine."

"This is all my doing. I've no idea how to solve the predicament since Darrell still believes you pose a threat to us. I cannot tell him why I know this isn't true without betraying my involvement."

Edward's face contorted. "No, please, you mustn't tell him. He'd never forgive you."

"I presume you're correct. I wouldn't want him to learn of Catherine's involvement either. I promise you, I'll find another way to fix my blunder."

"Abigail, you mustn't think you've done anything wrong when you've helped me enormously. For the first time in ten years, I want to live. You've restored in me the freedom to enjoy my life."

"You cannot be free in this prison, nor can you live happily in this God-forsaken darkness."

"It may be difficult to accept I'll be content here until you understand the true prison was my mind. Even in this darkness, there's a kind of light in my heart, due entirely to your wisdom and compassion."

"While this is good to hear, it doesn't set things right. I must find the means to end your confinement."

"I beg you, don't say or do anything which may anger Darrell. Likely it will be of no use. Once he's reached a decision, he rarely rescinds it."

"I've no desire to hurt anyone, Darrell least of all. A way out of this will emerge eventually. In the meantime, I may offer you consolation by continuing our visits."

"Nothing would please me more. I'll look forward to your company whenever my brother is away."

"He won't leave for some time; however, we could meet as we have tonight."

"You mustn't consider it. No matter how much time must pass, I'll be satisfied knowing you will return."

"There's little risk of my discovery when the hour is late."

"I won't have you take the slightest risk. It's simply not worth it."

"If I sense any danger, I could abandon the plan."

"Supposing you can manage it safely, how do you propose we'll spend our time? I won't be able to play for you."

"I've noticed you enjoy books, as do I. Perhaps you would read to me."

"I could... what am I saying? I cannot, and I will not. The answer is no."

"You cannot prevent my coming here."

Edward shook his head. "Promise me you won't come if there's the slightest indication of danger. If a mouse roams the hallway, you must call it off."

"You have my word. Unless I spot a mouse, I'll see you tomorrow."

"This isn't the occasion to be flippant."

"You're quite correct. Truly, I'll be exceedingly cautious."

"Once more you've proven how selfless and tenderhearted you are, although I'm discovering you may be as stubborn as you are kind."

"Contrary to my appearance, I have a substantial capacity for stubbornness," Abigail said. "Of this, you may rest assured."

*****

Abigail was finally able to sleep. By the morning, she felt much better. She joined Darrell for breakfast to find his temper had eased, which revived her sense of optimism. He'd begun to make their plates when Catherine surprised them by entering the dining room.

"Good morning, Catherine. You're up and about early," Darrell said.

"I woke prior to the usual hour, and thought I'd join you for breakfast if you don't mind."

"We would never mind." Her brother helped her to a chair. "May I prepare a plate for you?"

"Please."

"I take it you slept well?" Abigail asked.

"Very well, thank you. Darrell?"

"Yes, my sister?"

"Would you permit me to dine with Edward this evening?"

"Presently, I cannot allow it."

"Please, Darrell, it's been a while since our last visit."

"I've given you my answer."

"Why do you deny me?"

"There's no need for me to provide a rationale when I render a decision."

"While not the need, an explanation seems a reasonable request," Catherine said.

"Edward has caused me a great deal of worry recently," Darrell said resignedly. "I fear he's up to something, which is why I cannot permit you."

"*Up* to something; what gave you that idea?" Catherine asked.

"Yesterday, he approached me with a petition I find highly suspicious."

"What sort of petition?"

"The specifics are inconsequential. The pertinent point is my fear he'll take advantage of any situation he could use to his benefit."

"How could he, when I'll be accompanied by Jake and Eleanor?"

"It may not make a difference. I've instructed them to exercise additional vigilance. They're to enter only together, prepared to handle a dangerous incident. To this end, any form of distraction would be ill-advised."

"Darrell, you're alarming me."

"Which is why I'd intended to say nothing of it. Don't fret, dearest sister. It's possible I'm being overly cautious. Either way, I have the matter well in hand."

Since Catherine seemed on the brink of pressing him, Abigail discreetly motioned she should let the subject drop.

A short while later, Darrell folded his napkin and placed it on the table. "I'm sorry to rush off, dear ladies. I have a business complication which demands my attention."

He gave Abigail a kiss, and his sister's shoulders a squeeze prior to departing.

"What on earth was he talking about?" Catherine asked.

"Edward sought Darrell's permission to leave the north wing. He wants to live with us," Abigail explained.

"He wants to return to us? And naturally, Darrell refused. My poor, dearest brother; to think he had the courage to ask, only to be rejected. He must have been devastated."

"I thought that would be the case also. I was distraught to the point I couldn't sleep and decided to pay Edward a visit."

"Do you mean to say you went to the north wing with Darrell in the house? Have you lost your mind?"

"The hour was late; after one-thirty."

"Whatever the hour, it's beyond my comprehension you would do this. As it's said and done, tell me how he seemed."

"Thankfully, much better than I feared. He said he thought it likely Darrell would deny him and claims he'll be fine. I told him since I'm responsible for the situation I'll find a solution. Until then, I intend to visit him as often as I can."

"With or without Darrell in the house?"

"With or without."

"Will you visit Edward tonight?"

"I plan to."

"I believe you've gone entirely daft. I guess I'm daft too, for I'd like to tag along, if I may?"

"You're more than welcome."

"What time shall we meet?"

"Let's stay with one-thirty. The house is dead at that hour."

"One-thirty," Catherine said. "I'll see you then."

*****

When the clock chimed at the arranged time, Abigail cracked opened her door.

Catherine was awaiting her in the hallway. "I've checked the house. No one's about."

After they crept to the north wing, Abigail unlocked the door. "Be careful inside. The sconces aren't lit at this hour."

"We could light a few."

"We mustn't. Jake may notice they've burned lower than the others."

"I wouldn't have considered it. Sound thinking on your part."

Edward stood when they entered his library. "Catherine, Abigail. How nice you both came."

"It's wonderful to see you, my darling brother. Darrell has forbidden my visits, he claims for my safety; therefore, I may visit only at this hour. Abigail told me you asked his permission to live with us. I'm furious with him for denying you."

"He assumes I'm being deceitful. Given my past behavior, how can he be blamed? The fault for his reaction is my own."

"Your fault indeed," Catherine retorted. "As usual, he's being completely heartless towards you."

"Don't say that, and don't be upset. This has been my home for ten years. I'll be happy here."

"How can you?"

"You can't be truly happy," Abigail said. "We must prove to Darrell you're well enough to leave."

"I doubt it's possible. Please, Catherine, help me persuade her not to try."

"I haven't the ability, and frankly I haven't the desire."

"Don't worry, Edward, I'll do nothing rash. There must be a way out of this dilemma. I will find it," Abigail said.

"Our outwardly placid sister has within her an indomitable streak, does she not?" Edward asked.

"High-spirited is a better description. It may, in fact, be her finest quality."

Abigail laughed. "If you find this surprising, I guarantee it surprises me all the more. Edward had agreed to read to me tonight. Does that sound good to you?" she asked Catherine.

"I'd love it. Although Abigail is our literary scholar, would you allow me to choose the book?"

"Being the reader, I should have a say in the selection," Edward joked.

"The two of you should decide together," Abigail suggested.

She watched as the siblings bantered back and forth playfully, and their joy solidified her resolve. *This is the happy household we must have. No matter how long it takes, by whatever means necessary, this family will be reunited!*

7

For all its precise measurement, the passage of time often seems to vary significantly. When bored, lonely, or in the anticipation of a pleasurable event, one may have the perception it's crawling by at an agonizingly slow pace. Under different circumstances, usually, when it's the least convenient or pleasing, time may seem to slip rapidly from our grasp. These occasions can be frustrating, for although one may wish it were so, nothing can prevent time's relentless and perhaps merciless progression.

After several weeks had flown by, Abigail found herself in the latter circumstance, still no closer to resolving the state of affairs at Rochester Manor. Throughout this time frame she and Catherine had continued their visits with Edward, usually on alternate nights, to provide him with frequent companionship, and yet obtain adequate rest. While these meetings were beneficial, Abigail knew she wouldn't be satisfied until a permanent solution was found.

In the wee hours of the morning following one of these visits, Abigail was returning to her room when she stopped dead in her tracks. Darrell was standing at her door, his hand raised as if he was about to knock.

"Darrell?"

He lowered his hand and glowered at her. "Why are you up and about at this hour?"

"I was…I couldn't sleep…and I hoped…"

"Yes?"

"I thought a glass of wine would help to sedate me. I went to the kitchen to fetch one."

"Where is this glass?"

"I've drunk it."

"Do you imply you finished it in the kitchen? You must have drunk it straight down."

"Although I did it was hardly a full pour; just a few sips."

"Therefore, against my advice you risked a fall, the chance of which doubled due to the consumption of spirits?"

"Wine isn't a potent drink, particularly in a small dose. As you can plainly see, I'm not unsteady."

"The darkness alone could have caused you to stumble. If you required something, you should have summoned your maid."

"I didn't wish to disturb her over a small matter."

"You didn't wish to disturb her. Explain to me why you have a maid if you won't call upon her for assistance? And I would have you know the possibility you may fall is no small matter to me."

"Please, Darrell, don't be distraught. With the moon full, the hallways may be negotiated easily."

He huffed as he rubbed his forehead. "A friend you may not wish to disturb; however, your maid isn't a friend, as you seem to regard her. You must never again behave so foolishly, full moon or not."

"You have my word; going forward I'll ring for Mary."

"Thank you. At times I have the impression I'm raising a child."

He escorted her to her room. "May I come in?"

"Of course. What brings you here at this hour? Has something happened?"

"Nothing has happened. In light of my intent, perhaps I'm the one who deserves to be reprimanded."

"Why do you say this?"

"My purpose is less than honorable. I've been unable to sleep as well, fighting an impulse I shouldn't act upon. After many hours, I could contain myself no longer. I've come to beg you to give yourself to me, and permit me to take you, here and now."

"We wouldn't wait for our wedding night?"

"With your upbringing, you may consider it highly improper. But engagement is a mere step away from marriage; proof of one's devotion. We wouldn't be the first to share our love prior to our nuptials, I assure you."

"I've no doubt we wouldn't. I…"

Abigail felt the same longing and was on the verge of granting her consent when the implications dawned on her. Once they'd begun their relations it would be unsafe to visit Edward unless Darrell was away, and so they must wait for the marriage bed. She assured herself by then the difficulties between the brothers would be resolved.

"Your hesitation leads me to believe I've offended you."

"You haven't in the least. I can't explain the reason for my hesitance."

"You're nervous, my sweet."

"I suppose I am, just a little."

"Perhaps more than a little. I won't press you into a decision you weren't prepared to make. When our first encounter takes place, I want you to feel you may give yourself to me fully, without reservation."

"I understand your desire more than you may think. I've been experiencing sensations which are likely similar to yours. While a part of me wants to say yes, at the moment my preference is to wait."

"Very well, my love, we'll wait until you're comfortable. Whether our first liaison occurs on or before our wedding night is in your hands. I believe this is unqualified proof I haven't forgotten the promise I made to you long ago."

"The promise?"

"My vow I wouldn't unleash the wolf until the appropriate time."

"I *had* forgotten. Perhaps the full moon has served to heighten your instincts."

Darrell laughed softly and pulled Abigail closer to kiss her gently. "I'd best leave before I weaken."

He walked towards the door.

"Darrell?" she called out.

He turned with a hopeful smile. "Yes, my darling?"

"You do know how much I love you."

"That I will never question. Sleep well, my sweet."

"Good night, Darrell."

When he'd departed, Abigail placed her hand to her brow. *That was nearly a disaster. Had he given into temptation earlier, he may have caught me exiting the north wing. This is becoming torturous. If I don't find a solution soon, I'll be in danger of losing my mind.*

Overcome with exhaustion and frustration, she collapsed onto the bed.

*****

In the morning following breakfast, with Darrell otherwise engaged, Abigail took a long walk about the property, to think more clearly and ease her troubled mind.

While all was peaceful when she'd left, upon her return the condition was entirely different. She heard an altercation taking place in the study and walked in its direction to investigate. The inflection in Darrell's voice was forceful to the extent he could be heard from behind the door. Whoever was with him was incurring a full-scale chastisement.

The door opened and Catherine emerged. She rushed past Abigail, her eyes bright red and her face excessively wet.

She was about to follow Darrell's sister until he motioned for Abigail to enter the study. Her shoulders stiffened as she went inside.

"Darrell, why are you upset with Catherine?"

"*This* arrived today." He grabbed a note from his desk which rustled when he waved it in the air.

"What is it?"

"A letter from Laura Kensington, Catherine's dear friend."

"It was addressed to you?"

"It was addressed to her; however, I read it immediately."

"Why would you?"

"I review all communications which enter or leave the estate, prior to their delivery."

"You read them, regardless of the addressee?"

"It's imperative I do, as the head of a household that's far from typical."

Abigail's head joggled as she stared at him in disbelief. "I don't understand."

"Don't observe me in this manner. I must employ precautions to ensure the family's safety."

Stunned as she was, it was apparent there would be no benefit in pressing him to explain further. "May I ask; what did Laura write you found offensive?"

"After the usual text concerning the gratification of their recent visit, there was a paragraph pertaining to Edward. It relates how pleased she was to hear of the vast improvement in his mental condition. She wondered whether he now resides outside the north wing, and even suggested he accompany our sister when she next visits. It comes to light Edward's request to leave the north wing wasn't his alone. Obviously, Catherine encouraged, if not instigated, the idea."

"How did Laura learn of this?"

"Catherine sent a letter to thank the Kensingtons for their hospitality. In it, she described this fabrication regarding Edward. Since the servants would route the letter to me first, she had the impudence to post it herself; a small wonder considering the content. I assume she had designs to preempt a return letter from reaching me. That scheme failed."

"How do you intend to deal with her?"

"I've banished her to her room for two weeks. I may never again grant my permission for her to visit Edward."

Abigail's heart constricted. "This seems a harsh course. Are you certain it's necessary?"

"It may not be harsh enough. No one, including you, may visit Catherine during her punishment. Her maid will deliver all meals to her room and attend only to the absolute necessities. Although you and Catherine have become close, I insist upon your complete support."

"You'll have this if you've no doubt the penalty is appropriate."

"I haven't the slightest reservation it's for the best. And now, if you'll excuse me, this affair has put me behind in my day's work. I'll join you for tea."

"Certainly," Abigail agreed.

Darrell gave her a peck on the cheek before she departed.

Abigail trudged to the conservatory, where she sat in disillusionment. Even its cheerful environment did nothing to alleviate her anguish. Catherine had warned her life could be difficult in this household. With the current turmoil Abigail now understood more fully her concern.

Poor, dear Catherine, she thought. *How could Darrell sit there and inform me in a nonchalant manner he reads every correspondence, as though indisputably he has the right. Precaution indeed; his true purpose is to maintain control over us. Thank goodness I didn't send the letter to Father and Mama in which I spoke of Edward. On the other hand, it may've been for the best. Perhaps it would've been preferable if he'd broken our engagement, had he been so inclined.*

Abigail stared out the window, while her hopes for the future seemed to drift out of reach.

*****

Following the episode with Catherine, the household deteriorated into a bleak state. To make matters worse, Jake was ordered to keep the staff on alert day and night for prohibited activities, as if they were guards in a prison. Since Abigail could no longer safely continue her visits with Edward, she requested Eleanor slip him a note of explanation. Afterward, Eleanor told her this was a conclusion with which Edward emphatically agreed.

Outraged by his mandate, Abigail made no attempt to hide her disdain from Darrell. She spoke to him only as etiquette demands and avoided his company whenever possible. He was clearly aware of her opposition, and yet he offered no indication of remorse or charity. As the days passed, the strain between them increased.

The conditions were bad, to the point Abigail thought it impossible they could worsen, until a week later when Mary entered her bedroom in a state of severe distress.

"Mary, whatever is wrong?"

"Miss, I don't want to burden you with another problem, but I'm horribly upset. There's no one else I can turn to."

"You need never hesitate to approach me. Take a seat and tell me what's happened."

"It's my roommate, Annie, of the kitchen staff. She's in a terrible, *terrible* way."

"What way is this?"

"Do you remember me telling you she fell in love with one of the gardeners, that nice boy Harry?"

"I do recall; are they no longer happy with one another?"

"They are, or I should say they *were* happy, very happy, until…"

"Whatever you have to relate, I'll hold in strict confidence."

"Annie's in an awful pickle, miss. You see, she's expecting!"

"Oh my, this could be trouble. Has she informed anyone else?"

"Yes, Mrs. Williams just now, for soon enough she'd have no choice. When the master gets wind of it, he'll sack them for sure. They're both from the local orphanage with nowhere to go. Once they're set out of the house, the only question is whether they'll freeze or starve to death first. I'm scared, miss. Not merely for them; it's likely their baby will never be born."

"This I won't have. Hopefully, Mrs. Williams will persuade the master to grant them leniency. If she cannot, I'll have a word with him."

"Miss, I'm sorry. I'm asking too much of you, but there's nothing else I can do."

Abigail patted her arm. "You don't ask too much. Any difficulty I may sustain would be insignificant compared to that of Annie and Harry, should the master elect to cast them out. If he does, I believe my parents would take them in. They'd never tolerate cruelty of this nature."

"Oh, miss, you would do that?"

"I would. Let us approach Mrs. Williams immediately before she notifies the master."

They dashed down the stairs. When they were in the foyer, they saw the study door open. Eleanor stepped out.

"I'll handle this from here," they heard Darrell instruct.

"As you wish," Eleanor said. She closed the door and walked in the opposite direction.

"What'll we do, miss? Annie must be in there."

"I'll interrupt them."

Abigail started towards the door, but Mary tugged her arm. "Maybe you shouldn't. I wouldn't have you hurt due to this mess."

"I'll be fine. You may wait here…"

The door opened again. This time, it was Annie who exited. "Thank you, master, thank you, a thousand times over."

Darrell stood in the doorway. "There, there; fetch your young man. I imagine he'll have a question to ask me."

Mary and Abigail regarded each other in astonishment.

Harry, who was waiting close by, joined Annie. Together, they returned to the study.

Darrell ushered them in. Not long after, they reemerged.

"Sir, we can never repay you, but I promise we'll work hard, extra hard to try," Harry offered as he clutched his hat.

Darrell shook his head. "That won't do. Annie must have her duties lightened to obtain more rest."

"Thank you, master. In her stead, I'll work twice… three times as hard."

"Which won't do either since you must have time to take care of Annie, and soon your child as well."

Harry bowed his head. "Bless you, master, you're too kind to us."

"Yes, bless you, sir, again and again," Annie chimed in. She curtseyed and kissed Darrell's hand.

"There's no need to make a fuss," Darrell said. He gave Annie a hug, and Harry a pat on the back. "All will be well. Congratulations to you both. You may be dismissed to spread your news."

"Thank you, master," Harry repeated. After he took Annie's hand, the two youngsters scampered towards the kitchen.

Darrell took note of Abigail and Mary walking towards him.

"May I be excused, miss?"

"Of course, dear Mary."

Mary regarded her master sheepishly as she scurried past him.

"Harrison has explained the situation, I gather," Darrell said.

"She has. Harry and Annie seemed elated. What did you decide for them?"

"I granted Harry my permission to ask for Annie's hand. They'll marry in a few days at the local church. As she has no father, I'll give the bride away. I've provided them with a dowry to meet the necessities of a child. Once wed, they'll reside in an apartment reserved for the married servants."

"This was remarkably generous of you, when the situation may be viewed as grounds for dismissal."

"They're good children, and hard workers, who merely succumbed to their love. It would be unconscionable to cast them out for this reason."

"You mustn't brush this away as a course any master would choose. It was uncommonly compassionate. I regret I had my…"

"Doubts; is this what you'd intended to say?"

"No…it isn't…"

"Your hesitation indicates it's true. I presume Mary solicited your help, supposing I'd be cruel to these youngsters, and apparently you of all people agreed. Why would you entertain this idea when you're aware I understand their desire? Do you consider me an uncaring man?"

"Indifference isn't generally characteristic of your nature."

"Not *generally;* I should hope you wouldn't identify this trait in me at all." Darrell's expression was pained. "You haven't concealed your viewpoint that I was overbearing regarding Catherine's infraction, the probable cause of your callous inference. Being a reasonable man, I'm willing to admit I may've made a misjudgment. It's conceivable Edward induced her to accept his self-proclaimed improvement. He could have coerced our sister as an unwitting participant in a scheme he's been hatching."

"I find that unlikely. Catherine is a perceptive woman."

"She is, except in her appraisal of our brother. Through no fault of her own, she has a vastly contorted perspective of Edward's mentality. With this in mind, it's reasonable to grant her the benefit of the doubt. You may inform her I've rescinded her period of confinement."

"I believe this is a prudent decision."

"While I may not always share your opinion, I do value your observations. In the future, I would prefer you'd confront me with your concerns rather than judge me harshly."

"You're correct. I should have expressed my objection openly, instead of engaging in a tactic which doesn't solve anything."

Darrell took Abigail's face into his hands. "I'm glad we've had the opportunity to clear the air. Unfortunately, I must excuse myself, for I've work to attend."

"I'll see you at dinner?"

"Of course. Until dinner," he said and kissed her.

Abigail went directly upstairs. She tapped on Catherine's door.

Catherine blanched when she opened it. "Abigail, you mustn't be here. Darrell would be furious."

"Don't be alarmed. I'm delivering a message from Darrell."

Catherine sneered. "A message? I'm not certain I want to hear it."

"I believe you will since this is good news. May I come in?"

She stood aside for Abigail to enter. "What news do you have?"

"Darrell has come to realize his judgment of you was unfounded. He's consented to end your detention."

"This is a surprise. I've never known him to change his mind about anything. What prompted him?"

"He believes your brother has deceived you as part of some plot and has determined Edward is ultimately responsible for your actions."

"That's not good at all. I'd prefer he would continue to blame me rather than place the culpability on poor Edward."

"It is a shame this was his line of reasoning."

"What did Darrell conclude regarding my visits with our brother?"

"He didn't address the matter specifically. I suspect he'll maintain it's too dangerous."

"Naturally he'll continue with his convenient excuse."

"We don't know for a fact Darrell's intentions are self-serving. And you never know, he may yet allow you."

"I won't hold my breath."

"It remains to be seen. I have additional news, which should please you a great deal."

"That would be nice. What is it?"

"You've heard the rumors Annie of the kitchen staff, and the gardener Harry have fallen in love?"

"Indeed yes, it's a topic the servants never seem to tire of, or at any rate my maid doesn't."

"Their talk may now cease. Harry and Annie are to be wed on Saturday."

"How is it possible when they're without money or family?"

"It would seem Annie is expecting."

"Ah, the gossip *is* true. Surely Darrell dismissed them. Is this why they'll marry? Where and how will they live?"

"Mary approached me a while ago and begged for my assistance. We presumed the worst as well until we discovered Darrell has arranged for them to marry. He's agreed to provide them with a dowry and the ceremony, and he'll give the bride away. Following their nuptials, they'll reside in the quarters with the other married servants."

"Thank heavens for their sake he's being generous. If only he'd treat our brother with the same benevolence."

"Perhaps one day he will. Before anything can happen, he must be convinced of the improvement in Edward's mental state."

"Given the extent of Darrell's animosity, it may not make a difference."

"I find this hard to believe. Be that as it may, with proof Edward no longer poses a threat Darrell would be forced either to release him or provide solid grounds for his refusal."

"The design has merit but for one key point; how do you propose to prove Edward's sanity?"

"Frankly, I've no idea. There must be a way. I'm determined to find it."

"I hope you do, my dear sister; I hope you have the capability to enact this miracle."

"I won't rest until I do. I'll leave now so we may dress for dinner."

Catherine grinned. "Dinner in the dining room will be an agreeable change, I must say."

"I'll see you then," Abigail said and smiled in return before she left the room.

*****

With the announcement of the upcoming wedding, the dismal fog surrounding Rochester Manor had lifted. Following Catherine's release, the guard duty ended. Soon, the house was bustling with activity of a pleasant nature. As time was short, every member of the household was involved one way or another in the preparations for the ceremony. Given the added assistance, all was in readiness by Friday.

At ten o'clock the following morning, Darrell walked Annie down the aisle to take her vows with Harry. Mary had accepted the role of bridesmaid. The groom's close friend, Peter, stood for him. The bride was pretty in her charming white eyelet gown, her veil ornamented with fresh flowers. The groom was aglow with unconcealed adoration when Darrell presented Annie to him. He placed a fatherly kiss on her cheek before taking his seat next to Abigail.

After the ceremony, the assembly returned to Rochester Manor, where Eleanor and her staff had prepared a banquet for all to enjoy. Prior to the close of the festivities, Darrell surprised the happy couple with a stay at a nearby inn to spend the week on honeymoon. The youngsters were in tears as they expressed their gratitude for all he'd done on their behalf.

When the celebrations ended, Darrell and Abigail retired to the parlor.

"It was a lovely day, was it not?" Abigail reflected. "I must give the staff credit for their prompt organization. Didn't Annie look pretty?"

"She did. I understand you assisted with her dress appreciably."

"Hardly, since I'm not skilled at sewing. Your gift of the honeymoon was incredibly thoughtful. Everything you provided was of far greater consequence than my small contribution."

"My only feat was to pay the inn a visit, and hand them my money."

"Your *only* feat; none of this would have been possible without your generosity. I must say, your escort of Annie seemed a natural thing. It had me dreaming of the day you may walk our daughter down the aisle."

"It would be wonderful. I hope it will take place with more than one daughter. I'd love a large family."

As he spoke Abigail's smile faded, and her eyes welled.

"Dearest, is anything the matter?" he asked.

"This is dreadful, how is it I never considered the possibility?"

"The possibility of what? What's upset you so?"

"Surely you're aware there's a fundamental reason I've no brothers or sisters. I wasn't my parents' only child; I was the only infant my mother carried who survived. If I have a similar condition, you may never have the family you desire. You mustn't risk your chance for happiness. We must break our engagement."

Darrell placed his arm around her shoulder. "My darling, you mustn't consider it. While it's my hope we'll have a sizeable family, it's not a requirement to secure my happiness. *You* are my life. Together we'll welcome the children we're blessed with, as all couples do."

"Yet suppose I cannot bear children. I'm certain you'd come to regret our marriage."

"I shall never regret our marriage. If to be childless is our fate, we'll have each other."

Abigail's tears trickled, and Darrell wiped her cheeks.

"Don't cry, my sweet. Life offers no guarantees. I would claim I'm more familiar with this fact than most."

"This is true," she admitted.

He poured her a glass of wine. "Drink this, my darling." She took a sip.

"Please," he said and raised her chin gently. "You must accept my love for you will never diminish."

"You are such a kind man. I love you with all my heart."

If she hadn't been entirely convinced before, Abigail was convinced now. Benevolent was the true nature of the man she loved. Catherine, she believed, had to be wrong about his intentions regarding Edward. When Darrell was provided with evidence his brother was well, Abigail had no doubt he would forgive him and release him from the north wing. For her, it was no longer a question of if, it was a question of how; how to obtain the necessary proof.

*****

Tired as she was, Abigail pondered the issue well into the night. When the breakfast hour arrived, she attempted to listen while Darrell spoke. Engrossed in her contemplations, she couldn't grant him her full attention.

"Have you heard what I've said?" he asked.

She regarded him blankly. "Forgive me, I'm afraid I haven't."

"Your thoughts have been elsewhere this morning. The question of your ability to have children is yet troubling you, I presume?"

"Oh, yes, it is."

"My darling, to put your mind at ease we should consult with the physician. He may be able to provide you with a level of comfort."

"The *physician*, my gracious how obvious, *this is the answer.*"

"I'm glad you agree. I'll call for him straight away."

"And after he's seen me, he could examine Edward, to provide us with an evaluation of his condition."

"Edward, what has he to do with anything?"

"Since the day he requested his release from the north wing, I've wondered whether he spoke the truth regarding his purpose. While we may hypothesize, only a doctor is qualified to ascertain his mental state. We owe it to Edward to have him properly diagnosed."

"I disagree. Edward is exceptionally clever. He's apt to have the ability to deceive the doctor as well as us."

"Won't you concede a professional evaluation is worthy of your consideration? This is your brother we speak of. Isn't his welfare of critical importance to you?"

Darrell hesitated as he thought the idea through. "You are correct. Naturally, my brother concerns me. It is time we had his physical and mental condition reviewed. When I notify Dr. Hardin, I'll request he also examine Edward."

"This is wonderful. It may make all the difference to the household."

"Again, my darling, I find your insight invaluable. When the doctor provides his diagnosis, we may put the matter to rest, and worry about it no further."

She grinned shrewdly. "It will be a relief to have peace of mind. I'm yet a bit hungry. I believe I'll have another crumpet."

"Allow me to fetch it for you," Darrell said.

"Thank you," Abigail accepted. "You are indeed the most thoughtful man."

*****

Three days later, at a little past two in the afternoon, Abigail listened ecstatically when the physician offered her his prognosis.

"My dear, you appear perfectly fit. Given the results of my examination, along with your description of your bodily functions, in my opinion, you're as capable as any healthy woman to bear children."

"This is reassuring to hear. Thank you, Dr. Hardin. Now, I believe you are to see Edward?"

"I am. It's been a while since my last visit. My examination of him is long overdue. Goodbye, my dear."

"Goodbye, Doctor. Thank you again."

After he departed, Mary entered to help her dress. "You seem happy, miss. The news must be good."

"It is. The physician has determined it's probable I'll have children."

"How marvelous! You must be relieved."

"Indeed I am. The master will be pleased as well. I want to inform him without delay."

"I'll hurry then, miss." She secured the last button. "There, I'm finished."

"Thank you, Mary."

Abigail gave her a hug before she bounded down the stairs and knocked on Darrell's study door, disappointed to discover he wasn't there. She was about to begin a search when she came across the footman.

"Mr. Phillips, have you any idea where the master may be?"

"He escorted the doctor to the north wing."

"Oh. When he returns, would you request he join me in the conservatory?"

"Of course, miss."

Abigail wandered there and sighed in contentment as she lay on one of the chaises. Having waited a long time, she had almost fallen asleep when Darrell entered. His appearance was disturbingly grim.

"Darrell, what's wrong? Didn't Dr. Hardin relate the good news?"

"He did, my dearest. I'm happy his report of you is encouraging."

"My report; what of Edward?"

Darrell sat by her and took her hand. "My darling, I'm sorry. The prognosis of Edward is not good."

"Not good? Is his physical health unsound?"

"Edward is fit in a physical sense. What's distressing is the doctor has determined his mental condition hasn't improved substantially."

He handed the doctor's note to Abigail. His findings were so startling she read the page several times, particularly the final paragraph which related:

Following my analysis, factoring in each aspect of my examination, while I have observed a slight improvement in his mental state, in my opinion, Mr. Lewis is not of sound mind and thereby is incapable of functioning in the world of his own volition. In his best interest and the safety of the household, I recommend his confinement continues. I do suggest a reevaluation of his health, both physical and mental, be performed on a yearly basis.

Abigail's hand went limp and she dropped the page. *His conclusion isn't possible,* she thought.

"My love, I was convinced you'd find this upsetting. You were hopeful the hearsay of Edward's recovery would be corroborated. I regret you've been disappointed. As I've advised, my brother is ingenious. My presumption he's deceived my sister must be the case."

"Darrell, this account cannot be accurate. May I speak with Dr. Hardin?"

"No, my dear, he departed some time ago. My sweet, sweet Abigail; you want the best for everyone, and the situation is grievous. Goodness, you're pale. May I bring you a glass of water, or perhaps wine?"

"No, thank you. I'd prefer to be on my own awhile."

"Certainly, dearest. I have business to attend. I'll see you at tea. You do appear ill. Shall I summon Harrison?"

She shook her head. "Rest is what I need, which I may obtain here."

"Very well, my darling."

Darrell kissed her hand and left.

Abigail lay back on the chaise. *This doesn't make sense. There's no good explanation unless Edward has pulled the wool over my eyes. But if he has, why hasn't he taken advantage of my gullibility? He's had every opportunity. Something doesn't add up here. I believe a trip to the north wing will be in order tonight.*

*****

The candle on the table of the north wing library flickered. Edward looked up from the book he was reading. "Abigail, what are you doing here? Why did you come when the condition is dangerous?"

"With the guard duty ended, you've no cause for concern," she said.

"Guard duty or not, I'm highly concerned. You should have waited for Darrell to leave."

"This couldn't wait."

"How could something be urgent?"

"I've read the doctor's report."

"I see," he said matter-of-factly.

"Edward, what occurred during the examination? What led Dr. Hardin to reach the wrong conclusion?"

"I was nervous; it would seem unnaturally so. I had great difficulty answering his questions. For whatever reason, I couldn't formulate a coherent sentence. I simply babbled on in a nonsensical way."

"You've always spoken clearly with me. If you were tense, we must have the doctor return. He needs to reexamine you when your mood is calmer, and you're better prepared to address his inquiries."

"He plans to return in a year, which will give me ample time to prepare."

"We cannot wait for a year to pass."

"I doubt we'll have the choice. Darrell will deem a visit prior a waste of everyone's time."

"Then we'll wait for him to leave, and have the doctor see you without your brother's interference."

"It won't make a difference."

"Why ever not?"

"The doctor's analysis is correct. I'm not sufficiently recovered to face the world on a daily basis. I need more time."

"Darrell put the idea into your head."

"Truly, he didn't. You must understand there are places and things outside the north wing to which I may respond irrationally."

"What makes you think that? You've already faced the outside world."

"If you'll recall the interval was brief. I encountered one room only."

"You adjusted remarkably well during your short visit if *you'll* recall. Given the opportunity, you'll overcome the obstacles we've yet to confront."

"You don't know this with certainty."

"While I don't, the physician could play a crucial role. He could guide you through the rough waters."

"You presume the doctor will change his assessment. It isn't going to happen."

"He will if your coherence returns. I suspect Darrell caused you to be nervous. Did he say or do something to upset you?"

"No… he didn't."

"Edward, don't hide the truth. If Darrell has done anything improper, you must tell me."

He fidgeted. "There's nothing to tell."

"You're lying. It's apparent you're distressed."

"Why do you suppose I'm lying? Why should you speak harshly of the man you intend to marry and make ugly allegations when you would pledge to him your undying love and devotion?"

"It wasn't my intention to speak ill of him. I'm aware there are issues between the two of you Darrell won't disclose. They need to be addressed."

"If you love him as deeply as you claim, why don't you trust him implicitly?" Edward asked snottily.

"I do trust him, only I want the family to be whole. I want everyone to be happy, Darrell especially."

"If you have any interest in my happiness, you'll leave at once and never return," he said, his voice uncharacteristically stern.

"Edward, what's wrong? You sound aggravated with me."

"I'm worried about you. Don't you realize, if you continue your visits, eventually you will be discovered."

"As always, I'll be careful."

"No, I'll tolerate your recklessness no longer."

"There's little risk when Darrell is out of the house; at least permit me then."

Edward seated himself in a huff. "Very well, come when Darrell is away. I grant my permission *only* when he is. You must promise me."

Abigail's eyes filled with tears.

"*Promise me,*" he repeated.

"You have my word," she said.

"A brother should consider his sister's welfare more than his own, isn't that true?"

"I've never had a brother," she reminded him. "Would you have me relate your wishes to Catherine?"

"She is also my sister, is she not?"

"She is. Edward…"

"Don't attempt to change my mind. I'll block the door if need be. Please, I'd prefer it if you left." He took Abigail's arm and pulled her roughly out of the room. "Goodbye now," he said bluntly.

"I'll miss you, dreadfully."

"As I'll miss you," Edward admitted.

"We'll see each other when next Darrell travels," Abigail said.

"Until then," he said.

Although she offered her hand Edward didn't take it; instead, he gave her a motion of dismissal.

Abigail's shoulders were slumped in dismay as she made her way down the corridor. When she arrived at the doors, she glanced back to find Edward's expression had changed. She wasn't sure if she imagined it, but it appeared he may be apologetic—perhaps on the brink of calling after her. When his eyes met hers, he turned away and entered the library. She exited the north wing and with a heavy heart took the key from her pocket to secure the doors.

8

A troublesome incident may lead to obsessive contemplation, particularly if the matter cannot be promptly addressed. During the course of the next ten days, Abigail had been preoccupied with thoughts of her last meeting with Edward. His belligerence he'd claimed was due to his concern for her safety, and that point she didn't question, but the explanation seemed incomplete. His comments regarding Darrell had puzzled her, not so much what he'd said, it was the sarcastic way he'd said them. She regretted she hadn't followed him to the library to clarify the meaning behind his remarks, particularly since his expression when she'd left contradicted his ill-temper.

Several days later, Darrell notified her he was compelled to depart at the end of the week. Abigail was secretly thankful, since that would give her the opportunity to confront Edward.

The day prior to Darrell's departure, Abigail was taking a stroll through the gardens with Catherine. They saw Eleanor hurrying towards them, her cheeks red and her breathing labored.

"My gracious, Eleanor, you're shaking," Catherine said. "Is something wrong?"

"Not in the least." She paused to catch her breath. "You may scarcely believe our luck. When Darrell leaves in the morning, Jake will accompany him."

Catherine's jaw dropped. "You cannot be in earnest! How did this come about?"

"Darrell's valet has taken ill. Since he cannot endure the trip, Jake will take his place."

"This is amazing news," Catherine exclaimed.

"I'm sorry to hear the young man is unwell," Abigail said. "Is his condition serious?"

"It doesn't appear to be. He should make a full recovery," Eleanor said.

"How marvelous he was stricken at an optimal time."

Abigail smirked at Catherine. "That isn't nice to say, but it would be wonderful for Edward to spend time away from the north wing if we can convince him to comply."

"He'll have no choice. I'll drag him out of there if need be," Catherine said.

Eleanor's eyes grew wide. "I have an idea."

"What idea?" Catherine asked.

"Until I work through the particulars, I'd rather not say." Without further comment, Eleanor bustled off in the direction of the house.

"What do you suppose she's contemplating?"

"I haven't the slightest notion," Abigail said. "We'll have to wait for her to tell us."

Upon the girls' return, a note from Eleanor had been left for them. She requested they meet in her private parlor after tea.

When teatime ended, Darrell went to his study to finalize the preparations for his trip. Abigail and Catherine then rushed to Eleanor's quarters.

She smiled at them. "Have a seat, my dears. With most of the details in place, I'll reveal what I have in mind."

"Please, tell us," Catherine said. "The suspense is unbearable."

"While Darrell and Jake are away, I have arranged for Edward to spend the *entire* length of their absence outside the north wing."

"How is this possible?" Abigail asked.

"Edward will pose as a guest of the house. To avoid suspicion, he'll play the part of a relative of yours come to visit," she told Abigail.

"Won't the servants recognize him?" she replied.

"Most of the staff has never laid eyes on Edward," Eleanor explained. "The exception is Mr. Phillips, who knew him as a child, and has on occasion seen him as an adult. I've confided in him our plan. He's agreed to participate."

The idea worried Abigail. "Oh, Eleanor, I'm aware he's a kind man, and yet do you think this was wise? Are you certain we may trust him?"

"We may trust him implicitly. Although he loves all of the children, he has a great deal of sympathy for Edward. Mr. Phillips was thrilled to hear of his improvement. He consented without hesitation to support us."

"Will we be able to convince Edward?" Abigail wondered.

"I've spoken with him," Eleanor said. "He has agreed."

"From the sound of it, you have the essentials ironed out," Catherine said.

"But for one crucial detail; Abigail must supply us with the identity of a relative. While we could invent one, a genuine relation who's unlikely to visit would be preferable. You never know; his name could slip out when your family is here for the wedding."

"I have a cousin who may fit the bill perfectly, a Mr. Brandon Wilson. His family located to America when he was a small boy, and I haven't seen him since. They've sent word they're unable to attend the wedding; however, I could claim he paid me a surprise visit. Though apparently a rare occurrence, Mr. Wilson has traveled to England on matters of business. No one will have a reason to question my word."

"He would seem the ideal candidate," Catherine said.

"It should work well," Eleanor agreed. "The day following Darrell's departure, I'll sneak Edward out of the north wing at an early hour and make the announcement your *Mr. Wilson* has arrived."

*****

Two days later, Abigail was in a sound slumber when she heard a soft knock on her bedroom door. "Come in," she called out.

Mary entered in a highly animated state. "Miss, I'm sorry to rouse you early, but your cousin, Mr. Brandon Wilson, has arrived. He's awaiting you in the library."

Abigail yawned and sat up. "You don't say. What a nice surprise. I suppose I should dress straight away."

Mary helped her to the dressing table. "The maid who told me he'd come, Sylvia that is, went on and on about him. She thinks he's most handsome."

"Oh?"

"You don't agree?"

"I wouldn't know. I haven't seen him since we were children."

"May I come with you to the library, and have a peek?"

Abigail found this amusing. "Of course, you may."

Mary completed the preparations at a hectic pace. "There, miss, I've finished."

She snatched the dressing chair from under Abigail and shuffled her out of the room.

At the library's entrance, Mary stood on tiptoe to peer over Abigail's shoulder. "Goodness, Sylvia didn't exaggerate, did she?"

"Not in the least."

Abigail was amazed by Edward's appearance. His attire, which had previously been dated, was of the latest fashion, accentuated by a posture he held taller than usual. He wore an eye patch as well which created an astounding transformation to his face.

"Have a lovely visit, miss." Mary giggled as she left.

Abigail closed the door. "Edward, you look wonderful."

"Thank you, Abigail."

He rushed to her and took her hands.

"Have you been well since our last meeting?" she asked.

"I was about to offer my apology for that night. My behavior was unforgivably boorish."

179

"Not unforgivable, it was only out of character. You worried me more than anything. I'm glad you agreed to leave the north wing. When Eleanor related her plan, I was convinced you wouldn't. You said you were fearful of what you may face."

"To an extent I still am, but I wanted to see you. I was concerned you'd come to despise me. I wouldn't blame you if you had."

"I could never despise you. You were simply out of sorts, I believe, from the doctor's examination, and perhaps there was more to it…"

They were interrupted when Catherine entered the room.

"Dear brother, don't you look well."

"Thank you, my dear sister. It's all a result of Eleanor's efforts."

The door opened again, and Eleanor joined them. "Good morning, my dears. There are a few crucial points we must discuss. Please, take a seat."

They sat in a line, and Eleanor stood before them like a teacher ready to recite a lesson plan. "This is a momentous occasion. You could easily become emotional. Keep in mind at all times you're not alone in the house. A servant could interrupt without warning or overhear your conversation; therefore, you must be mindful of what you say or do. You mustn't engage in any affection which could be deemed inappropriate. Remember also to address each other in the proper manner. If you were to slip, even for a moment, all could be lost."

"We'll remember," Abigail said.

Edward and Catherine nodded in agreement.

"Good. Breakfast will be set out in about twenty minutes," Eleanor told them.

After Eleanor left, Catherine sniffled.

"Catherine, what's wrong?" Edward asked.

She took her handkerchief from her pocket. "Nothing."

"Then, why are you crying?"

180

"Seeing you outside the north wing, sitting here with us, it's too much. I thought this day would never arrive."

He put his arm around her. "My darling sister."

Abigail's eyes filled with tears as she held Catherine's hand. They were on the verge of an emotional eruption when Eleanor returned. She shut the door quickly.

"In heaven's name, what did I tell you not five minutes ago? Supposing one of the maids was with me. If you're incapable of controlling yourselves, I'll arrange for *Mr. Wilson's* sudden departure."

Catherine gasped. "Please, Eleanor, you mustn't! The fault was entirely mine. It won't happen again, you have my word."

"Children, children." Eleanor shook her head. "Wipe your eyes and collect yourselves. I won't give you another chance."

*****

An individual's need to become reacquainted with a home they'd never left would be unthinkable for most people. This was by no means the case for Abigail; she was keenly aware of the challenges Edward was to face. During his first days of freedom, she was on high alert for signs of trouble. As Eleanor had advised, a lapse on Edward's part could spell disaster not only for him; it could impact the entire household.

Tense moments had transpired on a frequent basis. Oftentimes he would stare, seemingly at nothing. No one appeared to notice, except for Abigail, who believed images of Emily had been haunting him. Fortunately, he'd been able to maintain his composure. As time passed, incidents such as these had lessened.

During this interval fog and rain had persisted, conditions which weren't of any help to raise one's spirits. Forced to remain indoors, Abigail, Edward, and Catherine spent their time playing card games, chess, and reading.

By the morning of the fourth day, the skies had cleared. The weather was warm and bright, and the household mood followed suit.

Edward arrived at breakfast to find the ladies were already there. "You two appear jovial this morning."

"Of course, we are," Catherine said. "It's a gorgeous day. At last, we may venture outside."

Edward looked troubled. "You'll excuse me, Miss Lewis. I've no desire to join you."

"Why not?" his sister asked.

"We may come across…that which I could not bear to encounter."

"You're referring to the tree?" Abigail speculated.

"Yes," he said grimly.

"The thought hadn't occurred to me," Catherine admitted. "It's a long way off, over the ravine. We could easily avoid it; we just won't head in that direction."

"I'm sorry; I'm not up to an exploration."

"I believe we must. The servants would find it odd if we never left the house. It may raise suspicion if we don't acquaint our *guest* with the property," Catherine said.

"A valid point," Abigail agreed.

Edward reflected for a moment. "Very well. If we remain on this side of the ravine, I'll come with you."

Catherine smiled. "We'll go nowhere near there."

After breakfast, they went to the rear of the house. Catherine exited onto the courtyard and held the door open for the others. Abigail was by Edward's side, as for the first time in ten years he stood at the threshold of an exterior door. He had the appearance of someone about to enter an abyss when he took a step out of the house. He looked up and the sunbeams lit his face.

"I promised myself I wouldn't cry," Catherine whispered. "I hope no one else can see my tears. How suspicious they would be to spot me in such a state."

Edward extended his arm to her. "May I offer you my escort, Miss Lewis?"

"Thank you, Mr. Wilson," Catherine said as she placed her hand on his arm.

Abigail followed while they walked the garden path. Edward seemed contented until they neared the north wing. There he stopped and regarded the structure with an odd expression.

"We shouldn't have come this way," Abigail said.

"It's fine, only I haven't seen my wing from the outside since the windows were bricked. I should have anticipated it; how strange it looks."

"My thought exactly when I encountered it for the first time," Abigail said.

Catherine harrumphed. "Strange indeed. One of these days I'll take a hammer and knock out these bricks myself."

Edward obviously regretted he'd ignited Catherine's ire. "Let's continue with our stroll," he suggested.

The tension eased as they ambled amongst the sea of flowers. While they wandered through the various plots, the siblings shared memories of their youth. In short order they were romping about like children.

Catherine ran ahead of Edward. "I'll bet I'm still faster than you."

"You were never faster." He hurried to grab his sister. The two of them stumbled to the ground.

Catherine tried to squirm from under him. "Don't you dare tickle me." He tickled her anyway, and soon she was giggling uncontrollably. "Please, stop!"

Edward chuckled as he helped her rise.

Abigail's eyes widened when he stalked towards her, his hands raised. "Don't you consider it."

He ignored her plea and pulled her onto her back. She was now the prey to his frivolity as she laughed along with him.

"Release my sister at once," Catherine said jokingly.

Edward stood. Grinning mischievously, he lifted Abigail onto her feet. With their faces close, he gazed into her eyes. His mood became sober while he yet held her waist.

When she took a startled step backward, Edward dropped his hands in embarrassment.

Abigail checked her pendant watch. "It's nearing luncheon. We should return to the house."

"We could use the trail," Catherine said. She indicated a natural path which circled the perimeter of the grounds.

They agreed to her suggestion and strode along the uneven terrain. Not long after they came upon a hill, at the top of which were boulders to be traversed. Edward helped his sister, and then turned to offer Abigail his hand. Before she could take it, he straightened himself and froze as the color drained from his face.

Catherine looked back. "Oh no!"

Abigail couldn't fathom what had unnerved them until she peered behind her to see a huge oak off in the distance. With a large rock embedded near its base, she determined this was no ordinary tree, this was *the* tree.

"Emily, oh my God no, *no!*" Edward fell to his knees. "What have I done? Emily, wake up, please *wake up!*" he said as he rubbed the grass.

Catherine knelt next to him. "Edward, I'm sorry, I'm so sorry; I should've recalled it could be seen from here." She attempted to put her arms around him.

He pushed her away. "Don't touch me!"

She silently appealed to Abigail, who placed her hand on his back.

"Leave me alone," he hollered.

"Please, Edward, let us help you," Catherine implored, to no avail. "Abigail, what'll we do?"

She shook her head. "I've no idea."

The girls' attention was captured by one of the gardeners. Although a fair distance away, he was evidently aware something was wrong. He dropped his tools and rushed in their direction.

"Edward, you've been seen," Abigail alerted him.

He continued to wail, tugging at his hair.

"Please, Edward, stop," Catherine beseeched.

Abigail panicked when the man drew near. "Are you badly injured?" she bluffed, loudly enough for all to hear.

She hurried to intercept the gardener and arrived at the base of the hill just as he did. "My cousin's ankle has been turned. Fetch Mrs. Williams. Have her bring bindings. Mr. Phillips should come as well. Mr. Wilson will require help down the hill."

The man tipped his hat before he left to do her bidding.

Abigail returned to Edward's side. "The situation is serious. Now you've been spotted, more are bound to come."

He lay on his side, apparently unable to hear while he stroked the ground. "Why, Emily, why did this happen to you? It should have been me."

Eleanor and Mr. Phillips approached, with many of the servants following them.

"Edward, they're coming. You must return to us now," his sister urged.

"Wait here; we don't need a crowd," Eleanor told the others.

When she and Mr. Phillips had climbed the hill, Catherine discretely pointed at the tree.

Eleanor glanced in that direction and indicated she understood. She knelt close to Edward while he continued to fuss. "Enough of this, young man," she whispered. "We're not alone. If you don't cease this behavior, it might be our undoing." When he didn't respond, she pulled him to a seated position. "Do you see what you've done? You've placed us in danger."

Concern crossed his face as he surveyed the many eyes upon him.

"Don't worry," Abigail said in a low voice. "No one heard you distinctly. I've claimed you were injured. You must cooperate if they're to believe this."

He acknowledged her and permitted Mr. Phillips to wrap his ankle.

Eleanor stood to address the servants. "The injury isn't serious. We have things well in hand. Return to your duties at once."

Mr. Phillips helped Edward rise. Together they negotiated the steep decline.

At the house, several of the maids were awaiting them in the parlor.

"Your assistance isn't required," Eleanor said. They left and she secured the door behind them.

On the brink of fainting, Edward collapsed onto a chair.

Eleanor poured brandy into a snifter. "Drink this," she told Edward as she handed it to him.

He took the libation with trembling hands, choking a bit when he swallowed.

Eleanor collected the glass. "Rest will do you good. Mr. Phillips and I will take you to your room."

"Should he be left alone?" Abigail whispered to her.

"I'll stay until he falls asleep," Eleanor said.

After they'd left, Catherine covered her eyes. "This was my fault. I don't know what I was thinking. I'd forgotten the tree could be viewed from the top of the hill. I'll never forgive myself if he's unable to recover."

"Whatever happens, you're not to blame," Abigail said.

Catherine shook her head.

Abigail put her hand on Catherine's shoulder. "Only time will tell. The best we can do is remain hopeful. We must collect ourselves, for we're expected in the dining room shortly."

"How can you consider eating? I couldn't swallow a bite."

"Appetite or not, we must make the effort. Since the staff was told the injury is minor, it will create suspicion if we're overly upset."

Catherine begrudgingly complied. Twenty minutes had passed when Eleanor entered the dining room. She informed them Edward had fallen asleep. He hadn't yet spoken, and so there was nothing further for her to report.

When they'd finished their luncheon, the girls spent the remainder of the afternoon in the library. Any activity they engaged in was of little distraction. For them, the hours crawled by at an agonizing pace.

As teatime neared, they had yet to hear a word.

"Why have we heard nothing further?" Catherine grumbled.

The door opened. To their relief Edward entered, accompanied by Mr. Phillips. When he'd assisted Edward to a chair, Mr. Phillips departed.

"My dear…Mr. Wilson," Catherine caught herself. "How are you feeling?"

"I'm doing well."

"Have you found it in your heart to forgive me?" his sister asked.

"What have I to forgive you?"

"I promised we wouldn't go near the tree, and then like a fool led you up the path where it was in full view. You'd think I would've had better sense."

"You've done nothing wrong. It is I who must beg pardon for my behavior."

"Behavior which was understandable, under the circumstance," Catherine said.

"It was a terrible shock for you," Abigail added.

"I cannot deny it was, and yet when Eleanor brought to my attention I'd placed all of you in danger, it dawned on me how selfish and thoughtless I've been. Not merely today, for some time now," he said. "Dwelling on the past cannot bring Emily back, but it could have hurt the people I love who are here. From this day forward, I'll focus my attention on the present; on the kind individuals who've granted me their love and compassion, without reservation."

"Ed…Mr. Wilson, it's wonderful you've come to this conclusion," Abigail said.

Catherine's eyes were misty. "I'm so proud of you."

There was a knock at the door. A maid entered with the tea tray. Catherine turned away from her, ostensibly to hide her emotional state.

"I'll pour for my cousin today. You may be excused," Abigail said.

"Yes, miss." The girl curtseyed and left.

Abigail locked the door behind her.

"Thank you, Abigail," Catherine said. "Today I'd prefer to spend time with my *brother* rather than your cousin."

*****

Following dinner, due to their exhaustion, the ladies retired early. While Edward claimed he was grateful for the chance to attain additional rest, Abigail sensed he was apprehensive to be on his own.

Abigail found the comfort of her bed welcoming; however, the moment she slipped under the covers, her thoughts were filled with concern for Edward. She knew sleep would be impossible until she confirmed he hadn't relapsed.

She tiptoed to the east wing and listened carefully at each door. When she heard a noise coming from one of the rooms she knocked.

"Abigail," Edward said upon opening the door. "Why are you here?"

"When we said good night, I had the impression you weren't ready to retire. I cannot sleep, and thought I'd join you for a while unless I'm disturbing you?"

"As a matter of fact, I was reading. Please, come in."

"Thank you. This is a pleasant room, yet it must be strange for you to stay here."

"It is. Of course, I've never slept in one of these guest rooms. I'm also unused to the moonlight. I've found it difficult to fall asleep."

"I can well imagine."

"Shall I read to you?"

"That would be nice. I see from the placement of your mark you're well into the book you're reading. Perhaps you'd prefer to finish it, and read to me another time?"

"No, no; I'll gladly begin another. The only other selection here must have been left by a previous visitor. I'm unacquainted with the author." He handed the book to her.

"I'm not acquainted with his work either."

"Would you rather choose from the library?"

SUSAN BUTLER

She returned the book to him. "This will suffice."

He indicated two chairs on either side of a small table. As he read it was clear the story chiefly concerned romance. Edward glanced at Abigail for permission to continue. Although the subject matter wasn't entirely appropriate, so far it wasn't provocative. She granted her approval.

"Philippe enticed Anita to join him in his bedroom," Edward narrated several pages later. "He pulled her gown to her shoulders. As she displayed no reluctance, he kissed her neck passionately, slowly lowering the silky garment to her waist, exposing her…" he stopped, his expression stunned. "I beg your pardon; I'd no idea the content of this book was unsuitable." He reviewed more of it silently. "I fear it doesn't improve."

"It doesn't sound as though it would."

After he'd scanned further, the book slipped to the floor and landed near Abigail's feet. Edward knelt to retrieve it, his face close to her body. He was fixated on her nighttime attire, regarding her in such an uncharacteristic manner she drew back and crossed her arms.

He took his seat and stared at his lap. "We could fetch another book."

"No, it's late. We ought to say good night."

"Yes, I suppose we should."

Edward assisted her to the door. He took hold of the knob but didn't turn it.

Abigail folded her arms again. "We'll meet at breakfast." Her glance at his hand signaled her desire to leave.

He hesitated before he opened the door. Once he had, she made a hasty exit.

"Abigail?"

She turned around. Edward held out his hand to her. She didn't offer hers in return.

"You do believe I was unfamiliar with the subject of that book?" he asked.

I'm overreacting. He thinks of me as a sister only, Abigail convinced herself. "I believe you."

She extended her hand which he took gently, placing upon it his usual delicate kiss.

"Good night, dearest Abigail."

"Good night, my dearest brother."

His smile was affectionate when he closed the door. Was it a bit too affectionate for a brother? she wondered, her concern renewed as she walked to her room.

*****

Abigail deliberated about the situation with Edward for some time after she'd gone to bed. Given their history, she concluded any change in his behavior had to be a product of her imagination. Before long they would become siblings through marriage, and she could think of no reason he should have come to view her in any other way.

She awoke to a beautiful morning. After she dressed, she entered the dining room to find Catherine and Edward awaiting her.

"What shall we do with ourselves today?" Catherine asked. "We must continue to take advantage of this lovely weather, don't you agree? Perhaps a drive into town would be entertaining for our Mr. Wilson."

"I would enjoy it immensely," Edward said.

"Let's depart after luncheon," Catherine suggested.

"Thank you, Miss Lewis."

Abigail felt slighted they weren't of a mind to consult with her. "It will be fine," she said curtly.

Following breakfast, they moved to the courtyard, where they played a game of cards to pass the time. At one point, Abigail looked up from her hand to see Catherine gazing at her peculiarly. Abigail then glanced at Edward, who averted his attention so abruptly she presumed he'd been staring at her. Although she attempted to persuade herself otherwise, when similar incidents happened, she believed her previous conclusion had been wrong—Edward's regard of her had unquestionably changed.

After they took luncheon outdoors, they headed to the carriage. Edward walked with a feigned limp as the servants would expect, using a cane for support. When they were boarding, Catherine groaned and touched her forehead.

"Is something wrong, Miss Lewis?" Edward asked.

"My head is throbbing. Possibly I've had too much sun. I'm afraid I'll have to miss our drive."

"We could postpone until tomorrow," Abigail said.

"I won't hear of it," Catherine said. "Tomorrow could be rainy. You mustn't waste a beautiful day on my account."

"We could delay awhile in the hopes your pain will ease," Abigail suggested.

"Recovery from a headache is most uncertain. It could persist throughout the day. The two of you should go ahead."

"Truly, we wouldn't mind," Abigail said.

"No!" Catherine's insistence was adamant to the extent the driver peered over his shoulder. "Your cousin's time with us is limited. It would be wrong to deny him the pleasure."

"As you wish. We'll leave as planned," Abigail told the driver.

"Please feel better, Miss Lewis," Edward said.

Abigail and Edward were seated, and the driver cracked his whip. When Abigail turned to wave goodbye, her eyes narrowed in suspicion. Catherine appeared strangely pert for a person supposedly in a good deal of pain.

While they drove, Edward was unmistakably relishing his first outing in many years; although, Abigail suspected his interest was focused more on her than the scenery. With her uneasiness building, she tried to divert his attention to the landscape, attempts that were short-lived at best.

They arrived at the town's center and Edward used his cane to disembark. When they were out of view of the driver Edward flung it in the air and caught it on the way down. "This is far more comfortable. It's surprisingly difficult to hobble when one doesn't need to."

Abigail laughed and he smiled as he offered her his arm. She accepted it, relieved his manner now held no suggestion of any unbefitting familiarity.

Several hours passed while they strolled along the streets and wandered into the shops. They shared with each other items which delighted them, frequently giggling like children on a treasure hunt. This was the kind of behavior typical for siblings, which convinced Abigail his brotherly attitude had returned.

When tea time arrived, they came across a quaint inn with a dining room, welcoming the opportunity to rest their feet. The room was crowded, with many tables occupied by families. Abigail was entertained by their interaction until she saw Edward's mood had dimmed.

Poor Edward, she thought. *I can imagine what he's contemplating. If Emily hadn't fallen, he'd likely be married, and perhaps he'd have children of his own. It must be difficult to witness the sort of life he was denied by a cruel twist of fate.* She rubbed his arm gently. He squeezed her hand in response.

After tea, they returned to the carriage. Abigail reminded Edward to resume his limp. She pretended to assist him by holding him under the shoulder.

"How are you feeling, Mr. Wilson?"

"I'm doing well," he said. His somber expression didn't support his claim.

She sat by him in the carriage and covered his hand resting on the seat with hers, using the folds of her dress to conceal the deed from the driver. Edward smiled, seemingly consoled by her act of kindness.

Upon their return, they prepared for dinner, and then met Catherine in the library.

"Good evening, Abigail, Mr. Wilson."

"Good evening. Did your headache pass?" Abigail asked her in a skeptical tone.

"Blessedly it has. Did you have a pleasant journey?"

"The trip was nearly as lovely as my company," Edward said. His forward gaze of her had resurfaced.

The maid who'd entered seemed to take note. "Dinner is served," the girl announced. She snickered as she departed.

While they dined, it seemed to Abigail all eyes were fixated on her. She felt awkward, like a nervous animal reluctantly on display. For her, dinner couldn't end soon enough.

"Would you ladies allow me the pleasure of reading to you tonight?" Edward asked.

"That would be lovely, Mr. Wilson," Catherine accepted.

"Shall we retire to the library?" Edward suggested.

"Yes, lets," Catherine said.

Abigail was annoyed her input had again been excluded. Since she could see the staff was prattling, she said nothing, for fear her objection would only make matters worse.

Catherine stopped at the library's entrance. "I'm afraid I've spoken out of turn. That headache has fatigued me. I believe I'll retire instead."

"Perchance a chapter or two would aid your sleep," Edward said.

"Thank you, Mr. Wilson, but no, at the moment the comfort of my bed is beckoning."

"Good night then, Miss Lewis," he said.

"Good night, Mr. Wilson. Good night, Abigail."

"Good night, Catherine. I hope you'll fall asleep quickly, given you're so very worn out," Abigail said in a tone of irony.

"I'm sure I will," Catherine said and left the room.

Edward escorted Abigail inside the library.

He closed the door. "Would you care to make the selection tonight?"

"I would, thank you." She went to browse the bookshelf.

"Thank *you*, Miss Parker, for sharing the beautiful day with me."

"I'm glad you enjoyed yourself."

"I hope you enjoyed our outing."

"I did, very much." She handed him a book and took a seat on the sofa. "I was concerned about you at tea. It seemed difficult for you to confront the families at the inn. I imagine it was akin to a slap on the face."

"It was troubling to witness the sort of life I may never have."

"Undoubtedly you were imagining Emily, and the family you may've had together."

"It wasn't her I imagined."

"It wasn't? I was certain it must be. It's a relief to hear I was mistaken."

"We are of the same mind, then?"

"I don't take your meaning."

"Emily didn't enter my mind. It was you I thought of, and you alone."

"Me; why?"

Edward sat next to her and took her hands into his. "I love you, Abigail. When you touched my arm at tea and held my hand in the carriage, I suspected you felt the same. Now you've confessed your relief I'm no longer consumed with thoughts of Emily, I'm certain of it."

"Edward, I'm sorry, but you've misunderstood my intentions. I sought to provide you comfort; nothing more. I was relieved you hadn't envisioned Emily since it dispelled my concern you were having painful thoughts about her, and the life the two of you may have shared."

He released her hands. "Then, you don't love me."

"I love you as a brother and a friend. The man to whom my passionate love belongs is Darrell."

Edward grimaced. "What a fool I've made of myself. I should've known you'd never entertain a life with me in lieu of my brother. He has in abundance the qualities a woman seeks in a man, the qualities I lack."

"You mustn't think this. You've many wonderful attributes. Any number of women could love you and desire marriage with you; it simply cannot be me."

"The notion was absurd. I'm aware of how deeply you love Darrell. Nevertheless, I've hoped you loved me as a woman loves a man, for if you don't, no one will."

"That's not true. During the past few days, you've proven your ability to function in the world. We'll have the physician return as soon as possible. He'll conclude you may be released from the north wing. Once you're away from there you may begin a new, full life. You'll be able to find happiness."

"Your belief this could take place, while naïve, is undeniably sweet."

"Why do you speak as if it's impossible when clearly it's not?"

Edward smiled faintly. He touched her cheek. "Part of why I love you is your unwavering trust and determination you have the ability to help me. If you'll excuse me, I'd rather not read tonight." He walked to the door. "Good night, dearest Abigail."

"I don't understand why you doubt me. In time, I'll prove how wrong you are."

"Good night," he repeated and left.

Abigail sat in bewilderment. *How did this happen? Why did he come to believe I'm in love with him? It was Catherine. She didn't have a headache this afternoon, and she wasn't so terribly tired this evening. Her purpose was to bring Edward and me together. I'll have her know not only did she fail in this; she humiliated her brother in the process. I hope she'll be happy with herself,* she thought in irritation.

She departed the library, snarling as she climbed the stairs to her bedroom.

*****

Abigail entered the dining room for breakfast to find Catherine waiting alone, grinning like the cat that swallowed the canary.

"Good morning, Abigail," she said.

"You appear quite well and pleased with yourself this morning," Abigail snapped.

"Pleased with myself?"

"Yes, your smirk of self-satisfaction says it all."

"What an unkind remark."

"Unkind indeed. I've come to realize your headache and fatigue was feigned. You wanted Edward and me to spend time alone."

"And now you make an untoward allegation."

"Continue your attempt to pull the wool over my eyes if you will; however, you're not fooling me, not one bit."

"Then I may as well admit, what you suspect is true."

"Such impertinence. Did you sincerely believe you could instigate a romance between Edward and me?"

"There was no need to instigate that which had already begun."

"For Edward perhaps, but not for me. I was forced to hurt him last night when he confessed the sort of love I don't share."

"You do share the same love."

"I love him as his friend and sister, nothing more."

"You needn't deny your deep affection. It's obvious the love you hold for him isn't the love of a sister."

"That isn't the case at all."

"Abigail, as your sister and confidant, there's no need for you to hide your feelings from me."

"I'm not hiding my feelings."

"You most certainly are."

"What, may I ask, has you convinced of this?"

"Lately, when you've looked at Edward it hasn't been in the manner of a sister. You've had the longing gaze of a woman who's utterly in love."

"Whatever you assume you've witnessed, you're wrong. If you weren't, what do you expect could be gained here?"

"I want Edward to have the love he deserves. I want my brother to be happy."

"And what of your other brother; would you have me abandon Darrell?"

"As a matter of fact, I would."

"You cannot mean it."

"Oh, but I do! Darrell may select from any number of women. He'll become engaged to another without difficulty.

Edward's only chance for happiness is you. Since you're in love with him, you shouldn't resist emotions which cannot be altered."

Abigail shook her head. "I'll listen to no more of this." She left the room fuming.

Edward, who'd been about to enter, regarded her with concern. "Miss Parker, what's wrong?"

She stopped without looking directly at him.

"Please, tell me what's upset you," Edward said.

"We must discuss it in private."

She led him to the parlor and shut the door firmly behind them.

"You're angry with me, aren't you?" he asked.

"Not with you; with Catherine. She *lied* about her headache yesterday. She didn't have one; she invented it to have us spend time alone."

"Why would she?"

"Apparently, she hoped to spark a relationship between us, even at Darrell's expense. You must be honest with me; did you have any involvement in this?"

"You have my solemn word I did not. I would never deliberately hurt you or my brother. My intention was to apologize for my conduct. I value our friendship above all else. I hope you can forgive me."

"Dearest Edward, of course, I forgive you. We'll put the matter behind us, for I wouldn't want to lose…"

Before she could finish her statement, Eleanor entered without knocking. Wide-eyed and out of breath, she was obviously in a state of panic.

"Gracious, Eleanor, whatever is the matter?" Abigail asked.

"Darrell has returned! He's exiting the carriage as we speak!"

"Heaven forbid!" Abigail exclaimed.

"Edward, you must return to the north wing," Eleanor said. She glanced out the window. "Dear Lord, it's too late;

197

Darrell's about to enter. I'll attempt to delay him while you find a place to hide." She rushed into the hallway.

Abigail surveyed the room frantically for a solution. "The windows?" She ran towards them. "Oh no, you cannot escape here. Jake is standing by the carriage. He has a clear view of this side of the house. The furniture won't cover you fully. Where can you hide?"

"Eleanor," Darrell said. "May we please discuss this later? I'm longing to be with my beloved."

Abigail's heart was pounding. After a desperate search, the only possibility became apparent.

"The door?" Edward asked.

"It's our only chance. Please, hurry!"

He raced to the wall and stood where the door would hide him when opened.

"My darling Abigail," Darrell said as he entered the room.

He approached her in such haste, he didn't close the door. Abigail breathed easier with Edward concealed.

Darrell gathered her into his arms. "I couldn't tolerate being without you a moment longer..." He stood back, holding her by the shoulders. "Dearest, are you unwell?"

"I'm well, though surprised you've returned early."

"It doesn't appear to be a pleasant surprise."

"On the contrary, I'm most pleased."

"Pleased? You're shaking, and pale as a ghost."

"The result of my excitement."

"You're unnerved, not excited. Why is this?"

"I wish I'd received prior notice of your arrival. I would've taken additional efforts with my appearance."

"If you weren't traumatized, you'd appear as you always do. Something is terribly wrong here."

When she didn't speak, he went to the door, presumably to close it for privacy.

"Darrell!" she cried out in the hopes of preventing him.

His hand grazed the knob when he turned around, moving the door sufficiently to expose his brother. Darrell must have seen her staring past him and glanced back. Edward had pulled the door in time to cover himself.

"Abigail, you're alarming me. Explain your condition at once," Darrell insisted.

"I have something to confess."

"What could you possibly have to confess?"

She shook her head.

"Tell me what this is regarding before I go mad."

"I'm afraid you won't forgive me."

He again headed to the door, and Abigail braced herself for his rage. When he closed the door she was relieved, for Edward was no longer there.

Darrell's patience was plainly wearing thin. "Sit here." He indicated the sofa. "You will now tell me the truth."

She hesitated to concoct a story.

"*Abigail!*"

"We had a guest…"

"Yes, continue."

"He arrived the day after you departed. Since he gave me no forewarning of his visit, I couldn't obtain your permission for him to stay with us."

"Who is this person?"

"A cousin of mine. He moved with his family to America, several years before my parents and I left for Vienna. He was in the vicinity on matters of business, when an unexpected opening developed in his schedule. He'd learned of my whereabouts from the announcement of our engagement. Neither my cousin nor his family can attend the wedding, and he wanted to wish me well. He offered to register at the inn, but I said he must be our guest. It was wrong of me to suggest it without your consent. I'm certain you'll be angry with me for my insolence."

"Abigail, I'm not angry. You should know had I been here I would've extended him the same courtesy."

"I thought you would; still, I shouldn't have permitted him lodging in a home where I'm not yet mistress."

"You'll be mistress soon, and you're hardly an underling. This is your home. I trust your judgment implicitly."

Tears of relief trickled down her cheeks. "A huge weight has been lifted from my shoulders."

Darrell pulled her into his embrace. "My darling, there's no need to cry. Please now, tell me, where is this cousin of yours?"

"He departed early this morning. It's unfortunate since I imagine you would have enjoyed meeting him."

"Undoubtedly I would have. It's a shame I missed him so nearly. Fortunately, my business was resolved promptly, and I was able to schedule a seat on the next train. In addition to being in a hurry, I wanted to surprise you."

"It is a surprise; a wonderful surprise."

"This is the response I was hoping for."

Darrell helped Abigail rise, his eyes smiling as he kissed her. He then escorted her to the hallway where Eleanor was waiting.

"You needn't bother with an explanation," he said. "Abigail has told me of her cousin. I have no objection to his stay. Dearest, will you excuse me? I must freshen myself."

"Certainly," Abigail said.

When he was out of sight, her legs buckled.

Eleanor rushed to support her. "My poor child. I'll help you to the dining room."

"Edward?" Abigail asked.

"He's returned safely to the north wing."

"Thank the dear Lord. Have you alerted Catherine?"

"I have. She fled to the boudoir."

"This was nearly a disaster, far too near."

"Someone was looking out for us today."

"I can hardly breathe."

"Perhaps a cup of tea, my dear?"

"Please."

"I could slip a little something into it, to calm your nerves."

"No thank you, Eleanor. I must keep my wits about me."

She delivered the tea to Abigail. "If you're better, I'll return to the kitchen."

"Thank you; I'll be fine," she said.

Eleanor left the room.

I'll be fine when I discover where on earth I've placed my good sense, Abigail thought. *What'll I do now? I wouldn't risk losing Darrell, and I wouldn't risk hurting Edward. Someone is bound to be hurt, however, unless I solve this dilemma soon. If nothing else, I'm at risk of losing my mind!*

9

Frustration, when mixed with desperation, is often a highly volatile brew, leading to actions one wouldn't typically undertake. Abigail had become entangled in this sort of circumstance, and she was about to learn first-hand how serious the consequences can be.

She was seated on the sofa in the parlor when the clock chimed three. Although three in the morning was usually a time when all were asleep, she had no idea what had possessed her to be so imprudent; how foolish she'd been to have Edward meet her outside the north wing. Now, there was little doubt she was going to pay a high price for her lapse in judgment.

Darrell had been awakened and had discovered her whereabouts. He was heading to the door behind which Edward hid, as he'd done hours earlier. She made every attempt, yet Abigail was unable to speak or move, helpless to prevent Darrell from taking hold of the knob. The door creaked when he opened it with a surreal slowness until inevitably her secret was revealed.

"Why are you here? How did you escape the north wing?" Darrell shouted at his brother. His attention shifted to Abigail. "You did this!" he accused her, his eyes filled with a fiery rage. "I should have known in the end you'd betray me!"

He turned towards Edward, Darrell's hands raised, his fingers curled threateningly as he closed in on him.

"Don't do this," Abigail pleaded. She shrieked when he took hold of his brother's throat. "Please, Darrell, don't hurt him; *release him, I beg you!*"

Abigail tried to stand, but her muscles wouldn't respond. She could only writhe in horror until she bolted upright to find herself in bed. It took her a moment to realize she'd only been dreaming.

"What's wrong with me? This is the third time tonight I've had the same nightmare," she cried out.

Her pulse was racing as she lay back. She wondered if she'd be able to fall back to sleep, or if she really wanted to—fearful she may suffer through a fourth repeat of the gruesome dream.

As a matter of course she did sleep, her next awareness someone's touch of her shoulder. It was Mary, who was standing over her.

Abigail sat up slowly. "It's morning already?"

"Yes, it is. My goodness, miss, you've surely had a bad night."

"It's noticeable?"

"I'm afraid so."

"I'd like to hide it as much as possible. Do you know of any remedy?"

"Cucumbers or tea brighten the eyes. Would you like me to fetch some?"

"If you would, please."

"I'll return soon. You can rest a bit longer while they take effect."

Although Mary's treatment did improve her outside appearance, on the inside Abigail was in turmoil. She took a deep breath and tried to calm herself before she entered the dining room.

"Good morning, Darrell," she said.

He scowled at her. "Good morning."

"You appear upset. Is anything the matter?"

"Perhaps you can tell me."

"What could I tell you?"

"I would like you to explain a troubling report I received from Jake this morning."

She swallowed hard. "What did he report?"

"He overheard the gossip of the kitchen staff. It would seem many of the girls find your cousin most handsome."

"Why should that perturb you? They oftentimes prattle about that sort of topic."

"That's not what unnerves me. Their other opinion, however, does; their belief you've become infatuated with your attractive cousin."

"What a preposterous notion. It's the typical idle speculation engaged predominately for amusement."

"Were it the perception of a few silly girls, I wouldn't give it a second thought. When several members of the more mature and level-headed staff have made the same observation, this I cannot ignore."

"The idea is ludicrous. I cannot imagine what led them to such an absurd conclusion."

"Evidently, it began with a mishap in which your cousin was injured, and you came to his aid."

"What is the fault in offering assistance to someone who requires help?"

"Usually nothing. It's my understanding the two of you became close as a result of the accident; a little too close apparently."

"I wasn't the only person who tended to him. We were all concerned about his wellbeing. What I cannot fathom is why you'd entertain nonsense. I'm disappointed you've allowed yourself to be deluded by a rumor, when you must be aware stories of this nature spread swiftly, with or without warrant."

"Normally I wouldn't pay attention to hearsay, but your panicky reaction upon my return lends a great deal of credence to the account. And the servants didn't expect your cousin to depart yesterday. They were under the impression he was to remain quite a while longer."

"He was called away unexpectedly. Eleanor hadn't the opportunity to notify the staff prior to your arrival."

"What was the reason for his convenient departure?"

"There was a family emergency. His mother, my aunt, has been afflicted by a severe illness."

"If it's true, why didn't you tell me this yesterday?"

"I didn't think of it. I was flustered if you'll recall. Why he left didn't seem important. I was afraid you'd be angry with me regarding his stay."

"Or you may have urged him to leave for fear I'd discover the truth; you've fallen in love with him."

"Darrell, he's my cousin."

"Cousins have been known to marry."

"He's a cousin I hadn't seen since we were small children. This supposed love would have had to develop out of the blue."

"You've heard of Florence Nightingale, the nurse who fell in love with her patients? There are instances when love can arise out of nowhere."

"It didn't happen for me. I hoped to ease his suffering, which was the extent of my involvement."

"Not merely, it would seem. I've learned afterward the two of you took a trip to the village without an escort."

"Catherine had planned to join us, an outing that was her suggestion. As we were about to depart, she developed a headache and elected to remain at home. Even so, my cousin and I were never alone. The driver served as our escort during the journey, and then we were in a public setting. Please, Darrell, you must believe you've no call to doubt me, none whatsoever."

He clutched her arms and pulled her closer. "If you speak the truth, look into my eyes. Swear to me you don't love him."

"You have my solemn word; I am *not* in love with my cousin," she said without flinching.

He smiled and wrapped his arms around her. "I believe you, my dearest Abigail, I *do* believe you. I'm sorry I questioned you harshly. I had to be certain the rumor was false."

"Darrell, you've no call for uncertainty. I love you desperately. That will never change."

"I must have been off my head to imagine anything else. My panic and jealousy prove how deeply I love you. I simply couldn't survive if I lost you."

"The same is true now as it has always been; my love for you is eternal. You'll never lose me."

"If you'll forgive me for my doubt, we may start the day afresh."

"I forgive you."

"Thank you, my darling." Darrell took Abigail's hand and kissed her on the cheek. "Let me help you to a seat. Tell me what you're hungry for so I may prepare your plate."

*****

After breakfast, Abigail went in search of Catherine. She found her seated in the garden. "May I have a word with you?"

"You appear out of sorts," Catherine said.

"I am, and it's a small wonder. I had an unpleasant encounter with Darrell this morning. Did you discuss with your maid, or anyone else, your notion I may be in love with Edward, or my cousin as they know him?"

"Heavens no. Why do you suspect I would?"

"Jake overheard gossip to this effect, which he related to Darrell. Your brother grilled me regarding its validity."

"That was rotten of him. I give you my word it wasn't due to me; I've said nothing."

"How then did the hearsay start?"

"If the servants said something it was of their own accord. Obviously, it isn't me alone who's noted the change in your feelings."

"My feelings haven't changed. I'm in love with Darrell."

"Continue with your futile protest if you will. The day will come you'll accept the truth."

"The day will come *you'll* accept the truth; the day I marry Darrell."

"Let's not argue about this," Catherine said. "It's Edward we should discuss. I'm worried about him."

"Eleanor has assured me he's doing well, and yet I hate to think of him back in that dankness. We must find a way to end his confinement permanently."

"How do you propose we accomplish this?"

"The next time Darrell leaves, we'll have Dr. Hardin return. Edward has made such strides; he'll find no alternative but to revise his diagnosis."

"A good idea. In the meantime, we should visit Edward when we can. Possibly tonight."

"With rumors running rampant about the household, it's ill-advised," Abigail said. "We must wait for Darrell to depart."

"He's mentioned no travel plans in the near future. If we don't see him soon, it could be very hard on Edward. He may regress significantly."

"Perhaps; however, we cannot be reckless. The doctor will approve his release; then the matter will be solved once and for all. No more occasional visits or outings. Edward will have all the time he requires to recover."

Catherine appeared doubtful. "I hope you're correct."

"At the moment, belief is all I possess. We must cling to faith a solution is close at hand."

*****

Three weeks later, Darrell hadn't the need to leave town, and it was clear Catherine's perseverance was waning. Abigail implored her to remain patient, assuring her it wouldn't be much longer before he'd be compelled to travel. So far, she had complied, but as the days passed, she'd been harder to convince.

It was of no help Darrell had repeatedly denied Catherine his permission to visit Edward. Ironically, he'd cited the physician's testimony for justification. Catherine hadn't bought it; she was convinced his stance was a punishment against Edward instead of a precaution for her. Her frustration was at a peak, and like a volcano rumbling in the distance, it seemed only a matter of time before trouble would erupt.

The volcanic atmosphere exploded on what had otherwise been a placid day. Abigail and Darrell had returned to the house following an afternoon drive. She'd excused herself to wash and was on her way to meet Darrell in the study when Catherine stormed out. The wall shook when she slammed the door behind her.

"Catherine, what's happened?" Abigail asked.

"Darrell will speak with you next. I've told him you've no knowledge of this. You must corroborate my story. Say you had no involvement. Promise me you'll deny everything."

"But, Catherine, deny what?"

"I haven't time to explain. Give me your word you'll do as I say. You cannot help me by telling the truth. I'll never forgive you if you do."

"I don't understand."

"You don't need to understand. You need to promise me!"

"Whatever you wish. You have my word."

The study door opened. Darrell summoned to Abigail, and Catherine ran off.

She entered the room trembling. "Catherine is beside herself. Has she done something wrong?"

"Wrong hardly describes her infraction. As you know, on numerous occasions she's been defiant in regard to my authority. Still, her audacity today is beyond shocking."

"What has she done?"

"On my way to the study, I caught her sneaking out of the north wing. Obviously, she was unaware we'd returned from our drive."

"I simply cannot believe it. How was she able to enter?"

"She had a key to the north wing on her person. When I asked how she obtained it, she admitted to pilfering Eleanor's. She had a duplicate made before it went missing."

"I can't imagine what possessed her to do this."

"Certainly, I couldn't. You must be truthful with me; did you provide her assistance in this treachery?"

"I didn't. I'm completely stunned."

"It was your idea we take a drive. If you were in conspiracy with my sister, it'd be better to confess now than have me discover you've lied."

"I swear to you she did this of her own accord. How do you intend to deal with her?"

"I've confined her to her room while I deliberate the matter further."

"May I be of help?"

"You may help by granting me your support."

"Naturally you'll have this. Might I pose a suggestion?"

"As ever, I value your input."

"Catherine has confided in me her desire to visit Edward more frequently. He is, after all, her brother. The desperate measure she undertook may indicate you should reconsider your position."

"Our brother is unwell. I restrict her for her own safety."

"Are you convinced he remains dangerous?"

"I've no call to think otherwise. You've read the doctor's prognosis."

"Edward had every opportunity to take advantage of Catherine today, yet she was unharmed."

"The fact nothing transpired on this occasion doesn't prove there's no risk. Given his instability, a level of danger will persist."

"If you're concerned you could allow her to visit with Jake and Eleanor, perhaps on a scheduled day each week. Settling the matter permanently would alleviate the aggravation for you both, which in my opinion is a course far preferable to punishment."

"At the moment, I'm hardly of a mind to placate Catherine. Under any circumstance, it would displease me if she met with him more often."

"Why is that?"

"Her desire to see Edward upsets me."

"What do you find upsetting? I'm certain she means you no offense."

"I don't owe you an explanation for my standpoint."

"Please, recall our agreement when I elected to honor our engagement. You promised you'd no longer keep secrets from me."

"My position is a private affair rather than a secret."

"These seem one and the same."

"Frankly, you'd prefer it if I didn't divulge the truth."

"Why wouldn't I want the truth?"

"In this instance, you may find it hurtful."

"I'd prefer to be hurt rather than endure the dark."

"You must trust me; it would be better for you to remain unaware."

"How can it be to my benefit, when my suspicion alone will cause me harm?"

Darrell frowned. "Since you won't relent, I'll tell you. Bear in mind, I divulge this at your insistence. The fact is, I resent my brother for killing Emily. I'll never forgive him for it."

"Why do you allege he killed her? By your own account, it was an accident."

"An accident which resulted solely from his reckless behavior."

"You speak as if it was his intention."

"Intention or not, the consequence was the same. His behavior is indefensible."

"He was a child of twelve, and they were merely playing."

"His age doesn't exonerate his actions. The accident could have been avoided had he used common sense. I've never recovered from the agony Emily's death has caused me."

"It was a tragedy anyone would find difficult to bear. Nevertheless, after ten years the time is long overdue to put the incident behind you."

"For me, this cannot take place."

"Why not?"

"I've explained myself sufficiently. I suggest you let the matter rest."

"I no longer can. I won't be satisfied until you tell me the entire truth."

"You don't want to learn the particulars, I assure you."

"If I'm to understand your position, you must reveal everything."

"Since this is your stipulation, so be it. The truth is Emily should have been *mine*. As the eldest, *I* should have been betrothed to her, but our parents didn't agree. Edward and Emily played together and enjoyed each other's company; absurd reasons to deny me my birthright. Had they made the proper decision, Emily would still be alive and *my* wife."

Abigail was shaken to her foundation. "Did you love her?"

"How could I love her, when she died very young? In any event, it makes no difference. It's rare for a man of my stature to enter a marriage based solely on love."

"You've told me love is of great importance to you."

"It has become so, now I've no option but to marry for love alone."

"Therefore, if you had the option, you wouldn't have become engaged to me."

"Indisputably, I would not."

She winced at the bite of his words.

"I warned you the truth would be hurtful."

"While you were correct, it's best I've learned of your doubts before we are married. If you'd prefer to find someone more suitable, you needn't consider yourself bound by obligation. By all means, break our engagement."

"Abigail, don't do this. I could have easily lied to you, yet I did not. As a result of Emily's demise, Catherine and I were forced to accept our fate and adjust our priorities. I've come to appreciate it's preferable to marry for love."

"With this supposed enlightenment, if you could choose who would you marry, Emily or me?"

"The question is impossible to answer. Had I the opportunity, I may have grown to love her. No one may be certain of their feelings if their reality were altered."

Abigail's eyes narrowed as she glared at him.

"Don't view me sternly. You did insist I speak my mind."

"Although I did, it doesn't lessen the sting."

"You mustn't fault me for being honest at your command, and you shouldn't doubt the depth of my love for you. Emily is gone. You are the only woman I've ever loved. You've given me a happiness I hadn't thought possible. I would never break our engagement, for I'd be lost without you."

"I'd never doubted it previously."

"Please, my darling, we've departed from the purpose of this conversation. The events of the past have nothing to do with you or the love between us. I didn't want to harm you. I'm sorry I have."

"You gave me fair warning your confession would be painful. It has, however, answered a great many questions. If you'll excuse me, I'd like to be alone for a while." Abigail walked to the door.

"Don't leave in anger."

"Primarily it's strain I feel, not anger."

"Promise me you won't allow what I've divulged to stand between us."

"Eventually I'll come to terms with it, but it's been a shock. At the moment, I'm exhausted. I need to rest."

"Rest then, my dearest. We'll put the business behind us, and never speak of it again. You'll find nothing between us has truly changed."

"I suppose not." She knew this was a lie. Things had changed to such an extent she doubted her feelings could be rekindled.

Darrell placed a kiss on her temple. "I'll see you at dinnertime."

"Dinnertime; yes."

Abigail left the room and closed the door. On the verge of weeping, she covered her mouth and staggered towards the conservatory. Halfway there she stopped and leaned against the wall, tears dripping over her palm.

She looked up with a start when the piano in the north wing began to play. The music surrounded her, like the warm embrace she desperately needed. Abigail's crying ceased as the truth coursed through her like an intoxicating drug. "Catherine was right, she and the staff saw what I could not," she whispered. "I *am* in love with Edward."

*****

Nearly a week into Catherine's confinement, Abigail was seated alone on a garden bench, the afternoon sun washing over her as she inspected the note Mary had delivered. Despite her annoyance to find the seal had been broken, she hoped this letter from Anna would provide her with some comfort. She unfolded the page to read:

3 September, 1888

Dearest Abigail,

Where on earth are you hiding? We've heard nothing from you in ages! While we understand the distraction your handsome and charming man must induce, this doesn't seem an adequate excuse to neglect us, don't you agree?

Don't worry darling; I merely tease you. The purpose of my letter is to end the incessant chatter of Gerta and Elsa. They've driven me to the brink of madness with their relentless inquiries regarding the style and color of dress we should acquire for the wedding. I beg you for relief by writing back to me at once. Please relate your preferences and spare no details or the two of them will never cease with their questions.

Setting aside all flippancy, I'm aware of how very hectic your life must be as the ceremony nears. I hope you're remembering to take good care of yourself. We all miss you terribly and are looking most forward to our upcoming visit.

All my best to my dearest friend.

Yours, Anna

She refolded the page carefully and stared into the distance. If ever she was in need of Anna's friendship and counsel, this was the occasion. Unfortunately, after Catherine's fiasco, Abigail had learned better than to request advice via a letter. Since Darrell would have read this urgent plea from Anna, Abigail knew he'd be expecting a reply soon. Even if she were bold enough to post a clandestine letter, she thought the chances were slim any possible response from Anna would bypass Darrell's scrutiny.

Abigail returned to the house, her plan to compose a decidedly cheerful note. When she'd begun to climb the stairs, she heard a ruckus originating from the ladies' wing, and hurried to find Catherine's bedroom door open. Her clothes and belongings were strewn haphazardly as she and her maid sorted frantically through them.

"I've told you I've no use for this," Catherine groused. She yanked the item from her maid's hand and threw it on the floor.

"I'm sorry, miss," the girl said.

"This dress must remain until I return," Catherine added.

"What's going on here?" Abigail asked.

"Is it not plain enough, I'm packing," Catherine told her.

"Packing, for what reason?"

"Darrell is sending me into exile."

"What do you mean?"

"In a few days, I'm to depart for our aunt and uncle's home, to live with them indefinitely."

"That cannot be. Darrell wouldn't send you away with our wedding so near."

"You think not? Then you're mistaken. *Graciously,* he will permit me to return with my aunt and uncle for the ceremony."

"Why would he do this? Is it intended to be a punishment?"

"Not merely a punishment, he wants to be rid of me."

"I'm afraid you've lost me."

"Several days ago, Darrell came to my room to discuss the situation with Edward. He informed me our visits would be severely limited. Should I protest, he threatened to end them entirely. I blew my temper and told him as an adult I'd see Edward whenever I please. I said he could no longer prevent me, but he's proven me wrong."

"Miss?" someone said. They turned to discover it was Mary. "The master wanted a word with you, the minute you returned from your walk. You're to meet him in the study."

"How convenient. I'd like a word with him as well," Abigail said.

She walked brusquely to his study and entered without knocking.

"Abigail, I'm glad you're here," Darrell said. He attempted to hold her.

She dodged him by folding her arms, regarding him with contempt. "Catherine tells me you're casting her out of the house. How could you do this with our wedding date approaching?"

"It's regrettable you spoke with my sister before I could explain the circumstance. I knew she would describe my decision as a punishment when it's nothing of the sort."

"I'm perfectly willing to hear your explanation now."

"Please, Abigail, take a seat."

She glowered at him while she sat.

"Yesterday, I received a letter from our uncle." He retrieved a communiqué from his desk. "They've offered to have Catherine live with them, to attend a prominent school near their home. Since I will soon marry, my uncle suggested it would be agreeable to have Catherine settled as well. As you know, a scholastic setting is an ideal place for a woman of refinement to acquire a proper suitor."

"There are schools far closer. Why should she attend one at such a distance when she could live at home?"

"Regarding marriage, Catherine suffers from the drawback I faced; Edward's illness. They believe an introduction into their society will be her best chance to procure a husband."

"What prompted them to make their suggestion at this particular time?"

"They were recently notified of an unanticipated opening in the fall semester."

"Why must she begin in the fall? You could delay her entry until the following semester."

"Unfortunately, this cannot be. What she will learn in the second semester must be preceded by the first."

"Then why not wait until she may enroll the subsequent year?"

"Apparently attendance at the school is highly coveted, and they're fully booked two years hence. It was by pure chance one of the young ladies withdrew due to illness. You must agree it would be foolish not to take advantage of this rare opportunity."

"Education is always valuable," Abigail said.

A knock came at the door.

Darrell called out his permission to enter. "Ah, Jake. Eleanor has informed you of Catherine's journey to my Uncle Charles' home?"

"She has," he said.

"I would like you to accompany her and her maid. I've sent a cable alerting them of your arrival."

"As you wish, Darrell," he said and left.

"It would seem the plans for Catherine's departure have been set," Abigail said.

"They have. It was a difficult decision, my darling, one I didn't make lightly. I've determined it's for the best. I hope ultimately you'll be happy for her."

"Although I am, I'll miss her dreadfully. I've been counting on her assistance with the wedding and the household."

"That's understandable, and yet we must put her requirements ahead of ours, isn't that true?"

"Yes, of course. I'm relieved to learn punishment wasn't your intention."

"Catherine's misinterpretation isn't surprising given the coincidence. As always, I have her best interest at heart."

"Naturally you would. If you don't mind, before this arose, I'd intended to compose a letter to Anna."

"Please do so, my darling. I have work to attend myself."

Darrell assisted her to the door.

"I'll meet you at tea," he said and kissed her forehead.

Abigail returned to Catherine's room, to find she was alone.

"Abigail, come in. I'll be interested to learn what Darrell has told you."

"He explained you're to attend a school near your aunt and uncle's home, to better your education and meet prospective suitors."

"His plan sounds utterly magnanimous, does it not? I don't believe his purpose is to benefit me, not for a moment."

"He had the letter from your uncle in his possession. I've no call to doubt him."

"With his mind set, it hardly matters. My primary concern here isn't myself; it's Edward. Promise me you'll continue your efforts to help him."

"Rest assured it will be my priority."

"Is anything else on your mind? You look pensive."

Abigail considered confessing her newly discovered feelings for Edward. Given the current situation and her own confusion, she determined this was ill-advised. "Nothing, other than I want you to know how much I'll miss you."

"As I'll miss you, my dear sister." Catherine dabbed her eyes with her handkerchief. "It's possible some good may come of this. A neighbor of my uncle has a son who's always been nice to me. As I recall, he's quite handsome. With any luck, he remains unattached," she said with a grin.

"If he proves to be a good man worthy of you, I hope it is the case."

Abigail smiled and gave Catherine a tight hug.

10

Goodbye, the simple, commonplace word used on a daily basis, often with little thought, unless it conveys not merely separation but also a sense of loss. At those times, it can be the most difficult, painful word to speak. Abigail and Catherine had said this sort of goodbye, both so filled with emotion neither of them could say the word clearly.

Tears filled Abigail's eyes as she and Eleanor watched her drive with Jake into the breaking dawn. Darrell, who'd been called away to London, wasn't present. He'd conveyed his best wishes via a note, which in her fury his sister had torn to bits.

Catherine leaned out the carriage window to extend a final wave. After they waved back, Abigail and Eleanor returned to the house.

"My dear child, you appear miserable," Eleanor said. "Perhaps a trip into town would lift your spirits."

"With Darrell and Jake gone, I'd planned to visit Edward."

"You've plenty of time. At this hour he'll be asleep, and then he'll need to bathe and dress. You may as well have some amusement rather than wait here. I'll order the small carriage for you."

Abigail changed into her travel clothes. Soon, she was on her way. She stared at the seat where Edward had once sat and thought of their jaunt into town. "I wish you were here with me now," she whispered.

When the carriage arrived at the village, every place she went, every shop she entered reminded her of Edward. In the hat shop, she caressed the brim of the style he'd modeled, grinning as she recalled how he'd played the part of an arrogant, aristocratic man. In the dress shop, she found the stunning gown she'd held to her body and remembered how his face had glowed with admiration for her.

Absorbed in such daydreams, Abigail was startled when someone touched her arm. She turned to discover a woman in her middle years, dressed in nice albeit unassuming attire.

"Excuse me, my dear. Aren't you the young lady who's engaged to Mr. Darrell Lewis of Rochester Manor?"

"Indeed I am."

"It's a pleasure to meet you at long last. Allow me to introduce myself; I am Sarah Hamilton."

"My name is Abigail Parker. May I inquire how you recognized me?"

"I live nearby and am well acquainted with Mrs. Williams, with whom I meet here in town now and again. I had been fast friends of Mrs. Lewis for years. There was a time when I dined at Rochester Manor frequently."

"Then the pleasure is mine."

"Mrs. Williams has given me so detailed a description of your appearance, I knew at once it must be you. She adores you. Whenever we visit, she carries on and on about your many attributes. She tells me you've made a tremendous difference to the household."

"How kind of her to say."

"It's been ages since I've seen the family. The poor dears; such dreadful tragedies they've suffered. Please tell me, how are they getting on?"

"*Fairly* well."

The woman raised an eyebrow.

Abigail hadn't intended to fuel her curiosity and therefore changed the subject. "How were you acquainted with Mrs. Lewis?"

"We were at school together during the time she was known as Alison Carter. She was a most beautiful and dear young lady. Her family was far more prominent than mine; nevertheless, we'd been friends from early childhood. When she married into a grander situation still, with her benevolent nature, my station in life was inconsequential to her. She continued to extend me every courtesy, and we remained close."

"How wonderful to hear. I wish I could have known Mr. and Mrs. Lewis."

"They were uncommonly lovely people. Mr. Lewis had a heart as tender and generous as Alison's, and their children, every bit as beautiful and sweet as their parents. It was the worst day of my life when the carriage accident took them from us, and another shock for those poor children yet recovering from their young neighbor's demise. It must have been doubly traumatic since the incidents happened in such a brief span of time."

"A brief time span?"

"I consider it brief, with the carriage accident only a few months after Emily's fall."

Abigail regarded the woman in shock.

"You're familiar with the circumstance?" Mrs. Hamilton asked.

"This detail was unclear to me."

"I'm rather surprised. I suppose it must be difficult for them to speak of distressing trials."

"They rarely discuss either incident."

"Of course, of course. I've interrupted your shopping. I should allow you to continue."

"I wasn't seeking anything of importance. I enjoyed meeting you."

"It was my good fortune I met you. I wish you the best of luck with your upcoming nuptials."

"Thank you, Mrs. Hamilton."

"Goodbye, my dear," the woman said and walked away.

Abigail stood motionless, thinking it may turn out to be her own good fortune they had met. With the timing of his parents' death yet another deception, she wondered what other lies Darrell had told. As the recent events filtered through her mind, the image of him holding the note from his uncle materialized. It occurred to her he hadn't handed the page to her; she'd accepted he'd divulged its true content. *I'd like to read that letter. I hope he didn't discard it.*

She exited the shop, her skirt bustling while she rushed towards the carriage. Her face was red from the exertion when she boarded.

"Return me to the house as swiftly as possible," she instructed the driver.

Upon their arrival, Abigail was thankful she encountered no one as she stole directly to Darrell's study. After closing the door quietly, she rummaged carefully through the pile of papers on his desk. She recognized the note she sought by the seal. Her heart pounded when she sat to read:

6 September, 1888

My Dearest Nephew,

Aunt Constance and I are in joyous anticipation of your upcoming nuptials. We are requesting our arrival take place the preceding week, should this prove to be convenient. Your description of Abigail has us convinced she's a fetching and amiable young woman. We are looking most forward to meeting her.

We wish to suggest our dear niece accompany us upon our return, for we imagine life at Rochester Manor could become tedious for her, particularly in the early days of your marriage. Since we haven't had the pleasure of a visit from her in some time, we hope you'll both find the idea agreeable. It would be a delightful diversion for us.

Whatever you determine, we're filled with excitement regarding our visit and the ceremony.

As always, I remain your devoted,
Uncle Charles

The letter slipped from Abigail's fingers and floated onto the floor. "It *was* a lie," she whispered. Engulfed in outrage and stupefaction, she was debating how to deal with the revelation, until she heard footsteps heading in her direction. *It's Darrell!* she thought.

In a panic, she grabbed the note and darted under the desk as the door opened. When she realized her breathing was audible, she covered her nose and mouth. An object was dropped on the floor with a clang, before whoever was there drew near.

"Penelope!" she heard Eleanor call out from the hallway.

"Yes, Mrs. Williams?" the girl in the room replied.

"Save the master's study for tomorrow. Louise has taken ill. I need you in the kitchen. Leave the supplies there."

"Yes, ma'am," Penelope said. She closed the door behind her.

Abigail's chin fell in relief. As she crawled out of her hiding place some torn remnants of paper, barely noticeable under the desk, caught her eye. Upon gathering them, she saw they comprised a memorandum. Dusty and crumpled, she presumed they'd been meant to be disposed of and had likely blown under the desk. She was about to discard them when she recognized the doctor's handwriting.

She smoothed the segments, and pieced them together to read:

22 July, 1888

Mr. Lewis,

It is with reluctance I prepare my report in the manner upon which you've insisted. Although my findings have been exaggerated to comply with your wishes, please understand the vehemence with which I dissent to this misrepresentation made under duress. It's my sincere hope you'll abandon this course of action and accept my true prognosis. Edward has made vast strides in his mental outlook. While your reluctance to grant his discharge may be justified to a point, I firmly believe any threat of violence on his part is minimal. My recommendation is to release him from his confinement, with continual supervision initially. I beg you to reconsider your position, in which case I'll gladly render my honest assessment.

Dr. Robert Hardin

"Oh my God no; no, no, this cannot be!" Abigail wailed. She read the note several times as if with sufficient review the words would spontaneously transform. "Please, someone tell me this isn't true!"

Her stomach clenched painfully as she collapsed onto the floor and sobbed. Several minutes passed before she pushed herself to a seated position and wiped her face with the back of her hand while she searched around in confusion. The room no longer appeared the same; for her, it had become a foreign place.

In desperate need of guidance, her first inclination was to seek Eleanor, when the person she must confront dawned on her. After stumbling to her feet, Abigail snatched the memo fragments and shoved them into her pocket.

She flung open the study door and fled to her room. In doing so, she passed Mary, who hurried to follow her.

"Miss, you look horribly ill. Shall I call for Mrs. Williams?"

"No, Mary, you mustn't tell anyone you've seen me. If someone asks, you must claim you've no idea my whereabouts. Do you understand me; *no one* must know."

"I understand, but you're worrying me. Could I be of help in some way?"

"For the time being you cannot; just do as I say."

"Yes, miss." Mary looked alarmed as she left the room.

Abigail collected the key to the north wing. In a bundle of nerves, she made her way there. Her hand shook while she struggled with the lock until at last, the door opened.

Edward must have heard the racket, for he was standing nearby when she entered. "Abigail!"

She tried to speak; instead, she fainted and collapsed into his arms.

Upon regaining consciousness, she found herself lying on the sofa in the north wing library. Edward was kneeling beside her, rubbing her hand soothingly.

"My goodness, Abigail, what's wrong?"

"I found these in Darrell's study," she said hoarsely. When she handed him the scraps of the physician's note, he lowered his head ashamedly. "You knew of this!"

He didn't answer but sat on the floor, his back to Abigail.

"Why? Why did you keep this from me?" she asked.

"I was forced not to tell you."

"In what way were you forced?"

Edward shook his head.

"Please, you must tell me."

"Darrell ordered Dr. Hardin and me to do his bidding, and never disclose it. If we chose to disobey, he threatened to send me to the asylum, and ruin the doctor's reputation."

"Why would he…he wouldn't unless he loathes you utterly…which he does, *due to what happened to Emily.*"

"He told you this?"

She nodded.

"It's unfathomable he would. Why did he?"

"I confronted him recently regarding Catherine. I demanded he divulge the reason her desire to visit you offends him."

"I'm sorry. These are matters I hoped you wouldn't discover."

"What makes you say that?"

"I feared if you learned the truth, you'd break your engagement."

"In this you were correct. I do intend to break the engagement."

"Abigail, please, you mustn't."

"I must and I will. I refuse to marry Darrell."

"You're overwrought and rightly so; however, you shouldn't reach a catastrophic conclusion in the heat of the moment."

"Whether a moment, an hour, or a decade passes will make no difference. I won't marry a man who's capable of unabashed deceitfulness and cruelty."

"Cruelty isn't fundamental to his nature, and it isn't his intention here. He believes justice is being served."

"Justice? This isn't justice, but a travesty thereof."

"From his perspective it is; a position I once shared, if you'll recall."

"The condemnation you'd imposed upon yourself was primarily a product of *his* attitude. How despicable of him to lie to me about you, the doctor's report, and Catherine's arrangement with your uncle. With all of these infractions, and goodness knows what else, you would have me marry your brother?"

"I would, in fact, I beg you to marry him."

"Why are you so insistent upon it?"

"It's the only way I may be near you."

Abigail's head joggled. "You want me to wed Darrell because you love me?"

"If you love me, even if it's the affection a sister holds for her brother."

"Edward, I don't know what to say. The trouble is I no longer love you as a brother."

"Please don't hate me. I understand you're angry I withheld the truth. You must believe I had no choice."

"I'm not angry with you, nor do I hate you. My feelings for you have, however, changed."

"How do you mean?"

"I love you, not as a brother. I love you as a woman loves a man."

"Abigail, is this true?"

"It is. I'm in love with you, Edward. I want to be with you, always."

He looked joyful as he sat next to her and placed his hands on her arms, though his expression soon dimmed. "The thought of spending my life with you brings me a happiness I cannot describe; nevertheless, for us to be together, you must marry Darrell. I depend on him for all I require to survive. If that wasn't the case, I love my brother. I couldn't bring myself to hurt him more than I have."

"Hurt *him?* Given his treatment of you, how can you feel love or hold any sense of obligation towards him, particularly when he despises you?"

"While it may be difficult to comprehend, I have the greatest respect and admiration for my brother. He has every right to begrudge me. Contrary to appearances, I've no call to resent him. When he told me of your engagement, I was delighted he'd met a woman he loves dearly. You've made all the difference to his life. I mustn't destroy it by betraying him in a way which could be his undoing."

"Your generosity regarding Darrell doesn't change anything. I've lost all of my love and admiration for him. After the way he's behaved, I can no longer stand the thought of becoming his wife."

"For my sake, you must forgive him. Eventually, your anger will pass. I'm certain you still love him, more than you're willing to admit. It was, after all, you who taught me forgiveness is the answer."

Abigail harrumphed. "If you'd have me grant him the opportunity, there is a way Darrell could make amends, though it's doubtful he'll agree to my terms."

"What do you propose?"

"I'll request he summon Dr. Hardin to reexamine you without delay. If he consents and accepts the doctor's true diagnosis, my faith in your brother may be restored. In the event he refuses, I will break the engagement."

"Abigail…"

"His cooperation is improbable, yet this will be his one chance to prove he's the type of man I believed him to be."

"If he refuses and you leave him, you must abandon me as well."

"You seem to have forgotten how tenacious I am. Where there's the will there's the way. Should I break the engagement, I'll find the means for us to be together."

"While your steadfastness is a favorable trait, at times it worries me."

"You've no need to worry. However stubborn I may be, I've learned to be exceedingly cautious."

The clock alerted them the luncheon hour was near.

"I suppose I must leave. I'll have Eleanor relate Darrell's response."

Edward escorted her to the door. When Abigail hugged him, their faces met. With their desire to kiss one another apparent, she drew her lips toward his.

"Please, don't," he said.

She was tempted to proceed; instead, she gave him a peck on the cheek.

"I love you," she said.

"As I love you," he returned.

*****

At dawn the following morning, Abigail was awakened by a knock on her door. "Come in," she called out.

Her maid entered. "The master's returned, miss. He's requested you join him for an early breakfast unless you mind rising before the usual hour, he told me to say."

"I wasn't expecting him until later," she said with a yawn. "I'll dress at once."

When Mary had completed her preparations, Abigail went to the dining room.

Darrell gathered her into his arms. "Abigail, my dearest."

She smirked. "Good morning, Darrell."

"This is hardly a warm welcome. Are you ill?"

"Merely worn out. I had difficulty sleeping last night."

"Undoubtedly, you're missing Catherine. I am sorry, but it won't be long until she returns for the wedding."

"Catherine wasn't the reason I couldn't sleep."

"What was it then?"

"I'm still upset regarding our conversation about Emily."

"Why? I've apologized and assured you, I presumed beyond doubt, you are the woman I love. Emily doesn't factor into any equation pertaining to us."

"I believe she does. If you love me as deeply as you claim, you should no longer have call to resent Edward. The time is long overdue to put the past behind you. I want you to forgive your brother, for unless the past is rectified, I will continue to question your devotion to me."

"My position towards Edward has nothing to do with my feelings for you. Whether or not I had designs to marry Emily, her loss and the horror of her death created a torment I cannot escape."

"This deeply seeded bitterness within you must be overcome since it will hinder any relationship into which you enter. It's caused adversity between you and Catherine. Now, it's raised tension between us."

"How do you suggest I overcome a shock which haunts me endlessly?"

"First and foremost, you must accept your placement of the blame upon Edward is the underlying obstacle. In my opinion, your anguish has clouded your perception, which under the circumstance is to be expected. Perhaps your brother could have employed better sense, but Emily's demise was accidental. Your aversion to Edward cannot change what happened or bring her back. It's been a destructive force that undermines the wellbeing of this family."

Darrell walked to the window and stared outside. Abigail prepared to respond to his reaction which she was certain would be hostile.

He returned to her side, his expression not antagonistic in the least. "My darling, as usual, your insight is astoundingly wise. It is possible I've behaved irrationally where my brother is concerned."

"Do you mean you will offer Edward your forgiveness?"

"I will. You're entirely correct; the time is long past due."

"This is wonderful to hear. With your absolution, Edward will have the means to recover. We must then have Dr. Hardin return, for I'm certain he'll retract his former appraisal."

"I doubt this one deed will improve my brother's condition to such an extent."

"I'm convinced it will, though we must rely upon the doctor's sound judgment."

"A good point; I'll solicit the doctor's return."

"Please send for him soon. I'd be ecstatic if Edward could join us for the wedding."

"It would be agreeable, and a nice surprise for the family. I'll have Dr. Hardin arrive at his earliest convenience."

It occurred to Abigail the reason he'd been forthcoming could be he intended to continue with his blackmail. "I should be present during the examination, to provide you with my support."

"How kind of you to suggest. It will be comforting to rely on the strength of your character, whatever the doctor should decide."

Abigail was stunned. A moment passed before she was able to speak. "I'm delighted to be of help."

"My darling; you are remarkably easy to please. I haven't forgotten my promise to do so."

"I am pleased, beyond all measure."

"Abigail, my sweet, *sweet* Abigail. How I adore you and your wise, generous nature."

"I love you, Darrell; I *do* love you, so very much."

"Are you hungry, dearest? Shall we dine now?"

"Yes, let's. I'm quite hungry."

Abigail grinned widely as Darrell helped her be seated. It appeared at last Edward would be free, and everyone at Rochester Manor could be happy. Her smile faded when she recalled her confession of passionate love to Edward; now she wished she hadn't been hasty.

It was Edward who insisted I grant Darrell the opportunity to redeem himself, she thought. *He claimed this was the outcome he desired. I have no call to feel guilty. It could be awkward at first, but I believe our relationship will return to one of siblings. He's such a dear, tender man; it won't be difficult for Edward to find a woman who can love him in the way he deserves. He'll have his happiness, I'm certain of it.*

*****

That afternoon, Abigail was enjoying a much-needed nap when her maid woke her to prepare for dinner.

Mary handed her a note. "This is from Mrs. Williams. I suppose it's important. She said you must read it at once."

"Thank you, Mary; would you return in a few minutes?"

"Yes, miss."

What could this be regarding? Abigail wondered as she unfolded the page. It read:

Dearest Abigail,

I must advise you, under no circumstance visit the north wing anytime soon. Darrell has ordered me to turn over my key after I collect Edward's dinner. When Jake returns in the morning, they alone will have access. Darrell intends to enlist his help, along with his valet and Mr. Phillips, to keep the wing under observation day and night; he refused to explain why. He insisted I not tell you of the arrangement. Dispose of this note the moment you read it.

Yours, Eleanor

Abigail shivered. *My heavens, what is Darrell up to?*

She threw the page onto the fire and watched it turn to ash. She had no idea how to proceed. To confront Darrell, she would have to implicate Eleanor. With Catherine gone, there was no one else she could turn to for help.

Whatever is happening here, it cannot possibly be good, Abigail thought.

Despite the warmth of the fireplace, she shivered again.

*****

Days had passed. With no ability to obtain further information, Abigail hadn't a clue why Darrell had ordered the bizarre operation underway at Rochester Manor.

On the fourth night, the hour was late when a tap on her door startled her. She opened it warily.

"Why, Mr. Phillips," she said.

"Miss Abigail, may I have a word with you?"

"Certainly." When she stood aside to let him enter, she noticed his expression was grim. "Mr. Phillips, is anything wrong?"

"Unfortunately, there is; a state of affairs which is most distressing."

"Does it pertain to the guard duty?"

"It does."

"Do you know the purpose of it?"

"Not specifically. I do know Master Edward has been confined to his room since it began."

"Why is this of particular concern? He's confined to the north wing at all times."

"He's confined not merely to the north wing; he's been locked in his bedroom."

"What; why?"

"I haven't been told the reason for his detention. I learned of it only tonight. It's my understanding it will continue until the doctor visits."

"That cannot be! When Dr. Hardin was summoned, he advised us he won't be able to arrive for two weeks at a minimum."

"I've heard that, but there's a matter more worrisome than the length of the interval alone."

"What could be worse?"

"Master Edward has been provided with two candles for the duration of his confinement. Since he must use them sparingly, he's spending most of his time in total darkness."

"Merciful heavens, it's unthinkable cruelty! Why would Darrell punish him in this inhumane manner...?" A horrifying thought occurred to her. "Mr. Phillips, this isn't a punishment. Darrell's intention is to drive Edward mad, in anticipation of the doctor's return. Dear Lord, we must help him; do you know of a way we could help him?"

He smiled and removed a large number of candles from his pocket. "While not an ideal solution, these should make his confinement easier to tolerate."

"They will help. How will you deliver them? Do you have a key?"

"That is the purpose of my visit. Mrs. Williams informs me you have a key. If I may have it, I'll take the candles to Master Edward immediately."

"Can you go there safely?"

"As it happens, I'm on guard duty tonight."

Abigail held out her hand. "Allow me."

"Please, Miss Abigail, I must take them. We cannot risk your discovery."

"With you on duty, the chance is minimal."

"Mrs. Williams warned me you'd be stubborn about this. She insisted I don't relent."

"She's correct about my stubbornness. Unless you intend to take the key by force, I suggest you escort me to the north wing."

"Miss, I beseech you, I can deliver them without difficulty."

"You can offer all night; my answer will remain the same. I'm worried about Edward. I must see him."

"I could return and tell you how he's getting on."

"That won't do. He must be in desperate need of companionship. You cannot spare him much time since you must keep watch. It would be cruel to simply deliver the candles and leave."

"As you wish, Miss Abigail. Bring your bedside candle. It is my understanding none of the candles in the north wing are lit."

She grimaced. "Let's not waste another minute."

When they arrived at the north wing, Mr. Phillips handed her the stash of candles. "The bedroom key hangs by the door, the fourth room on the left. Should I detect any danger, I'll tap three times."

"Thank you, Mr. Phillips. Don't be concerned if I'm there for a while. I'll stay as long as I dare."

"Yes, miss."

Abigail entered into the pitch darkness, sliding her hand down the wall as she advanced. After counting to the fourth door, in the scanty light, she was forced to grope for the key. It seemed an eternity until she located it. Her hand trembled while she fiddled with the lock.

The lock finally gave way. She entered Edward's room slowly, holding the candle high for any chance to see. She cringed when she found him seated at the foot of his bed, fully dressed, hunched over in what appeared to be a comatose state.

As she stepped towards him, he regarded her strangely. "Emily?"

He's already begun to lose his mind, she thought. "No, Edward, it's Abigail."

"Abigail! You mustn't be here!"

"Don't worry. Mr. Phillips is on watch tonight. He's agreed to protect us." She set the light on the nightstand and knelt next to him. "Edward, my dearest Edward, I'm terribly sorry. I learned only a short time ago what Darrell has done to you. How are you bearing up? Are you well?"

He leaned forward and touched her cheek. "I am, now you're here. With your white robe and hair glowing in the candlelight, I thought you must be Emily, come to take me to Heaven. I was correct in my belief I saw an angel. There's no doubt you are mine."

Abigail smiled as she handed him the candles. "These may make this appalling situation a bit more tolerable. I should also fetch you some books to relieve the monotony. Or better still I'll find a way to duplicate the bedroom key so you may leave as you please."

"Thank you, Abigail. As always, you couldn't be sweeter to me."

Edward rose and placed the candles in his dresser drawer. When he turned back, she stood to find him fixating upon her person.

"You're incredibly beautiful in your night clothes, with your hair loose about your shoulders." He caressed her locks.

His fingers moved to the nape of Abigail's neck. An intense yearning crossed his face. She swallowed hard as her breathing became labored.

Edward dropped his hand and hung his head. "We must retire to the library."

"Perhaps we could remain here."

He appeared stunned when he looked up. "Nothing may ever occur between us," he said in a tone which lacked conviction.

"Edward I... want this, I want ... to be with you."

"You don't mean it; you'll regret it if we ... if anything ... happens."

Abigail shook her head. "I'll have no regrets. I've no longer any doubt with whom I'm in love, none whatsoever."

Edward's forehead wrinkled. He searched her eyes for a moment before he pulled her body against his and kissed her urgently. His hands brushed her shoulders, and her robe and gown slipped to the floor. Their frenzy mounted as she tugged off his jacket, and frantically unbuttoned his shirt. Once his clothing had joined hers, they tumbled onto the bed. He lay above her and met her gaze.

"Are you certain?" he asked in a hoarse voice.

"I'm absolutely certain."

Abigail extended her neck towards Edward, and he kissed her again. She felt the sensation of a tidal wave crashing over her. Any remaining sense of reason disappeared as their bodies entwined. No one else in the world seemed to matter as they yielded to one another, succumbing fully to the depths of their passion.

*****

Abigail opened her eyes. Blinking in the dim light, she slowly recalled where she was. She saw how low the candle had burned, and realized they'd fallen asleep. Edward hadn't yet awoken. When she placed her hand on his chest, he stirred and turned towards her.

It appeared he'd been struck by lightning as he bolted upright and grabbed his head. "My God, what have I done? I've betrayed my brother in the most heinous way possible!"

"In light of what he's done to you, what happened between us was hardly a betrayal."

"How can you say that? It's not only a betrayal, it's one we can't hide. He'll discover on your wedding night what I've done."

"There will be no wedding night for Darrell and me."

"Oh please, Abigail, you must marry him. I cannot be responsible for destroying his life a second time."

"He had his opportunity to win back my affection. Once again, he chose to lie. To think I was convinced he would forgive you when all the while he was hatching this horrendous plot to drive you mad."

"Then, you intend to leave us."

"I'll leave Darrell, though I've no intention of going alone. You must come with me."

"I can't do that."

"You mustn't remain here."

"You seem to have forgotten I have no income, no means by which I may support us. How do you imagine we'll survive?"

"Fortunately, my parents are charitable and sympathetic. I've no doubt they'll welcome you into our home. We may live with them until you secure a position."

"But Abigail, what position? I've no training which could grant me a post."

"Have you no inkling the value your mastery of the piano affords you? Vienna is an ideal city for musicians. With your talent, you could teach, or perhaps perform. It won't be difficult for you to become settled."

Edward's lips curled up for a moment and as quickly turned into a frown. "I want to join you; however, I cannot. I mustn't accompany you."

"What's preventing you? We've addressed the critical issues."

"Not all of them. The primary concern is Darrell. Alone he may resign himself to relinquish you, but with me involved he never will. You must abandon me."

"I won't do that."

"I'm afraid you've no choice."

"Haven't you learned I'm too willful to accept I've no choice? Suppose we were to escape and convince Darrell we've gone somewhere other than Vienna. A distant location would be best, perhaps America. He may well believe it since he's aware I have family there."

"No place will be too far for him to search. He'll travel the world if necessary. The risk of his locating us will always remain."

"As we've agreed, life is full of risks. To live happily, we must take this chance."

"Are you implying you cannot live happily without me?"

"I no longer can."

"Am I to understand, are you asking me to marry you?"

Abigail smiled. "If you'll have me."

"There's no questioning my desire to be with you, and yet this is insanity. If you were hurt, I'd never be able to forgive myself. I couldn't survive another incident in which I lost the person I love."

"We will have to plan our disappearance carefully. I refuse to leave without you, and so there's only one answer I'll accept."

"Yes?" he asked.

"Yes," she confirmed.

"You've proven one thing; you're every bit as daft as I am."

"That is undeniably true."

"If you're certain this is the course you want to follow, I'll leave with you."

Edward pulled Abigail back into his arms and kissed her passionately until they heard the clock strike two.

"Goodness, I must leave." She dressed hurriedly. "I'll have Mr. Phillips deliver a note when I have the particulars in place. Good night, dearest Edward."

"Good night, my sweet, sweet angel."

He kissed her once more before she left.

After she'd exited the north wing, Mr. Phillips approached her. "Miss Abigail, I was becoming concerned."

"I said I would remain a long while."

"You did, miss. How is Master Edward? Is he well? I imagine your visit helped him enormously."

Abigail grinned slyly. "I would claim I've helped him significantly. Mr. Phillips, I may require further assistance from you, if it's not forward of me to request a favor."

"Not in the least, miss."

"It's a substantial and dangerous assignment I would ask of you. I'll understand if you decline to participate."

"Whatever you require. I'm at your disposal."

"You are such a dear, kind man. Please come to my room, and I'll explain the situation."

*****

Abigail was startled by a light rap on her door. She read the clock to find it was one in the morning and then cracked her door open to confirm it was, as she'd expected, Mr. Phillips, her trunk, and luggage in his possession.

Although the previous two days had passed slowly for Abigail, they were now a blur. Mr. Phillips was stunned when she'd spelled out her plan to leave Rochester Manor, more by her intention to marry Edward than her desire to depart. While Eleanor wasn't entirely surprised, she was also unprepared for the enormity of the design. Eleanor and Mr. Phillips were, nevertheless, pleased to offer their help, delighted Edward would, at last, have the ability to lead a happy life.

Abigail's greatest concern hadn't been enlisting help; it was how she could hide her revulsion of Darrell until she could flee. She'd decided her best course was to feign illness and confine herself to the ladies' wing. This turned out to be an ideal solution. Not only was she able to avoid excessive contact with Darrell, when he'd paid her a visit her crankiness was easily accounted for.

During her seclusion Abigail had composed several correspondences, to instigate the deception she and Edward had traveled to America. With the train tickets purchased and the other essential components in place, packing their belongings was all that remained for her and Edward to make good their escape.

Mr. Phillips carried her luggage inside. "Good morning, miss."

"Good morning, Mr. Phillips. I was roused by your knock. I must have fallen asleep."

"It's as well you obtained rest. You should pack straight away, while no one will be the wiser."

"I won't delay. What time will you collect us?"

"We'll depart promptly at midnight."

"Midnight, then. I've wondered how you've managed to be on guard duty two nights together, without creating suspicion."

"Master Darrell's valet has kept watch the entire night several times this week. In his weakened condition, he suffered a relapse. No one questioned my offer to fill his shift."

"The poor man. At least there won't be any call for him to suffer further."

Abigail lifted the lid of her trunk. Devoid of contents, to her, it didn't seem empty; it was brimming with memories of the last time she'd packed her belongings. Overcome with emotion she became lightheaded and collapsed onto a chair.

"Miss Abigail, are you unwell?"

"I feel a bit faint. I'll be fine once I've sat a moment." She paused and attempted to regain her composure. "Do you recall, Mr. Phillips, aside from Robert, you were the first person I met upon my arrival at Rochester Manor?"

"I do recall."

"It was you who took me to Darrell, and it's you who'll take me away from him." Abigail's eyes filled with tears.

Mr. Phillips handed her a handkerchief from his pocket. "You'll forgive me, miss. Although I don't consider myself cold, I haven't much talent for comforting."

"Warmth may come in many forms. The compassion you've displayed by taking part in my plan requires more warmth than words could supply."

"My dear Miss Abigail, I'd do anything for you. Are you any better?"

"I am."

"Then I'll leave you to your packing. If I may have the key to the north wing, I will deliver luggage to Master Edward."

She took it from a drawer and handed it to him. "I suppose you may as well keep the key since we'll all depart together."

"Thank you, miss."

"Thank you, Mr. Phillips, not only for this, for everything you've done on my behalf."

"It's been my pleasure. You'll be greatly missed." He bowed before he departed.

"Tomorrow night, the life I'd expected to lead will be gone forever," she whispered.

Abigail returned to her dresser to remove some items. As she did, she caught her reflection in the mirror, shocked by how profoundly her image had changed. *Where is that unworldly girl, awkward and unsure, but filled with such hope and promise? How did everything so wonderful turn so horribly wrong?*

While folding an article, she saw her engagement ring and recalled her elation when Darrell had placed it on her finger. Abigail wept softly as she removed it and set it on her note to him. It now lay in wait on her dresser.

*****

When next Abigail opened her eyes, she discovered herself in close to total darkness, the only illumination a flickering candle close by. The condition baffled her since she'd fallen asleep to the light of a full moon. Stranger still, the surface she lay on felt hard, and she was unable to move her arms and legs. Lifting her head, she looked around in confusion.

"Where am I?"

"Ah, you're awake at last, my darling," Darrell said, looming over her. "You're in the north wing."

"The north wing; how did I come to be here?"

"Don't you remember joining me for breakfast, when you confessed the transgressions you've committed over the past months, in my own household, beneath my very nose?"

A wave of panic swept over her once she recalled awakening earlier to sunshine, and the message Mary had related.

"The master inquired after your health, miss. I told him as of last night you were better. He requests you join him for breakfast."

Not wanting to create suspicion, Abigail had complied. She remembered how peculiar Darrell's mood had been. It brought to mind the events which followed.

"Good morning, dearest," he said, in a manner not at all amiable.

"Good morning, Darrell."

He handed her a cup of tea. "I must say, the advancement in your health is remarkable, considering how ill you've been."

"It's a relief to feel better." She took a sip of the tea. "You appear upset. Is anything the matter?"

"What a coincidence. I was about to ask you the same."

"I don't take your meaning."

"Apparently, something *is* the matter. I presume this in light of the recent activity I've been acquainted with."

Abigail choked on her tea. "What did you learn?"

"It would seem Jake had difficulty sleeping last night. He was on his way to the library to fetch a book when he saw Mr.

Phillips carrying luggage upstairs. Given the odd hour, he followed him and witnessed as he delivered the bags to your room. Mr. Phillips then returned to the storage area. Jake watched him gather another trunk, this one he delivered to the north wing. Would you explain for what purpose you and Edward required travel cases?"

A sickening sense of defeat consumed her.

"You'll confess to me at once the meaning of this," he demanded.

Abigail sat, utterly demoralized.

Darrell took her hand and squeezed it hard. "Answer me!"

"I'm planning to break our engagement."

"Why; why would you do this?"

"I cannot marry you, Darrell. I no longer love you."

"What has caused your feelings to change drastically?"

"*You've* changed them. It's impossible for me to love a man with the capacity for abject cruelty."

"In what way do you find me cruel?"

"Not only are you cruel, you're cold and calculating. You had me convinced your uncle suggested the arrangement with Catherine until I found his letter. It was you who instigated the idea, not him."

"While that may be true, Catherine is hardly suffering. Why would you abandon me due to this?"

"I'm not breaking our engagement based on this incident alone. I also found Dr. Hardin's letter pertaining to Edward, the one you thought you'd disposed of. I was aware something was wrong regarding his opinion. I know for a fact Edward's mental condition has improved profoundly."

"How did you reach this conclusion?"

"Quite simply, it was *I* who initiated his recovery. From the moment you introduced me to your brother, I couldn't comprehend the reason after ten years his outlook was the same. When I observed your callous treatment of him, I wondered if your attitude was a hindrance to his recuperation. It's become clear this was a resounding yes."

"How did his supposed recovery take place?"

"Throughout these previous months, I've visited him frequently. Although it took some time, I was able to convince him of the truth you've refused to accept; forgiveness is the answer. When at last he forgave himself for Emily's death, Edward's perspective improved vastly. He became a changed man, the man he may have become earlier, but for the relentless blame you've imposed upon him."

"How did you manage to visit him?"

"It wasn't Catherine who stole the key to the north wing, it was I. She borrowed it from me the day you discovered her there."

"My, my, what a traitorous and disrespectful creature you've turned out to be, after everything I've done for you."

"Traitorous? You dare refer to me as traitorous, given the way you've treated your own brother?"

"Ah, my *dear* brother; what were your plans for him?"

"I intend to take him away from here, and as far away from you as possible."

"That will never happen. Edward will remain in the north wing while you honor our engagement. You will obey me in the manner I deserve."

"You cannot force me to marry you; neither can you prevent our leaving…"

This was Abigail's final memory prior to awakening in the darkness. "I do remember our conversation at breakfast, though I don't recall coming here."

"I'd added a sleeping powder to your tea," Darrell said. "When you lost consciousness, I carried you here."

Abigail recollected a lightheaded sensation prior to her blackout. Now fully alert, she determined her movement was restricted by bonds which secured her tightly to the dining room table. She heard a muffled groan, and raised her head as best she could, horrified to discover Edward, bound to the door and gagged.

"My brother has been kind enough to provide me with the details of your conspiracy. I've learned your intention wasn't merely to liberate him but to marry him as well."

"You didn't hurt him?" she asked.

"It wasn't necessary. The only thing required was my threat to harm you. Afterward, he became astoundingly cooperative."

"What do you intend to do with us?" Her voice had become raspy.

"I've any number of options at my disposal. I could, for instance, take you here and now, with my brother forced to watch. This seems a fitting penance, given his confession he's discharged you of your virginity." Abigail closed her eyes in mortification. "Yes, my sweet, dulcet girl, you denied your bed to your fiancé, and yet you permitted *him*."

Darrell leaned over to remove the unkempt strands of hair from her face. She trembled uncontrollably.

"My dearest, you needn't regard me pitifully. I'm saving this as a possibility for later, depending upon the decision you're about to make," he taunted.

"What decision?"

"You'll elect to proceed with our marriage, or should you prefer to refuse, you'll determine which of you will lose an eye." Darrell's matter-of-fact delivery made his threat all the more menacing.

He collected a butcher's knife from the table and placed the flat side on her cheek.

"Oh my God!" she cried out.

"Do I have your answer?"

"Darrell, you cannot do this. You're incapable of an act so brutal."

"Somehow, you're convinced that I am."

"No, no matter what else you've done, you'd never resort to this form of violence."

"You think not? You may want to think again. I'm entirely capable of an act of brutality, don't you agree, Edward?" Darrell turned in his direction. "Shall I tell her?"

"Mmnm, mmnm!" Edward mumbled, shaking his head forcibly.

"Dearest brother, you mustn't object. For Abigail to make an informed decision, she must learn the truth. You see, my darling, the fact is Edward didn't take his eye, I did."

Her forehead constricted painfully while she regarded Darrell in disbelief. "This isn't true! It cannot be true!"

"I assure you, it is. Now, you must choose. Will you marry me, or shall I employ the knife?"

"Please, Darrell…" she whimpered.

"Please, what?"

"Please, please don't do this."

"That isn't an answer," he said.

Abigail closed her eyes and shook as tears streamed down her face. "I cannot marry you."

"If you will not, whose eye shall I take? Will you lose one of yours, or allow Edward to be blinded?"

"You cannot expect me to choose."

"If you'd rather not I won't obligate you, in which case you'll both lose an eye."

Abigail stared at Darrell in horror. "Help us; someone *help us!*"

"Don't bother straining your vocal chords. Your voice won't carry past the corridor. The time for contemplation has ended. *Make your choice.*"

When she did not, he moved towards Edward. "Very well, since you refuse to decide I'll begin here."

His brother cowered when Darrell raised the knife over its intended target.

"No, *stop!* Take mine; take mine!"

Edward groaned, his head jerking violently.

"It's too late, Edward." Darrell returned to the table. He held the knife over Abigail's head.

"Take pity on us, Darrell. I beg you, show us mercy. I know you're capable of mercy!"

He stood back and lowered the knife. "Mercy isn't necessary. To avoid this fate, you only need marry me."

"What will become of Edward if I agree?"

"He'll remain in the north wing for the rest of his days unless you make any attempt to see him or help him escape, in which case I'll send him to the asylum."

"And if I offer my eye?"

"You'll be free to leave, although prior to taking your eye I'll take you, a scene my brother may relive whenever he lies with you. Won't the two of you make a charming couple with your matching disfigurements? You may wish to hide in the north wing. Being family, you'd be welcome to stay."

With Darrell's sarcastic remark and malicious attitude, it became clear to Abigail what she must do. "To live with you is the one outcome which will not happen. Take my eye."

Her body shuddered with the force of her weeping. Edward grunted piteously.

"You love my brother to the extent you'd make this sacrifice rather than marry me?"

"I *would,*" she said.

Darrell twiddled the knife with his fingers. "You cannot mean it; you will change your mind."

"I will not. I couldn't tolerate living with *you*. I'd prefer to undergo any form of torture than to become your wife. When this is finished Edward and I will leave, and I will marry him."

The knife slipped from Darrell's hand. "Then… I have lost you, I've lost you completely. Evidently, I've become a stranger to you. Did you truly think I would harm you in such a horrific way?"

Abigail's mouth fell open. "I wouldn't have, had you not persuaded me otherwise."

"It didn't require much to sway you. I suppose you also believe I would rape you, when I've wanted you desperately, but I've granted you only the utmost patience and understanding. You've come to view me as nothing other than a monster."

"How could I know you were bluffing? You're not a monster, only someone with a troubled soul. If you put the

246

past where it belongs, you can recover. This is what you need to do."

"Put the past where it belongs…how I wish I could." Darrell plopped onto a chair. "The day of the accident I became a stranger to myself. I became a monster, filled with such rage I must have lost my mind. I took a knife from the kitchen and found Edward in this very room. When I came at him, he stopped me, not to prevent me, but to agree an eye for an eye was a proper punishment. He vowed he wouldn't attempt to escape; he would remain still in order for me to proceed accurately. He lay on this table, and I plunged the knife…" He covered his eyes. Tears rolled down his cheeks.

Her brows furrowed. "Oh, Darrell."

He shook his shoulders and straightened himself. "The consequence of my act was a sight no one could imagine, and few could endure. My poor, defenseless little brother was screaming in agony. The blood was unfathomable. When I told him I would run for our parents, he pleaded with me to let the deed play out. I didn't intend for him to die and insisted upon bringing them. Before I left, he beseeched me, regardless of the outcome, to claim he'd inflicted the injury. He told me I'd done him a favor; that he couldn't have managed it himself and didn't want to cause me pain. After what I'd done, he didn't want to cause *me* pain.

"Being young and frightened, I did lie. Of course, I couldn't lie to myself. Day and night, I envisioned the scene, the torment of it relentless. I could hardly eat or sleep. I was nearing my wit's end when Edward made his first attempt to take his life. The day our parents were compelled to lock him away was a reprieve for me, since it was no longer necessary to face daily my atrocious act. As the fabricated tale was recounted over and over, it began to ring true. Eventually, my anguish subsided. At last, I was able to carry on with my life.

"Unfortunately, a consequence we hadn't foreseen occurred when word of Edward's madness spread amongst our social circle. One by one, those we'd considered our friends ridiculed and shunned us. It was no longer pity I felt for my brother but disdain. Although he was locked away for his own good, I became convinced he deserved his confinement.

"While Edward remained dangerously disturbed there was no option other than to continue his imprisonment, until seemingly out of nowhere, Dr. Hardin advised me he was making an astonishing recovery. Faced with the decision of granting his release, as you've discovered I took drastic steps to ensure this didn't happen. I presumed no one would question the false report I demanded the doctor submit; however, it comes to light you've had every reason for distrust. As a result of my obstinacy, I've lost you. Given my infractions, I deserve to lose my freedom. It's my turn to be punished."

"Please, Darrell, you mustn't think in this way. Punishment won't help anyone or change anything. Instead, you must forgive yourself, and your brother. When the past is rectified, the family may finally heal, and become whole once more."

"You regard this as a simple, straightforward solution, don't you? What you don't understand is this cannot take place. I've more to atone for than my brother. In addition to the deplorable way I've treated him, I'm responsible for our parents' demise."

Abigail's eyes widened in shock. "How is that possible? It was another accident, wasn't it?"

"Honestly, I doubt it was. As I've explained, I held our parents partly accountable for Emily's death; resentful to the extent I turned my back on them. In effect, they lost both of their sons. I can merely imagine how acutely this wounded them. The day of the carriage incident they were in an odd mood and said goodbye in a most peculiar way. When we received the news of their death, I alone was convinced of what truly happened: they didn't fall off that cliff, they drove off of it."

Edward whimpered.

"You were in too deep a state of self-loathing, and Catherine was too young to perceive it, though you must accept it was my abhorrent attitude that killed our parents," Darrell said to his brother, who was now weeping.

"Had you confided in me these matters, everything could have been different," Abigail said. "You mustn't carry the weight of your parents' demise on your shoulders, any more than Edward should carry Emily's. There's no proof it wasn't an accident. If you are correct, they made the decision to end their lives. All of you have suffered needlessly. The time to relieve yourselves of this pointless contempt and guilt is long overdue."

"If it was possible, it doesn't alter the fact I've lost you. The happy life I'd planned is gone, never to return."

"Your life isn't over. With your many attributes, you'll find another to love, perhaps more so than me."

"Please don't condescend. You're well aware you're the woman I love, the one person I want by my side. You alone loved me, truly loved me, for who I am, not what I am. Since I've lost you, it's no longer possible for me to live contentedly. I've no desire to live at all." He picked up the knife.

"Darrell, no, *no*!" she cried out. "This isn't the answer!"

"My sweet, lovely Abigail, how I adored you." He kissed her and gazed at her with a bittersweet smile.

"Please, Darrell, let me help you. If you release me, I can help you."

"I've already requested your help."

"When?"

"A few moments ago. I asked you to go forth with our marriage, and you refused."

"You asked me under duress. You'd frightened me enormously."

"Since you're no longer under duress, with the facts I've disclosed, will you change your mind?"

Abigail glanced at Edward. "I…"

"You needn't answer. I see in your eyes the love you hold for Edward, the love you used to feel for me, but no longer do. He is the man truly deserving of you, while I deserve penitence." Darrell stood next to Edward. "Although it doesn't account for much, I love you, my brother. It was never you I hated, I hated myself. I'm sorry, terribly sorry for the horrible things I've done." He kissed the scar he'd inflicted. "Please, take good care of her for me."

Edward groaned as he shook his head.

"He's trying to tell you he doesn't want to lose you, and neither do I. For our sake, you mustn't do this. You're not a monster, you're a good man. You've proven you are the man I fell in love with. I do love you, Darrell. I've always loved you, and I always will."

He cupped Abigail's chin and smiled. "I'll die believing this is true, for it's what I desperately wish. Goodbye, my dearest love."

Darrell placed the knife to his throat.

"I beg you, don't do this. I can help you; let me help you!" she implored and thrashed from side to side in an attempt to loosen her bonds.

"Forgive me, my dearest. There's nothing you can do. It no longer matters. Whether I use the knife or not, my life is over."

Abigail pulled at the ropes with every ounce of strength she had. "Please, Darrell, you must listen to me!"

Edward attempted to grunt his brother's name. He also made a frantic attempt to escape his bonds.

Darrell's eyes became blank as he entered into a trance-like state. Apparently unable to hear their pleas, he permitted the knife to do its worst. With one quick slash, blood streamed from his neck. A moment later, he collapsed onto the floor.

Abigail released a scream of excruciating misery from the depths of her soul, shouting for help at the top of her lungs. Muffled by the gag, Edward's guttural sounds of anguish were nonetheless as powerful. An unearthly clamor emanated from the room.

Eleanor, Jake, and Mr. Phillips came rushing in.

"What's happened?" Eleanor asked, clearly out of breath. "Darrell! What have you done!"

"Dear God!" Mr. Phillips called out.

Jake seized his own head, hollering while he paced frantically about the room.

Mr. Phillips cut Abigail loose from her bonds. He then went to free Edward. Despite Eleanor's use of her apron as a bandage, the loss of blood was immense. Abigail reached Darrell's side, barely in time to witness his eyes smiling into hers, before the last flicker of light faded from them. Moments later Edward was there, only to discover he was too late.

Abigail shook his shoulders in a desperate attempt to revive him. "Darrell, Darrell!" she cried. When there was no response, she crumpled onto his body.

Mr. Phillips pulled her up by the waist. Abigail resisted by bending over his arm. Although her mouth hung open, she was unable to make a sound. Everything inside her was clenching, twisting, constricting as an unbearable pressure mounted, creating wave after wave of searing pain. Her agony escalated to a rupturing point, until like a cannon firing a wail of torment exploded from her.

"No!" she sobbed. She wrenched away from Mr. Phillip's grasp and fell next to Darrell. "Please, God, no!"

After what seemed an eternity, Abigail felt the touch of someone's hand. When whoever it was tried to raise her, she clung to the sleeves of Darrell's coat. Two persons were required to unclench her hands before she was placed on her feet.

"Let me stay with him," Abigail pleaded, but couldn't prevent herself from being led out of the north wing. She had no perception of who it was until they were in her room.

"Miss, miss; can you hear me?"

She turned to find her maid. Abigail was eerily quiet, her face white as stone as Mary removed her blood-soaked clothes.

"Bathe her as best you can and put her to bed. Cover her with several blankets," Abigail heard someone instruct. "She's suffering from severe shock. She must be watched continually."

Abigail stood in dazed cooperation, with the sensation she was merely an observer while someone else was being attended. After several minutes she saw the floor grow near and slipped away into total blackness.

11

L ife is seldom a simple or straightforward journey.
Abigail Parker's life had not merely taken a detour, it
had diverted to a path she never could have anticipated and
would wish upon no one; a passageway mired in shadows and
immeasurable despair.

The train Abigail rode bound for Vienna lurched, rousing
her from her slumber in the same way it had when she'd
arrived in England months earlier. She rested her head on the
shoulder of the person seated next to her and closed her eyes.
The painful memories of her last days at Rochester Manor
entered her mind, beginning with her first awareness following
the catastrophic incident.

"Miss? Please, miss, you must take a little broth," Mary
said.

Abigail felt her place a spoon to her lips. Although not
fully cognizant she complied, choking as some of the soup was
consumed. Minutes later, she slid back into the darkness.

When she regained consciousness, it was nighttime.

"Fetch the doctor, Mary," she heard Eleanor instruct.

Not long after, he entered. He placed his hand on
Abigail's forehead. "The shock is abating."

Abigail searched the room in a panic. "Darrell; where is
Darrell?"

"He's been attended to," Eleanor explained.

"I had a nightmare…"

Eleanor sat on the bed next to her and rubbed her arm.

"It was a nightmare," Abigail continued. "It had to be a nightmare, for he cannot be…he isn't… please, tell me he isn't!"

The physician handed Eleanor a glass. "Help her drink this tonic. I've added a sleeping powder since she must yet rest."

"Please, Eleanor, no!" Abigail hollered and attempted to rise.

Dr. Hardin held Abigail by the shoulders to prevent her.

"You're to remain in bed, my dear. Drink this," Eleanor said.

She sputtered while the liquid streamed down her throat. Eleanor then pushed her gently onto her pillow, and Abigail drifted off again.

"Abigail?" she heard someone say.

She felt a hand and saw a figure sitting next to her, his face eclipsed by the sunshine.

"Darrell!" she called out.

"No, Abigail, it's Edward. Are you…how are you?"

She scowled. "Need you ask?"

"I suppose not."

"You'll excuse me; I want to be alone."

"You do accept what happened wasn't your fault?"

"*Obviously* I don't find myself at fault. It was my idea to leave Darrell; I broke his heart, why would I assume any blame for his actions?"

"I understand how you feel."

Abigail's lips quivered when she sat up. Seeing Edward's appearance of compassion caused her to weep.

She wiped her face. "Can you forgive me for my foolishness? How could I think I understood how you felt about Emily? I didn't; not in the least."

"I know," Edward said tenderly. He pulled her into his arms. "Only those who've survived such an ordeal can comprehend the misery."

254

"The pain is intense; it burns straight through my heart, and into my soul."

"An ache so acute it seems no measure of relief is attainable."

"Every bit of advice, all the guidance I gave you was utterly misguided. I hadn't the slightest inkling what I was speaking of."

"Although you couldn't fully appreciate my position, it doesn't follow your insight was mistaken."

"Mistaken doesn't begin to describe my unadulterated ignorance."

"You mustn't be harsh with yourself. Recall how immensely you've helped me."

"Edward, I feel sick, I'm going to be sick."

He grabbed the washing vessel from her dressing table and rushed it to her.

"Mary," he called out. "Mary!"

She ran in and hurried to the bed. "It will be best for you to leave, master."

"I'll return later," Edward said before he departed.

Mary patted her back while Abigail hovered over the bowl, and then left to attend to it.

Master? Abigail thought. *Of course; Edward is now the head of the household.*

Mary returned shortly thereafter.

"You must rest, miss," she said, handing Abigail another tonic. "You're to remain in bed until Dr. Hardin advises us otherwise."

Abigail lost consciousness too quickly to reply.

*****

When next Abigail awoke, the moon was shining in through the window. With her state of shock worn off, the horrific confrontation played in her head mercilessly. Unable to endure it she sat up and looked around the room. *What'll I do? Where will I go? Anywhere but here.*

She stumbled over to where her trunk had been. It had gone missing. She checked her closet to find her belongings had been replaced.

"Who did this?" she asked aloud.

Abigail was sorting through her garments, throwing them onto the floor when she came across her wedding dress. She froze in shock, until slowly, carefully, she removed the gown from its hanger. She stepped into the dress and placed the veil on her head before she turned to stare at her reflection in the mirror.

"I'm coming, Darrell," she whispered.

Abigail took a candle and glided down the stairs, silent as a ghost as she walked to the north wing. She tried the door which was no longer locked and entered the corridor in a hypnotic state. She went into the dining room and sat on the floor where Darrell had fallen. "I'm here, Darrell. I'll be your wife and stay with you always."

She caressed the spot that had been carpeted. "It's cold on this bare floor, isn't it? Shall we move to the library?"

Fantasizing she held his hand, she made her way there and lay on the sofa. "We should sleep." She cuddled a pillow and closed her eyes, smiling contentedly.

"Abigail," someone said.

She wakened, unsure how much time had passed. Given how late it was when she'd left her room, she assumed it had been many hours.

"Edward. How kind of you to visit."

"What are you doing in the north wing, dressed in your wedding gown?"

"It's lovely here, isn't it? Now I understand why you had no desire to leave."

"Lovely?"

"Indeed delightful. The darkness isn't gloomy and depressing, as I once thought. On the contrary, in here all that is beautiful may come true. We want you to attend the ceremony. I'm certain Darrell won't mind should you wish to invite Emily."

"Abigail, stop this. You're speaking complete nonsense."

"It isn't nonsense, and I'm not mad if this is your concern. It's mere imagination, yet everything here seems real."

"Enough of this; we're leaving." Edward took her hand.

She escaped his grasp. "I won't leave."

When he attempted to carry her, she clung to the sofa.

"You mustn't take me away. If I leave the north wing, Darrell will be gone."

"Abigail, Darrell *is* gone. It doesn't matter where you are; he cannot return."

"I want to be with him."

Edward sat next to her. "I'm sorry, Abigail. If we could turn back the clock, we would. We would have done anything to save him. We tried, desperately." Raising his sleeves, he revealed the bandages on his wrists. He then lifted her arms to display the similar bindings which covered her rope burns. "We would have sacrificed ourselves by any means to prevent him. He gave us no choice."

"I did have a choice. I made my choice, and it was his undoing."

"You did what you thought you must for my sake. In this sense, I'm to blame. If not for me, you and Darrell would've been happy. Had I insisted he send me to the asylum prior to your arrival, you'd never have known of my existence. I was too selfish to realize what I should have done."

"Please, Edward, don't say this. You've done nothing wrong, you never have."

"You've done nothing wrong either. You only ever wanted the best, for all of us."

"I did, but I failed miserably."

"If you feel this way recall what you taught me; forgiveness is the answer. You cannot honor Darrell by remaining in here."

Listening to these all too familiar words, Abigail nodded.

Edward stood. "Come now, we must leave. Everyone has been worried about you."

He offered her his hand. When Abigail accepted it, he helped her rise and led her out of the north wing.

*****

Another jolt indicated the train had arrived at the Vienna station, which returned Abigail's awareness to the present. She removed her head from her mother's shoulder.

Her mother helped her to the exit. "How are you, my darling daughter?"

"I'm fine," she muttered.

"It will be good for you to be home," her father said.

Once they'd disembarked, he left to collect their luggage.

Home will make no difference. After what I've done, nothing in my life will be good. I'll never again find happiness, Abigail thought.

Despite everyone's efforts to assure her otherwise, she was convinced she'd failed the entire family. While awaiting her father, she thought of the day Catherine had returned to Rochester Manor.

She gave Abigail a hug. "Dearest sister, you look dreadfully wan."

"I don't know how you can consider me your sister after what I've done."

"You've done nothing wrong. Edward has explained everything to me. If anyone is a victim, it's you. I can't imagine the terror Darrell inflicted upon you both. He must have gone mad."

"Undoubtedly he did, and it was my fault."

"Not at all. Darrell was obviously beyond help. If not for you Edward would still be suffering, locked away in the north wing, or even the asylum."

"We cannot be certain of this. I handled the matter in the wrong way. Had I been honest with Darrell from the start he'd still be with us. I should have found a way to convince him to reconcile with Edward. My decision to sneak behind his back was a huge mistake."

"Why would you entertain this absurd notion after the heartless and cruel way he treated Edward? You had no choice but to rescue him from unthinkable torment before he was driven insane."

"It should never have come to this. You warned me Darrell was disturbed, and a rash move could result in a catastrophe."

"You're extremely unkind to yourself. With Darrell set upon his vendetta, there was no other course to attempt."

"I wish I could believe this."

Catherine's image vanished when her father approached.

"We may proceed to the carriage," he said.

Abigail glanced back as he assisted her and her mother to board. She wondered if there was the faintest chance this carriage would transport her figuratively from her tortuous past. To her, it seemed highly doubtful.

*****

As Abigail had anticipated, her arrival at home didn't help her grim mood; in some ways, it made her worse.

She went directly to her room and glared at herself in her dressing mirror, spiteful of the individual she'd consulted long ago for advice. She recalled how she'd been seated at her dressing table at Rochester Manor when Edward came to visit at her request. It was to be their final conversation.

"Mary said you wished to see me."

"I did," Abigail replied. "I must tell you about an important decision I've reached."

"A decision?" he asked with obvious concern.

"Please, would you have a seat?"

He took one near hers.

"Edward, I regret to say we cannot marry."

His appearance was distraught as he began to answer her.

"It's nothing to do with you personally," she preempted him. "I can no longer be a good wife for any man. I will never marry."

"At the moment, your feelings are understandable. In time, your outlook will change. I'm more than willing to wait."

"Your wait will be in vain. I'm no longer capable of giving you the love you desire, the love you deserve."

"Even if it was true you needn't leave. You could remain, if only as a friend."

"That won't do. You've suffered too long to live with a woman whose heart is hopelessly bruised. I cannot make you happy in any sense. Whatever my role, I will only be a burden to you. You must find someone else, and you will."

"You would never be a burden. If you'd let me offer you my…"

"*No;* the situation has been settled. My parents will take me home."

"When will you depart?"

"My father has booked us passage on the morning train."

Edward hung his head. "I'll miss you enormously."

"As I'll miss you. I hope one day you'll find it in your heart to forgive me, for everything."

"There's nothing to forgive," he said. They shook with the force of their tears as he held her tightly.

With this memory, Abigail stared at the mirror before her and saw fresh tears stream down the face of a woman in perpetual misery.

12

Whereas Eleanor had once said resentment may be a persistent ailment when the wound is deep, Abigail was discovering depression has the potential to be downright debilitating.

During the three weeks following her return to Vienna, Abigail had spent the majority of her time isolated in her room, eating sparingly and sleeping less. Despite her parents' efforts to help, none of their attempts had remotely alleviated her despair. It was obvious they were becoming frustrated by her lack of progress.

One afternoon, Abigail was lying on her bed when her mother tapped on her door.

"Anna, Elsa, and Gerta are here to see you," Mrs. Parker said.

"Tell them to come another day," Abigail said.

"It's been weeks since your return. The time has come for you to rejoin your family and friends."

"Please, Mother, I cannot receive visitors yet. Permit me a few days more."

"I could grant you a few *weeks* more; nothing will change until you collect yourself and leave this room. You're to dress at once and come to the parlor." She closed the door firmly.

"How may I face my friends? How will I explain to them what happened?" Abigail whispered.

Despite her reluctance, she did as her mother instructed.

"Abigail, dearest," Anna exclaimed upon her entrance and gave her a hug. "My heavens; what have you done to yourself? You've become nothing but skin and bones!"

"It appears a slight wind could blow you away," Gerta said.

"Gracious sakes, Abigail, you look ghastly, simply ghastly!" Elsa added.

"Don't be unkind, Elsa," Gerta admonished.

"From what your mother told us, it's a small wonder the strain has taken its toll," Anna said.

"What happened to you is unimaginable," Gerta agreed.

"I'm glad now Mr. Lewis didn't choose me," Elsa said.

Gerta poked her with her elbow.

"Ow!" Elsa hollered.

"You mustn't say such things," Gerta said under her breath.

"I don't blame you, Elsa," Abigail said. "It was a nightmare no one should endure."

"We cannot fathom how Mr. Lewis's nature was patently opposed to the man he represented himself to be," Gerta remarked.

"Particularly given how incredibly handsome he was," Elsa said dreamily.

Anna and Gerta shot her a harsh glare.

"What's sad is his appearance wasn't a deception," Abigail said. "He was precisely what he appeared to be, but for his attitude towards his unfortunate brother. It was sheer folly for me to think I could help him, or anyone living in that household."

"From the sound of it, you did the best you could," Anna said.

Abigail pursed her lips. "Evidently, I didn't."

"Your mother said you rescued Mr. Lewis's brother, what is his name, Edward? Apparently, he's a most gentle and accommodating man," Gerta said.

"She told us you could've stayed at Rochester Manor with Edward. If this is true, whatever possessed you to leave?" Elsa asked.

Abigail frowned. "I've nothing to offer him, and categorically not marriage. I'm no longer fit to wed anyone."

The girls regarded one another in dismay.

"What an absurd conclusion," Elsa said.

"I'm sure she has her reasons," Gerta said through gritted teeth.

"Well now," Anna said to stop their bickering. "Your mother informs us you've been cooped up since your return. We must plan an outing for you."

Gerta smiled. "Oh yes; something fun like we used to do."

"We must get you out of this house," Elsa said.

"In a week or so, I may be ready…" Abigail started.

"Let's select a day," Anna interrupted. "Shall we say Wednesday? A new show is opening that night."

"That will be the very thing," Gerta agreed. "The theater is bound to lift your spirits."

"First, we'll dine someplace nice. We must find a way to plump you up," Elsa added.

Abigail shook her head. "Please, let's wait until next week."

"We won't allow it," Anna informed her. "You know one way or the other we'll convince you. You may as well save us the trouble."

"We'll arrive at your house early, to prepare you as we did for the…" Gerta caught herself.

"Don't worry. After what happened the last time, we won't overly adorn you," Elsa said.

Anna rolled her eyes. "Abigail needs her rest. We must leave."

"Thank you for calling," Abigail said. "I didn't realize how desperately I was in need of your friendship."

Anna gave her another hug. "Dearest, of one thing you may be assured; you may always count upon us. Good friends never let each other down."

*****

Although she once believed in the adage time heals all wounds, Abigail doubted any amount of time would assist in a case as devastating as hers. Her friends tried to help by taking her on frequent outings; however, each time any progress she made was short-lived.

The day she was to wed Darrell was particularly overwhelming. Abigail suffered nearly a complete relapse, plunging her into a state of despondency from which escape seemed impossible.

Unfortunately, the ensuing winter was unusually bleak, of no help to cheer a soul entrenched in a depressive state. Even Christmastime, a season she'd once adored, couldn't brighten her mood. Her mother entered her room on Christmas morning, to find her daughter was still in bed.

"Abigail, your father and I will soon open the presents."

Abigail pulled the covers over her head. "I don't want them."

"You have some, nonetheless. Please, join us when you're ready."

"I don't deserve presents. Give mine to charity."

Abigail was shocked when her mother yanked the blankets off of her.

"This attitude of yours has continued long enough. The time has come to put an end to it."

"I cannot change what I feel. How can I? How can I overcome my guilt, Mother, when what happened was my fault?"

"The underlying problem is your misguided blame. You blame yourself for finding the means to help Edward, but not Darrell. The fault wasn't yours; it was the distinct difference in their attitudes. While Edward was reluctant and resisted help,

Darrell didn't *want* help. A person with Darrell's mindset will refuse guidance, despite how desperately it's needed. To recover, you must decide into which of these categories you fall. Considering the manner in which your father and I raised you, I presume it's the first. If you come to agree, meet us in the parlor, and we may all enjoy our Christmas."

When her mother left, Abigail sat up. Misguided blame; for her this was the key. She thought about how she'd given Edward the same advice, and his words came to mind; "…it dawned on me how selfish and thoughtless I've been. From this day forward, I'll focus my attention on the present; on the kind individuals who've granted me their love and compassion, without reservation."

Abigail rose and fastened her robe before heading down the stairs.

*****

Despite winter's seemingly endless bereft and lackluster condition, springtime did, of course, arrive, imparting its message of renewal and hope. With the support of her family and friends, as the months passed Abigail's pain eased. She became willing not merely to rejoin life, but also to seek its enjoyment.

One particularly fine day, she and her mother were visiting the local shops in search of Easter apparel, when Abigail came to a sudden halt. In front of her was a store where pianos are sold and repaired. Through the window, she saw the same type of instrument Edward had played in the north wing.

Abigail pressed her hands to the glass. For the first time since her return to Vienna, she recalled with fondness the many hours she'd spent with Edward. Her heart felt heavy, not due to past horrors, but with an urgent longing to be near him.

In the days that followed, most of Abigail's thoughts centered upon Edward. Soon, she could think of little else. Several nights later she lay on her bed and imagined him lying next to her as he had in the north wing. She sat up when the truth struck her in the heart, shocking her like a bolt of lightning.

I want to marry him, she thought. *I must marry him!*

Abigail leaped out of bed and ran to her desk, believing there was no time to waste. She was about to write a letter until she stopped to consider her options.

Perhaps I should send a cable. No, they're ever so impersonal. This is the occasion for a letter; although, a cable will arrive faster...but will it arrive in time? After the way I've treated him, Edward may not want me back. He may already be engaged, or even married. I won't survive if he's found someone else.

"Calm yourself," she said aloud. *Write the letter and beg his forgiveness. If he has found another, I'll extend my best wishes for his happiness, though I'll never again be happy.*

While she wrote, Abigail's hand trembled to the point she continually made mistakes. Words also eluded her, and she crumpled page after page until the floor was covered with a blanket of paper that resembled a snowdrift. "This is useless, utterly useless!" She threw her head on the desk. The page on it became saturated with her tears.

Although it seemed only a minute had passed, Abigail rose to find the dawn was breaking.

Calling on her utmost determination, she took a fresh sheet of paper and continued. She'd written a few words when the piano in the drawing room rang out.

Mother, why are you playing so dastardly early? I won't finish my letter unless the racket ceases, and it must go out in today's post.

She scowled when the playing continued until the tune caught her attention. "Huh! It isn't...it cannot be. It's not possible."

After securing her robe Abigail raced down the stairs. Her mother was standing in the foyer.

"Mama?" she asked.

She grinned slyly. "He told me of his desire to see Vienna one day. I suspected the time had come."

266

Abigail leaped into her mother's arms. "How did you know? How could you possibly have known?"

"It isn't difficult for a mother to see into her daughter's heart." She gave her a kiss and pointed towards the drawing room.

Abigail went there, pausing at the entrance. With his back to her, she wasn't convinced this was the man she prayed it would be. She entered the room and crept to the piano.

"Edward?" she asked, her voice so cracked it was almost a whisper.

It was Edward who rose, hardly recognizable given his gain of weight and color.

He pulled her into his arms. "Abigail."

"Oh, Edward, Edward you're here; I can't believe you're here!"

He smiled. "Yet here I am."

"Have you forgiven me then?"

"My darling, I'd nothing to forgive you."

"There was much to forgive, particularly my abandonment of you. I left in such a callous way."

"I understood why you thought you must leave."

"Even so, it was cold and unfeeling of me. I behaved as if I was the only person suffering Darrell's loss. He was your brother, yet I didn't offer you the slightest comfort. You tried to comfort me, but I ignored you. I'm certain by now you've found someone else. Why wouldn't you, when I insisted upon it?"

"Abigail, how can you think there could ever be another? I would wait an eternity for my angel who rescued me, who gave me back my life."

"There's no one else?"

"No, my dearest, there's no one else."

"I love you, Edward, from the depths of my soul. I can't fathom how you could still love me. Do you, love me at all?"

"Perhaps this will provide you with the answer." He took her face in his hands and kissed her passionately while tears filled her eyes. "I do have a question of my own, if I may?"

"If it's what I'm desperately wishing for."

"I'll be most embarrassed if it isn't. Abigail, will you marry me?"

"Yes, yes, a thousand times yes!"

Edward took a beautiful yet old-fashioned diamond engagement ring from his pocket.

"What a lovely ring," she said.

"Does it suit you? It was my mother's."

"It more than suits me, unless for you it will be a constant reminder of her."

"It will remind me of her, which is why I would have you wear it. You have the same kind and gentle disposition she possessed."

Tears rolled down her cheeks as Abigail lowered her head.

"Before I place it on your finger, I must tell you of several changes I've made. I hope they won't disappoint you."

She regarded him with concern. "What changes?"

"I've taken on rooms here in Vienna. I intend to make my permanent home here. I've brought with me Mr. Phillips and Mary, who've agreed to assist us."

"My goodness, this is wonderful!"

"Then, shall I?"

Edward offered her the ring. After she nodded elatedly, he placed it on her finger and kissed her once more.

"I love you, Abigail, so very much."

"As I love you."

"I trust you'll be glad to learn Rochester Manor will remain in the family. Catherine is engaged as well. Her betrothed has consented to live with her there."

"This couldn't be better news. Will she marry your uncle's neighbor?"

"Why yes, she will indeed. How did you know?"

"A lucky guess."

"I've made another decision, based on an idea you planted in my head long ago."

"What is that?"

"I intend to audition for a chance to play on the stage."

"How marvelous, Edward. Vienna will welcome you with open arms."

"I wish I were as convinced. I'm quite nervous at the prospect."

"You've no call to be nervous. They'll find your talent astounding, this I guarantee."

"Catherine has agreed to visit with her fiancé to attend our wedding which, if you have no objection, will take place soon?"

"I see no reason to delay. If the truth is told, I'd prefer a simple ceremony, far more than one that's elaborate."

"My sister has offered to send the invitations. I only need give her the date."

"How sweet of her. I miss our sister dreadfully; how is dearest Catherine?"

"She's busily engaged at the moment, overseeing a massive project. Prior to her marriage, Rochester Manor will be renovated entirely. She claims when we return for her wedding, we won't recognize the place."

"Likely she'd deny it, though undoubtedly she undertook this venture primarily for our sake rather than for her own."

"Given what I observed when I departed the drive, I believe you're correct."

"Why? What did you see?"

"She was hauling with determination a huge, heavy hammer."

"A hammer? What was she going to do with it?"

"I can't be sure, but I don't think we'll need to guess."

"We won't?"

"No, for she was heading down the path, the one that leads to the north wing."

The End

ABOUT THE AUTHOR

Susan Butler was born and raised in Saint Louis, Missouri.
She divides her time between nearby Saint Charles county
and Tampa, Florida with her husband, Brian.